MOO

MOO

*The Story of a Highland
Cow Called Floss*

Susan Jayne McAuley

authorHOUSE®

AuthorHouse™ UK
1663 Liberty Drive
Bloomington, IN 47403 USA
www.authorhouse.co.uk
Phone: 0800.197.4150

This is a work of fiction. Names, characters, businesses, places,
events and incidents are either products of the author's imagination
or used in a fictitious manner. Any resemblance to actual persons,
living or dead, or actual events is purely coincidental.

Published by AuthorHouse 08/26/2015

ISBN: 978-1-5049-8753-0 (sc)
ISBN: 978-1-5049-8758-5 (e)

Print information available on the last page.

Any people depicted in stock imagery provided by Thinkstock are models,
and such images are being used for illustrative purposes only.
Certain stock imagery © Thinkstock.

This book is printed on acid-free paper.

DEDICATION

To Hillside Animal Sanctuary, its founder, and all those who work for and support this fantastic place – thank you for being there for the animals.

To my beautiful horse, Copper, who, after putting up a brave fight, lost his life to catastrophic laminitis at Liverpool Equine Hospital on 7 July 2011. We miss you so much.

To the staff and pupils at St Norberts School, Crowle – for their kind support and for being the first to read and critique 'Moo'

And to all the animals which suffer unnecessarily at the hands of humans, may God bless them all.

CHAPTER ONE

He was her first baby, and as she tenderly licked the russet curls which spiralled down his little face and then touched his little pink nose with her own, Floss wondered what princely name she could give to her handsome young son. He was three days old already, and she still had not decided on a name. But why should she hurry? There was plenty of time to make up her mind. After giving him a loving lick, she made her way to the gate of her stall so that she could catch the attention of Prudence, the cow living opposite.

"Good morning, Pru," Floss said ever so loudly. She mooed and did most things loudly. "How's your little one doing today? My son is really looking forward to meeting her."

Prudence frowned and then snapped her head around. "Shh, will you! Daisy is suckling very nicely this morning, and I do not want her disturbed. Didn't I tell you not to interrupt us yesterday?"

"Grumpy cow," Floss mumbled under her breath. Prudence had obviously got up on the wrong side of her straw bed, as usual.

Floss decided not to let Prudence's rudeness spoil the enjoyment of the rest of the day and she quickly forgot the matter altogether as she swished a fly with her tail and turned to look proudly at her baby son again. He had tucked himself under her belly, where he felt safe and warm, and seeing him there made her smile. Her thoughts turned to the many wonderful times that lay ahead of them. April was almost done, and May's arrival would herald the freedom of summer – many carefree and lazy hours spent in the lush green meadows outside. Even now, she could smell the loveliness of the meadow: the freshness of the young shoots of green grass pushing through the earth, just waiting for them to graze it.

As she breathed in the scent through her imagination, she let her eyes close whilst she thought about how lucky they all were at the barn. Their owner, Joe Devlin, looked after them well, and they wanted for nothing. Even when they were stalled for the winter, their every need was attended to. There was always lots of soft meadow hay to eat, a lovely thick bed of straw to lie on, fresh water, and on occasional days, for a very special treat, sweet haylage to tuck into. Not that any of these things could ever replace the first shoots of that delicious spring grass which waited for them outside – yum yum.

The comforting feeling of her small calf nuzzling her udder briefly interrupted Floss's happy daydreams, and soon she felt the warmth of his lips suckling her creamy milk. Dreamily, she closed her eyes again; this time, her mind wandered, not to the future but to the past, to the day that Joe Devlin had introduced her to Beefy, the Highland bull that was her calf's father. How impressed she had been at their first introduction, very brief though it was. Beefy's muscles rippled as he walked, and his coat was of the silkiest golden hair that she had ever seen. And boy was he handsome, with a fine head set on a stout, strong neck. Joe had definitely chosen her youngster's sire well, and all of Beefy's attributes were evident in her offspring. Fine-looking of face, her calf was strong and tall for his age, with a shining russet coat and bright, clear eyes. Buds that would one day become impressive horns had already appeared on his head, and they were visible beneath the curls of his fluffy forelock.

The stall to Floss's right was the winter home of Ned, an extremely elderly but always very astute donkey. Ned's grey nose, which was covered in remnants of sticky chaff, suddenly appeared over the wooden rail.

"Good morning, Floss and ... erm ... cute hairy thing. Goodness, I wish you would get a name for him, Floss. 'Cute hairy thing', well, it doesn't sound so good."

Floss smiled, looking with fondness at the old donkey whose hairy chin now rested on the wooden rail beside her. Ever since her mum died, Ned had been the one who looked out for her. In fact, if it not for him, she was sure that she would not have survived.

She had been just four days old when tragedy struck. It was very early in the morning, not even light, when young Floss had awoke with a growling hunger in her belly. Crying out, she had searched for the comfort of her mother, Bella, but instead of finding her breakfast milk, she had discovered Bella lying cold and hard on the ground, unresponsive to her desperate cries. The humans – Joe Devlin and his wife, Glenda – had come along at that moment. Floss hadn't known much of humans at that point, but she would always remember how intense their sadness had been as they watched her huddling pitifully against her mother's motionless body.

"She's gone. Bless her. Oh, the poor little calf! What will we do with her, Joe?"

"She can't survive without her mother. She's just too young."

"We could try to hand-rear her, couldn't we?"

"Is it worth it, Glenda? It will be such a lot of work. Maybe it would be kindest to have her put to sleep."

"But look at her little face, Joe. She looks like a fighter to me. Maybe we should give her a chance, just for a few days."

"I don't know."

"Come on, Joe. Let's try for a few days."

"Okay. We'll try for a few days."

After her mother's body had been dragged out of the stall and away down the aisle, young Floss had not known what to do. In her distress, she had cried out and fought to follow, but the farmhands had held her back. After that, had come the slamming of the barn doors, and then she was all on her own in a cold stall, abandoned, trembling with fear, and crying uncontrollably for her mum.

And then, as if by magic, her guardian angel had appeared in the form of this big head that had thrown itself over the dividing rail of her stall. At first, it scared her witless and she had shrunken away from it, wondering what it could possibly be. Was it a funny-looking cow? But then she'd decided no cow could possibly look like that, not with that ridiculously long nose and enormous overstretched ears. The head had spoken then, introducing itself as Ned the Donkey. His voice was loud, but his words were kind.

Ned had been firm yet gentle with her, understanding her sense of loss but convincing her that even though her mum was gone, she must not give up on her own life. He had insisted that she drink the awful plastic-tasting milk that the humans brought to her, and then that she eat the hay she found so difficult to chew. Later, when they were turned out in the fields, Ned's guidance had continued, and he helped her to make friends with the other animals living on the farm. The weeks and months had simply flown by after that, and now, four years later, she had given life to her very own little calf.

Bringing herself back to the present, Floss said, "I haven't chosen a name for him yet, Ned." When her friend shook his long head, Floss added, "I know it's taking me a long time, but it's just such an important decision. Whatever name I choose is the one my son will have to live with all his life. I have narrowed it down, though, and the list is rather short now, so don't worry."

"That's good to hear," Ned said, his long face brightening. "We can't let him grow up thinking that his name is 'hairy thing'! And, my word, isn't he looking just like you?!"

"Oh goodness, Ned! Do you think so?" Floss gushed. "I thought he looked more like his dad."

But then again, she didn't have much of a clue whether he looked like her or not, because she had only ever seen her reflection in the often murky and muddy pools of rainwater out in the fields.

"Nah, he's definitely got more of your colouring. A gorgeous redhead, just like his mum."

Ned winked at her, and Floss felt her cheeks flushing. She gave him a shy glance, and then, even though she was sure that the hair on her face would hide the glow, she still turned away for a moment, just in case. She didn't want him to think that she was embarrassed by his compliments.

"Hey, watch where you are sticking your horns, Floss."

"Sorry, Gertie."

Floss uttered the apology several additional times as she hastily retracted the long horn that had found its way into the stall to her left. It had been the second time that week that she had almost poked the poor little goat's eyes out. The stalls were just so very small when you had such very big horns.

After checking that Gertie had not been injured, Floss turned towards Ned again. The donkey had summoned her son over to him, and the two of them were playing ear wiggle. It was a game that Ned loved because he could move his ears independently and in various directions, usually dependent on his mood, but sometimes just for fun. His substantial ears were at that moment horizontal to his head, and her son was in fits of laughter, trying hard to copy the donkey.

"Watch this, Mum," her son said, standing before her, a heavy look of concentration on his little face. His left ear flicked forward ever so slightly. "Did you see it move? Did you see it, Mum?"

"I did, and it was very good," Floss said, smiling at him.

Ned then joined in. "Your son must be the cutest thing I have ever seen," he said. "He is just like a little woolly bear."

Floss gazed at her offspring with adoration in her eyes. He was indeed the cutest thing ever, but then, as his mum, she would have thought so no matter what because that's what mums were supposed to do. He moved over to cuddle against her, and his soft brown eyes looked into hers with an affection shared only by a mother and her baby. One day, he would be a mighty bull, just like his dad, independent and strong. But for now, just for a borrowed time, he belonged to Floss, and she loved him so very much.

Chapter Two

"Cock-a-doodle-doo!" crowed Red the Rooster.

Very early one morning just a few weeks after the birth of her calf, Floss awoke to the familiar sound of the cockcrow. Although the confines of the barn prevented her from seeing the spectacularly coloured cockerel, she knew that he would be at the very top of the highest vantage point he could find in the yard outside, making sure that his voice travelled as far as he could project it.

A number of houses overlooked the farmyard, and before long, the cockerel's crowing prompted the appearance of grumpy, tired faces at some of the windows. The odd shout for him to shut up followed, and soon afterwards daylight began to filter into the barn through the small windows positioned at intervals along the roof. As the barn got brighter, the volume of the bird's crowing increased.

Floss watched Prudence force herself to her feet. She knew that Prudence hated the cockerel with a passion as she was always moaning about it. Her complaining was usually worse than the cockerel's noise and soon it began.

"How can a cow possibly get a good night's sleep with that din going on outside? And I'm absolutely starving. If the humans don't feed us on time, I really do not know how on earth they expect us to produce good milk for our young!"

At that exact moment, Daisy made a beeline for her mother's swollen udder. She had been waiting for Prudence to get up, and now that she had, the young calf tried desperately to get her milk whilst avoiding being trampled by her mother, who was traipsing around the stall looking for pieces of dropped hay.

"Well, isn't this just ridiculous!" Prudence said. "I simply cannot find a thing to eat. Humans! Why can't they get here when I have run out of food? Is anyone listening? I can't be the only one who is hungry."

Floss cast a glance at Ned. His face had creased into a frown where his eyebrows met in the middle. It was painful listening to Prudence groaning, and she imagined that it got on his nerves too. Maybe his big ears made it even worse for him.

"Will you please stop moaning about everything, Pru!" he shouted. "We all get hungry first thing in the morning. You going on and on about it every day just makes it worse. They will turn up; they always do. You will just have to be patient like the rest of us. And, anyway, looking at that tummy of yours! You certainly are not going to starve, not at least till next year, I should say."

Prudence gave her ample russet midriff a backwards glance. "It's just my baby weight," she retorted. "And who are you to talk? You haven't exactly got a six-pack, Ned. Have you looked in the mirror yourself lately?"

Floss switched off from listening to her friends arguing about who did or did not have the biggest belly and looked hopefully towards the barn doors. Bright sunshine was twinkling through the gaps in the wooden slats, a sure sign that a beautiful morning lay beyond. As the doors moved in the light breeze, her ears pricked up. Had she just heard the sound of a key turning in the lock, signifying breakfast's arrival? No. It was just the padlock jangling against the chain, and her tummy gave a long and hungry growl. The farmhand was indeed later than usual today.

Floss made her way to the rail of Gertie's stall and looked over it. The little goat was standing with her head over her gate, also gazing longingly at the doors.

"Gertie," Floss whispered, trying to get the goat's attention without Prudence overhearing. "Is the farmhand really late today, or is it me?"

"Yes, he is very late," Gertie replied, also in a whisper. "The sun's pretty high up in the sky now. I can tell from the way it shines through the windows."

"Well, that's it then." The loud voice was Prudence's. "I'm going to have to eat my bed, and it isn't going to be pleasant, not with all that tummy trouble I had last night."

"Ugh!" Floss grimaced at the thought, but she too wished she had been a little more discriminating with her own toilet habits; otherwise, she would have looked to eat her bedding also.

It was hours later, well into the afternoon, in fact, when keys finally did jingle in the lock. The animals rushed to their gates, eyes bright with the hope that their feed would soon be in front of them. But, as the doors pushed forward, letting the late-afternoon sunlight stream inside the barn, it wasn't Joe Devlin who stood there, and it wasn't one of the usual farmhands either. The long dark shadows cast into the narrow passageway were made by strangers, and the voice of the man who spoke first was hard and unfamiliar.

"The bull calf's in stall two. Can you get it, Burt?"

"What about my breakfast?" Prudence called out. "I'm hungry!"

"Oh, do shut up, Pru!" Ned said with a loud bray. "Never mind your breakfast. Breakfast time has been and gone. What are they talking about Floss's young one for?"

At first, Floss did not fully take in what the man had said, but then, as the meaning of his words sank in, panic began to spread within her. There was only one bull calf in the barn, and he was hers. Her eyes widened with fear as she gently ushered him towards the corner of her stall, placing herself in front of him to protect him.

Footsteps of one man came nearer, and when they stopped, Floss knew before she even looked up that he was at her gate. She swallowed hard as she looked him up and down. He was tall and skinny, with a gaunt unshaven face, and his eyes were narrow and mean. He slid the bolt of her gate open, and then he began to push the gate. Floss stared at him, not sure what she should do. As he came towards her, she lowered her head, making sure that her horns were pointing towards him.

The man stopped dead in his tracks. It seemed as if he realised taking the calf was not going to be as easy as he had expected. He backed away and looked over his shoulder.

"Dirty big horns on the mother of it, Bill," the mean skinny man said. "Can you come and give me a hand?"

The man called Bill gave a heavy sigh as he heard the shout. "Hold on," he said. Under his breath, but loud enough for Floss to hear, he grumbled, "Can't any of these younger men handle cattle these days? Do they always need help?" He looked about the barn. When he spotted an old pitchfork lying in the aisle, he smiled. "Perfect," he said as he bent over his enormous saggy belly to pick it up.

"Here, Burt, use this," he said, tossing the huge fork to the skinny man.

The pitchfork landed at Burt's feet, and he nodded approvingly when he saw the sharp prongs on it.

"This is a good match for the horns of a cow any day! Cheers, Bill."

With a weapon in his hands, Burt looked as if he must feel much bigger and braver now. He clasped the shaft of the fork and pointed the sharp metal spikes towards Floss's face. Soon the weapon was just an inch away from her, and as the man waved it precariously, she tried to push her baby as far back against the wall of the barn as she could

"Don't move, son!" she cried, wishing her bulk could break them out of the barn. "Ned! Please help us, Ned!"

Ned was already frantically pacing in his stall. As Floss shouted for his help, he began kicking out with his hind legs. The metal bars of his gate clanged noisily as his hard little hooves landed against them.

"Hee-haw, hee-haw!" the donkey brayed. "Leave my friend alone, you bully."

Burt turned his attention towards the donkey, and then, after dropping the pitchfork into the straw of Floss's bed, he made a wild grab across the partition, catching hold of Ned's head collar.

"You noisy donkey! I will show you what we do with noisy donkeys."

Using his other hand, the man smacked the defenceless donkey straight across his face, and poor Ned fell back onto his haunches. Burt then lifted his hand again.

"You leave my dear friend alone!" Floss cried.

Ned was paying the price for defending her, and Floss wasn't about to let this horrid human strike her friend again. It was time to get rid of that man's scrawny bones, and having had a moment to think, she worked out exactly how to do it. The man's narrow denim-covered bum was right in front of her. *Perfect,* she thought.

Floss took Burt completely by surprise by the force of the butt which was so hard that it propelled him straight into the air and over the partition. He came down head first in Ned's stall, where he lay with his face in the straw, fighting for breath.

The look on Ned's face as his attacker lay there, motionless, said it all. He was obviously keen for revenge and he smiled broadly at Floss before reversing his rear end towards Burt, who was just getting to his knees.

"Time for some equine education!" said Ned.

Wham! Ned's aim was right on target, and Burt's bottom received the full force of the donkey's revenge – not so defenceless after all. Up into the air went Burt, and this time, he did not land in nice soft straw, *oh no!* Floss watched with glee as his huge nose went skidding through a fresh pile of donkey dung and he did not stop moving until it squashed like a tomato against the wall of the barn. He didn't move very much at all after that.

Seemingly pleased by his efforts, Ned strutted cockily around his stall, braying loudly in response to the rapturous applause given to him by the animals.

"Talk to the hoof," he said, braying proudly as he placed a front hoof on top of Burt's head. "Talk to the hoof."

Floss looked over the rail of her fence and smiled at Ned.

"Nice job," she said. Ned smiled back at her, but their moment of glory was to be short lived. The other man, Bill, was already on his way to Ned's stall. The commotion going on had obviously alerted him that all was not well. When he arrived at the gate, his friend was hauling himself up the wooden rails, trying to get to his feet.

"Jeez, what's happened to you and what are you doing in the donkey's stall. Didn't I tell you to get the calf? We do not need the donkey."

No reply came from Burt. Floss could see that though he was standing now, he was very unsteady on his feet. He swayed precariously and both his eye balls crossed into the centres. Bill reached over the gate and grabbing hold of the top of Burt's jumper he pulled him towards the gate.

"Come on! Get yourself together, man. Can't you do a simple job like get a small calf? I've other things to do today besides babysitting you. Did you use the pitchfork?"

Burt was visibly trembling. "I tried to, but … the cow and the donkey, they … attacked me."

"I should never send a boy to do a man's job, huh! Right, then, I guess I shall just have to help you. We will go and get the calf together. Have you got that?"

Floss recoiled from the rail of the fence and considered what she had just overheard. They were going to try again. She couldn't imagine Burt being much of a threat though, not now. He was looking so sorry for himself and had stuffed his nostrils with what appeared to be loo paper. She was sure that it was loo paper as she had seen Glenda bringing rolls of it to the human toilet which was at the other end of the barn. Red spots of blood were dripping from the ends of the tatty shreds. She looked towards the other man, the very fat one. He looked entirely more determined than Burt did. She must make sure she kept a keen eye on his flabby butt. Her horns would sink into that just nicely.

The men left Ned's stall and made their way to her gate.

"Here they come," she said to Ned. "Are you ready to help me again?"

Ned nodded. "I'm ready," he said.

The gate to Floss's stall flew open and Big Chief Flabby Butt came in, followed by a very nervous-looking Burt. Floss concentrated on the bigger man and she ran for him, but he was surprisingly quick; he had already turned before she could get to him.

"Get it quick, Burt!" Bill shouted. "Close the gate. Close the gate."

Floss found herself hurtling head first into the closing metal bars. Dazed, she shook her head, and then she turned to look for her son, but he was nowhere to be seen. She pivoted around and around on her haunches, and then, panic-stricken, she rushed to her gate. The scene that greeted her made her cry out in distress. Somehow, they had got her baby from her stall and tied a rope around his head.

The men were dragging her son down the aisle of the barn, and though she could see that he was struggling against them, fighting them as hard as he could and frantically digging his little hind feet into the sand, his bottom was still sliding towards the barn doors. It seemed that the more her son struggled, the tighter the rope became. Twisting and turning, he began to scream out for her to help him.

"I'm coming, baby, I'm coming!" Floss cried.

Again and again, she ran at the gate, hitting it with her head and her horns. She then turned around and kicked at it with her hooves. But, although it clattered loudly and shook violently, it did not open.

A cloud of dust billowed down the aisle, and she knew immediately that the doors had been closed. Her calf had been taken from her, and all that remained of him were scuff marks in the aisle made by his struggling little feet.

It took a few minutes for Ned to find his tongue.

"I'm so very sorry, Floss," he mumbled. "There was nothing I could do."

Prudence then spoke up. "They always take the boys," she said.

Floss stopped screaming and looked anxiously across the aisle at Prudence.

"Wh-wh-what do you mean?'" she stammered.

"If you have a boy, the humans will take him very early in his life. It's happened to me twice. If you have a girl, you get to keep her for longer. Bull calves do not produce milk, you see, and so they are only good for one thing, and that is …"

Ned quickly interrupted. "Will you shut up, Pru? Floss has just had her son taken from her, and she does not need to listen to your silly gossip and rumour. And that is all it is, gossip and rumour."

"But I do want to listen!" Floss cried out, trembling with emotion. "I want to know exactly what Prudence thinks they are going to do with my poor baby."

"It's not gossip and rumour, Ned, and you know that it isn't," Prudence said. "Floss wants to know, and so I'm going to tell her. The humans think that bull calves are only good to make beefburgers and sausages out of. That's it, I've said it. And you know that it is the truth, Ned."

Floss's bottom lip began to quiver. She then started to wail.

"Yeah, and maybe steak pies as well."

"Oh no! No, they can't eat my son. I won't let them do that to him. I want my baby back. I want my baby back."

"Well you will have to manage without him now, because there's nothing you can do about what has happened," Prudence said. "You will just have to live with it."

"Yes, there is something I can do," Floss said. "I … I … can escape, and I can rescue him."

Prudence gave a sarcastic laugh. "How is a lowly cow like you going to rescue a calf from the big bad humans? You are being ridiculous, Floss."

Ned piped up, "And you are being a cow, Prudence. Just you leave Floss alone. Have you any idea how much your words are hurting her? You are being extremely thoughtless. You should be thinking yourself lucky that you still have Daisy."

"Calling me a cow is hardly an insult, Ned. Has it escaped your refined notice that I am one?"

Ned seemed to ignore her as he turned to look at Floss. "Don't take any notice of Prudence, Floss. Your calf is a very fine animal, and not all humans are bad. Someone will recognise your son's potential, and he will be okay. I am sure that he will be okay."

But Floss could not be sure that her son wasn't going to end up as food for humans, and although she listened to Ned's comforting words, they didn't help her to feel any better, and they did nothing to take away the sickness that lay deep in the pit of her tummy. She turned around and gazed sadly at the flattened straw where her baby had slept the night before, and she touched the patch with her nose, filling her nostrils with his scent. She could sense his little mouth on her udder, and she looked beneath herself, half expecting him to be there, but the feeling was just a memory, and her wasted milk dripped to the floor. Again and again, she cried out her pain for all to hear, and when she had no tears left, her heart began to thump in her chest like a hammer beating down on a nail. *Thump, thump, thump,* as if it was trying to escape her body. And then the whole barn started spinning around her head. Faster and faster, it went, like a merry-go-round. She began feeling sick, and then, as a dark fog cloaked her consciousness, her knees buckled, and she went crashing to the floor.

The trauma had been so terrible that Floss did not wake for two whole days. When she did, Ned's head was hanging over the partition rail, gazing down on her. She imagined that he had been there the whole time that she had been out of it. He was always there to look out for her.

"How is she?" some of the others cried.

"She has just opened her eyes."

Floss lifted her head from the straw and tried to focus on her friend. She felt light-headed and weird, like she'd just had a bad dream. Maybe that's all it had been then, a bad dream, and now that she was awake, if she turned around, her baby would be there, waiting for his breakfast. She dared herself to take a look over her shoulder, but there was just a large and very empty space behind her. It had not been dream; it had been real life, her life, which was now in ruins. Breathing a heavy sigh, she let her head flop back onto the straw, and then she willed herself never to wake up again, so that the pain would go away.

Ned cried out to her. "Floss, please do not do this to yourself. I love you too much to let you throw away your life. You haven't eaten for two days now, and if you carry on, then ..."

"Go away and leave me alone. I want to die whilst I can still see him clear in my mind."

"I will not let you die," Ned replied, all the while thinking of how he could give her the will to live again. "Please listen to me, Floss. You do trust me, don't you?"

Floss opened an ear. Of course she trusted Ned.

"Of course I trust you, Ned, but there is nothing that you can do to help me. I am sorry, but I just want you to leave me alone. I don't want to live without him, and if you love me, then you will understand that."

"Surely you are not just going to give in to them."

The comment made Floss lift her head just a little.

"What do you mean 'give in to them'? They have taken my son, Ned. I have nothing left to give in to."

"I mean are you going to give up on your son's life, Floss? Where there's a will there's usually a way; even for animals, this is true. And, you are no ordinary cow, Floss. You are a very special cow, so special that I really believe you can go out there into the big world and find him."

"But I am not special, Ned. I'm just a cow, an ordinary Highland cow."

"You're not just any ordinary Highland cow," Ned replied. "You are Floss, and remember that I watched you being born. I saw every second of how you fought to come into this world in the first place, and then how much you suffered when you lost your mum. But you fought hard for your life, Floss, and you made it. Despite the odds being stacked against you, you made it, and you even had a baby son of your very own. Was it all for nothing then? I do not think so. I do not for one moment think so. You are a survivor, and as your son has your blood, he will be a survivor too. Now get up and eat your dinner. It will give you the strength that you need to get out there and rescue him."

"Do you really think that I could do that, Ned? Rescue him, I mean."

"I wouldn't say so if I didn't think so."

And so Floss decided that she must fight for the son that she loved so much. Summoning every bit of strength that she could find in her weak body, she uncurled her hooves from beneath her and struggled unsteadily to her feet. Ned immediately nodded towards the corner of her stall.

"Your hay is over there. You must try to eat some of it."

Floss looked at the hay. She didn't feel like eating.

"Please, Floss, just try a little bit."

And so, she stumbled falteringly over to the rack and forced a few strands of hay into her mouth. It tasted bitter, almost like poison, but after she had swallowed the first mouthful, she pulled out another. And then, with each and every forced swallow, her strength began to return. As it did, there came with it determination – the determination that she would indeed find her son. The very first chance those humans gave her to escape, the very first one, she would be on her way.

CHAPTER THREE

As he walked through the pasture, looking towards the big old barn that he had played in as a child, Terry Devlin found it difficult to hide his feelings of sadness, but he knew that he must do so now, because his two children were at his side and he didn't want them to see his pain.

Just days earlier, his father had taken ill and been rushed into hospital. The doctors there had taken the family to one side, explaining that it had been a heart attack, probably brought on by the stress of running the farm. There had followed a family discussion, and the outcome had been that the farm had to go. It had been a painful decision, but Terry consoled himself with the thought that at least the money would buy his parents a lovely retirement cottage by the sea. This was something that his father had always promised his mother. And now the farm – a lifetime's work, love, and achievement – was to be broken up and auctioned off to the highest bidder.

And here he was, preparing to deal with the worst task of all: the sale of his father's beloved animals. He looked down at the list in his hand. There was a small herd of prized Highland cattle, six pot-bellied pigs, a hundred or so sheep, one old goat, and an old donkey called Ned. Terry stared at the donkey's name on his sheet of paper now, smiling as he remembered the animal with fondness. When he was a little boy, Ned had taught him how to ride, and though Terry had of course had the odd fall, the donkey had always looked after him well. Wondering about the donkey's age, he began to add up the years on his fingers. How the time had flown! Ned must be at least forty. Well, the little old boy would not be going to the auction, not after all the years of loyal service that he had given to two generations of the family. In fact, it had already been decided that Ned and the goat would be coming to live with Terry, as pets for his identical twin girls, Isha and Niamh, who giggled excitedly as they followed him into the barn.

The ears of the animals soon picked up the girls' lively chatter and laughter. They didn't see children often.

"I wonder why we're having this pleasure," Ned said, looking over his gate as the trio approached.

"I don't know," said Gertie. "But they seem to be heading straight for you."

Ned watched the twins approach his gate where the slightly taller of the two began leaping up and down calling his name. He could see that she was terribly excited. The man who had come into the barn with them came over then, seemingly to calm his children down.

"Hey cool it, Isha," he said. "Don't frighten the life from him before we get him home."

Ned stared at the man with the two little girls thinking that he had seen him somewhere before, and then it came to him. This was the small boy who used to ride him years ago. Terry was his name. He looked so different now, all grown up, but the green eyes and slightly crooked smile were the same. But what was it he had just said? *Get him home? What was that supposed to mean?* A worried feeling came to his gut as he thought about the words, and then he realised that there was only one conclusion: Floss's son would not be the only one to leave. Ned looked past the trio and down the aisle of the barn that he loved so much and then he sighed sadly, feeling that his heart would break in two. This had been his home for almost twenty years now, and all his very good friends were here. Why did humans have to go and spoil it?

Isha let go of the gate and grabbed her father by the hand. "Can we ride him now, Daddy?" she shouted, urgently tugging the hand that held hers. "Please, Daddy, please." Her sister joined in with the begging.

"Isha, Niamh, patience please, girls," said Terry, removing his fingers from Isha's grasp. "I have a lot to do today, and Ned will need time to settle at his new home before there's any talk of riding."

He reached his hand out and gave Ned's nose an affectionate rub. "Hello, old boy," he said. "Do you remember me? You and Gertie are coming to live with us. We'll leave later today. I only wish I had room for all of you, but unfortunately, I don't. I hate the thought of sending any of you to market, but I don't really have a choice."

He turned away from Ned then to look at his children. "Come on, girls. Help me tidy up the rest of the yard for your granddad, and then we'll come back and get Ned and Gertie loaded into the trailer."

Now apparently over their earlier excitement, the girls seemed calmer and more compliant. "Okay, Daddy," they replied, and they each grabbed one of his hands.

The three of them then began making their way down the aisle, arms swinging as they walked.

In the wake of the humans visit, the animals were left in worried turmoil. They had all heard of this place called "the market" – of course they had – but, as many of them had been born on the farm, they had believed it to be a fantasy place, something their parents had made up when they were small. The market was the place where their parents threatened to send them if they did not behave; nothing more than that.

Floss turned her head to look at Ned. She could see that the donkey had tears in his eyes.

"I don't think I can take any more of this," she sobbed. "They've taken away my son, and now they're going to take you from me too."

Ned hung his head. "Oh, Floss," he said. "I am an old donkey, and I truly thought that I would be living my days out here with you and the others."

"I thought so too. It looks like Terry is going to look after you, though. You and Gertie are going to live with him and the children. That has to be good news."

"Yes, I guess that I should be happy about that, but it seems little consolation. At the moment, all I can think about is how much I am going to miss you. You will always be my gorgeous red-headed girl."

"Oh, Ned," Floss replied, her red-rimmed eyes overflowing. "How am I ever going to cope without you?"

"You have to, Floss," Ned said in a serious voice. Clearly he was trying to be strong for her. "When they take you to market, it will probably give you the best chance you will ever get to escape. It is a hectic place, and humans don't always watch everything that is happening. Animals get loose all the time."

"How do you know?"

"I can't believe that I never told you this, but Joe Devlin bought me from a market, though it was many years ago."

Floss's head lifted. "No, you didn't ever tell me that. What was it like?"

"Oh, it wasn't that bad," he said. "Quite noisy, but nothing to worry too much about."

Floss looked at him quizzically, but he averted his eyes, and she felt sure that he was hiding something really awful from her. She could have questioned him further, but that would have made him uncomfortable, and so she chose not to.

"I feel so very afraid of what the future holds, Ned."

"What are you afraid of, Floss?"

Floss took a moment before answering. "I am afraid that if I do escape, I will not be able to cope on my own. And yet, I am also afraid that I will not be able to live with myself if I don't try to escape and find my son."

Ned smiled at her. "Fear isn't always a bad thing. Being afraid will help you to make the right decisions. It will keep you on your toes, and it will help you to stay alive. It's okay to be afraid sometimes, you know. I get afraid."

"You, afraid?" She had never seen him afraid of anything.

Just then, Gertie shouted to them. "Ned! Floss! They're on their way back."

Floss swallowed hard and looked fearfully towards the barn doors. To her horror, she saw that they had swung open and this time the children had head collars in their hands.

Terry made his way to Gertie's stall first and held his hand out to Niamh, the smaller of the twin girls, who passed him a small candy-striped head collar.

"Come here, Gertie. Come here, sweetheart," he said, speaking softly as he opened the goat's gate. "I borrowed this from the owner of a little Welsh mountain pony that lives next door. Let's see if it fits you well enough to get you into the trailer."

The head collar fit Gertie perfectly, and he fastened the brass buckle and offered the lead rope to Niamh. "Can you take Gertie out of the barn for me whilst I get Ned?" he said.

Floss watched the proceedings from her stall. It seemed as if the child did not want to lead Gertie as she was looking at the rope as if it had set on fire. Maybe the two girls both wanted a donkey? Her father pushed the rope at Niamh again and this time she took it.

"Hey," Gertie said butting the little girl gently. "You don't need to hold me that tight."

Niamh began to laugh. "Did you see that, Dad?" she said with a giggle. "She is playing. Oh, she really is quite sweet."

Niamh led Gertie from her stall, and as they made their way down the aisle, Floss turned to her most beloved friend, Ned. "I guess we ha._ to say goodbye then," she said, and she lifted her head above the dividing rail so that she could touch Ned's nose.

"Time has suddenly become so short," Ned said, his voice breaking. "But, before they take me from you, I want you to remember something for me. I want you to remember it forever. Remember that you will always be in my thoughts, Floss. Whilst there is breath in my body, I will be thinking about you. I want you to hold onto that thought, because it means that you will never be truly alone. I know that a wonderful and happy place awaits you, so you must not give up looking for it. Treat the animals you meet well, and judge all humans carefully. Not all humans are bad, and not all animals are good. Use your instinct. It will keep you safe."

Floss listened to his every word carefully, knowing how wise he was, but she wasn't entirely sure what instinct was; she certainly didn't think that she had any of it.

"It's hard to imagine my life without you. I need you, Ned. I can't do this thing alone."

"Yes, you can, Floss, and you must. You will always be in my heart, and so the humans cannot really part us – not ever. If it comes to the point that you are at your darkest or loneliest, always remember that, my Floss. I will always love you, and I will never forget you."

And then, they heard the sound of the gate clanging. Terry was already in Ned's stall.

"You two saying goodbye?" he said with a laugh as he came up to the donkey and gently curled his hand over his nose. "Come on then, my old friend. Let's get this head collar on you. It's time to go to your new home."

A gentle pull on the lead rope, and Ned followed Terry slowly from the stall. As they passed Floss, he paused for a second.

"Goodbye, Floss."

Floss could not speak, as her tears were choking her, and she stood with her head over her gate, watching Ned's every step until he reached the doors. And then, as the doors closed behind him, she found her voice, and she cried out his name, listening to his familiar hee-haw until it faded away. She was never going to see Ned ever again – she knew that – but she had the strangest feeling that his wisdom and his love were going to stay with her forever.

CHAPTER FOUR

Three days later, it was everyone else's turn to leave the barn. The animals were to be transported from Reading, Berkshire, to the auctions at Thirsk, North Yorkshire, which was more than 250 miles away.

The transport men soon had them queued up for loading onto a large cattle truck. It was the biggest truck that Floss had ever seen, and as she made her way up the ramp and into the gloomy interior, she wondered if she would ever see daylight again. As it juddered forward, she was thrown sideways against the partition that separated her from some of the other animals, and it caused her to yell out.

"You'll get the hang of it, Floss." The reassuring words came from Bess, a much older cow. She had been loaded before Floss and was a few spaces away from her. "Spread your legs and dig your hooves in. That way, when the truck stops or takes a tight turn, you will be able to balance yourself."

"Thank you, Bess," Floss called out. And then, as the truck rounded a bend, she tried digging her hooves into the rubber flooring, but it wasn't as easy as Bess had made it sound. There just wasn't enough room for her to spread her legs out, and once again, she was thrown sideways and then forward, causing her to hit her head on the side of the truck.

Prudence had been given the compartment next to Floss for the journey. The two cows had not spoken to each other since the day that Floss's son had been taken.

"Floss," Prudence whispered, swallowing hard. "Can I talk to you?"

Floss threw her a sideways glance. Was that cow actually trying to talk to her?

"I am not sure that you have anything to say that I want to listen to," Floss said.

"Well, I am going to say it anyway," Prudence replied. "I don't know why I said those things to you, and it is truly awful that they took your son. No animal should ever have their baby taken away, girl or boy."

"His name is Boris," Floss replied. "I chose the name just before they took him away."

"That's a great name. Are you really going to escape and try to rescue him, Floss?"

At that moment Floss caught sight of little Daisy peering from beneath her mother's tummy. She smiled at the little calf. Prudence was so lucky to still have her daughter. And then a thought came to her. It was not Prudence or Daisy's fault that her son had been taken. With that truth now in her mind, she let go of any bitterness she had held for Prudence. She did not want to hold a grudge especially as she might never see Prudence after they got to market. Besides, this overture of conversation was Prudence's way of apologising; Floss knew her well enough to know that.

"Yes, I am going to rescue my son," Floss replied. "As soon as I get a chance, I will be off and away."

"Well, I hope that you find him safe and well. I truly do hope that, and I think that you are very brave, Floss, very brave indeed," Prudence said.

At midday, the cows were still on the road. They had been travelling for over three hours, and the summer sun was high, beating down mercilessly on the metal roof above their heads and sending the temperature inside the truck soaring. The air had long since grown stale, and in a desperate attempt to ward off the hundreds of flies that were swarming around, Floss swished her tail angrily. They left her for just a second, but then they were back, clustering around her face. When she cast a glance at Prudence, she could see that her friend was having similar problems.

"I think I'm going to be sick," Prudence groaned as she desperately tried to blink away the three flies that were feeding from the corner of her left eye. "This is hell."

"I know it is," Floss replied, feeling thankful that cows couldn't vomit. A truck full of cow poo, with Prudence's sick on top, would have made matters a whole lot worse – that is, if they could be any worse.

It was about a half-hour later when the truck, which had been travelling level and straight for quite some time, suddenly swayed slightly to the left. Seconds later, it lurched to a standstill so violently that it sent the animals off their balance. It was the first time the truck had stopped in several hours.

Floss's stomachs did somersaults, and after she had steadied herself, she threw Prudence an apprehensive look.

"Have we arrived at the market?"

Prudence shrugged. "I do not know."

Floss lifted her head and tried to catch Bess's attention. Bess was the one most likely to know.

"Bess, can you hear me?"

Bess turned her head. "Yes, I can," she replied.

"Are we at the market?"

"I very much doubt it."

"How do you know?"

"Because if we were at the market, our driver would turn off the engine, but as he hasn't, we are probably not there yet. If you keep very still, Floss, you will be able to feel the vibrations running along the trailer floor and up through your feet."

Floss nodded as she felt the vibrations that Bess had described, and then she let herself relax a little. But the brief respite was soon interrupted by a very strange sound that started up all of a sudden. *Beep, beep, beep,* in rapid succession. Floss had never heard anything quite like it, and it sent a shiver down her long spine.

"Wh-wh-what's that?"

The sound of a giggle broke through the noise. It was Bess.

"It's nothing to worry about," she said. "Worry when you get to market but not before."

"But what on earth is that sound?"

"I believe it is a pelican crossing, and it explains why we have stopped."

Floss screwed up her face. "I didn't think we had pelicans in this country."

Bess laughed out loud. "It's not actually a pelican," she said. "Though why on earth the humans call it a pelican, I do not know."

"So what is it if it isn't a bird?"

"The noise is coming from a pair of poles, each with three lights mounted on it. When humans want to know if it is safe to cross a road, they sometimes need help, and so a little green man flashes to tell people who are walking that they can go in front of the cars. I've never understood it myself, but that's what they do."

"A green man!" exclaimed Floss, hurrying to put her eye to the air vent. She had never seen a green man before. "I can't see him."

"What?" Bess said, and then she started giggling again. "You are a daft cow, Floss. It's not a real man. I cannot believe that you actually thought you were going to see a green human."

"But you said that a green man flashes."

"It's a light, Floss, a little green light in the shape of a man walking. It tells the people that they can walk across the road."

There came a brief silence as Floss gathered her thoughts on the matter. "So, can you tell me some more about humans, Bess? You seem to know quite a lot, and it may help when I escape."

"What do you want to know?"

"Anything … everything," Floss replied.

Bess chuckled. "Hmm, let me think," she said. "Okay, there are two vital things that you must know. Are you listening too, Prudence?"

"Yes, she is listening. Go on. Go on."

"Most humans sleep when it is dark, and when it is cold, they have to light fires in their homes."

"They light fires? Why would they do something as stupid as that?"

"They have to light fires to keep themselves warm."

Floss frowned. *How strange.* Her hairy coat had always kept her nice and cosy, especially inside the barn. "I don't understand," she said. "Why can't they keep themselves warm like we do?"

"Are you ready for this?" Bess said through fits of laughter. "They can't keep themselves warm because they are bald. Can you imagine that? They have no hair."

"No hair!" Floss exclaimed. She had thought that all creatures had hair, except for birds of course, but they had feathers.

"No hair!" Bess repeated, almost choking herself with laughter. "They are as bald as coots under those pieces of fabric that they wrap around themselves. Well, that is, apart from the silly long bits they manage to produce on their heads, and some of them can't even manage to grow that."

Floss managed to laugh. There was an awful lot of bird talk going on at the moment. What with pelicans and coots, Bess had certainly lightened the mood. So humans were bald and needed fires to keep warm and flashing green men to tell them when to cross a road. How weak they seemed, needing these strange things. And then her mood became more serious. But if they were so weak, how were they able to control the lives and destinies of innocent creatures? Why was that? And what had they done with her poor innocent little calf? Was he still alive? Was he as hungry and thirsty as she was now? Was he missing her as much as she was missing him?

It was a further hour of mainly winding roads before the they came to a standstill again; but this time there was no engine noise, and no vibrations either. There also seemed to be a lot of activity going on outside the truck. Floss lifted her nose into the air. It had a strange and pungent smell to it, and it wasn't coming from inside. She took a deep breath, and then her eyes widened with terror. The smell was the smell of fear – the fear of many animals. Terrible noises began to fill her ears, cows calling out for their calves, lambs bleating for their missing mothers, and horses neighing at the tops of their voices, listening for a reply from friends that had been left far behind. Floss's gut plunged, and her heart pounded against her ribcage. This time, she did not need to ask Bess whether they had arrived at the market.

Above the sound of the animals, a man's voice was shouting, louder than any human voice that Floss had ever heard before. She felt Prudence nudge her, and turned her head to see that her friend was shaking.

"I am scared, Floss," Prudence said.

"You are not the only one," Floss replied. "My legs are like jelly. But we must be strong, Pru. We all have to be strong. We must stand up to them and show them just how brave we are. We must not give them the satisfaction of knowing that we are afraid."

"But it is difficult pretending to be brave when your insides are quaking."

"I know it is, Pru, but we can do this. We have to do this."

Floss lifted her head then so that she could see Bess. "Why is that man shouting numbers out so loudly, Bess?"

"The numbers are amounts of money. The humans take a look at you, and then they decide how much they want to pay for you. Whoever is willing to pay the most gets you. Money makes humans happy, and the more of it that they have, the happier they seem to be. It controls everything they do."

Floss looked puzzled. "Does it grow like grass and hay? Does it taste nice?"

Bess giggled. "Even when we are in the thick of it, you still make me laugh, Floss. I think most humans wish it would grow from trees, but it doesn't; and, no, you can't eat it. Some of it is made of paper, and some of it is made of metal. Didn't you ever hear coins jingling about in Joe's pockets?"

Floss thought about it for a moment, but the only jingling she had ever heard was from the bunch of keys that told her that dinner was on its way.

"What good is money if they can't eat it?"

"Beats me," Bess replied.

"I wonder if the humans will want to buy me with their money. Do you think that they will, Bess?"

"I don't think you need to worry, Floss. You and Pru are healthy young cows, and someone will pay good money for both of you. It is older cows like me who need to be fearful. Who is going to want me other than the burger man?"

Floss shot Bess a look of concern but did not get chance to respond, as the dreaded sound of metal grating against metal had come to her ears. A second later, daylight began to appear at the top of the ramp. As it came down, Floss turned her head towards the light.

"Come on then! Come on then!" said a rough human voice.

Struck rigid with fear, Floss squinted at the man whose dark outline was in silhouette against the brilliant sunlight. He was at the foot of the ramp, and she knew that he was shouting at her. She now wished that she hadn't been the last to be loaded, as this made her the first to have to get off.

"Come on. I haven't got all day."

This time, the man's voice was more insistent, and Floss leaned forward. She then placed a shaky front hoof at the top of the ramp, but when it moved and creaked under her weight, she quickly pulled it inside again.

"I can't go down. I simply can't do it."

She heard Bess call out to her then. "You'll have to go down, Floss. One way or another, they will make you, so you may as well go down now."

Floss swayed back and forth, trying to persuade herself to go down the ramp, and then, in panic, she launched herself into the air, missing the ramp entirely and landing with a clatter on stony ground. The shock went right into her feet, and by the time she had recovered, Prudence, Daisy, and Bess were already off the truck as well.

"That was awful," Floss said, trembling. "Are you okay, Pru? Bess? Is Daisy okay, Pru?"

"No, I do not think that I am okay," Prudence replied. "What if they take Daisy away from me? I just don't think that I can bear it."

Floss gave Prudence a solemn look, and then she cast her eyes down to the little calf who had tucked herself as far under her mother's belly as she could. But for the separate pair of eyes, they could have been just one cow. She felt sorry for both of them.

"I don't think that they will take her away from you, Pru," Floss said, trying to sound convincing. "After all, she is a girl calf, and they will know that she needs you."

Moments later, all seven cows were off the truck and a man hurried over and hung a rope around each of their necks. A numbered plate was attached to each rope. Floss stared down at the irritating foreign object and shook herself to see if she could make it fall off.

"What's this?" she asked Bess.

"That is your number. You do not have a name when you go into the arena; you are just a number to them in there, not a life, just a number."

Floss took in a deep breath. She wasn't sure that she wanted to know what her number was, but then curiosity got the better of her.

"What is my number, Bess?"

"455. Your number is 455."

"455!" Floss said. It didn't even sound special.

"Come on, come on."

Floss turned her head. Two men had come up behind and were driving them towards a small pen. As they entered it one by one, it seemed that there wasn't enough room for them all, and Floss found herself forced against the barriers. It had been hours since she'd had a drink of water, and her mouth felt like sandpaper and tasted stagnant. There were other pens around, and the animals in them were disappearing into a large barn. None were returning.

Floss gulped as two men came up to the barriers. It seemed that they were looking straight at her.

"Number 455. Come on, let's have it."

"They are coming for me," Floss cried out. "Oh, Prudence … Bess! Whatever is going to happen to us?"

Giving her two friends a lingering look, Floss soon felt a cane at the rear of her hocks.

Moments later, she was out of the pen and trotting down a corridor of metal mesh. And then, she was inside the barn. It was gloomy compared to the bright sunlight that she had left behind her, and for a few seconds, she remained rooted to the spot, trying to adjust her eyes so that she could see through the billow of dust that her hooves had created. It was then that she saw their faces. There were hundreds of them, and they had formed a ring around her. They were pushing and shoving at each other to get closer, and their eyes seemed to be eating into her, as if she was already on their dinner plates. Nervously, she spun around on her haunches, but their faces were everywhere, and their mouths all seemed to be talking at once. The loudness of their voices filled her head with confusion, and her heart thumped so hard that she felt sure that it would burst out of her body at any moment. So this was the place where her fate would be decided, the place where they had probably taken her son.

Her poor son! As she thought of him and how afraid he must have been, she began to get angry, and she snorted. It was time to show these humans just what Highland cows were all about. They were good and proud mothers, and this good mother was about to show them just what she thought of them. The fear left her then, as she headed towards the crowd and she galloped the circumference of the arena twice, sending dust up into their faces. She then returned to the centre and began to scrape her hoof in the dry earth. A second later, she charged towards a section of the crowd, and as she tossed her head, the humans fell back away from her. A collective murmur resonated through them.

"Come on you cowards," she said with a deep moo, opening her eyes wide and shaking her horns as if she could throw them from her head like spears. "I can stare too. Which one of you would like to make my day? Come on, don't be shy. Who would like to go first?"

"Feisty this one," the auctioneer called out. "So, come on, lads, how much you gonna give for her? It's a nice four-year-old, this. I have 300 pounds; do I see more? Fred, is that you bidding? Yes; 350. Do I see ten more? Yes; 360. Do I see ten more? Thank you; that's 370 now. Come on, take a good look at her. She's worth more than that. Fred, I thought you were after all of these Highlands today, but you'll not get this one for that. Come on, I'm giving her away. Thank you. That's 400 then. Yes; that's more like it. Any higher?"

Who was going to buy her? When was she going to make her escape? The thoughts whizzed through Floss's mind almost as fast as her hooves beat a gallop around the ring. The hammer fell at 450 pounds.

"Sold to Fred. Nice cow, that, Fred; a bit crazy, but nice."

The shouting ceased, and Floss returned to the centre of the ring, with her nostrils flared out wide and her hot sides heaving. What was going to happen now? They seemed to have lost interest in her. All except one, that is. A thin, long-haired youth, dressed in manure-stained overalls that looked as if they had once been blue, now made his way towards her. When he reached her, he poked her in the ribs with the long thin cattle prod he was carrying.

Floss glowered at him. "I wouldn't do that again if I were you!"

The youth gave her a blank expression, and then he prodded her again.

Floss shook her head at him. There would be no more prodding; not from his side, anyway. Slowly and determinedly, she began to march towards him.

Casting a glance at his pathetic stick, she shook her impressive horns. "I think I may have the advantage," she said. "Coming – ready or not."

The youth's jaw dropped, and his eyes opened so wide that Floss could see the whites against his dirty face. He took two steps backwards, looked to either side, and then cast a glance over his shoulder. It seemed to Floss that he was assessing whether he could reach the safety of the barriers in time. She could fair read his mind. "It's too far," she said with a loud moo.

Wow! Floss had never seen a human run so fast before, but then she considered that he had probably never been chased by a cow with horns like hers. To her dismay, he made it to the fence just in time, and then he threw himself over it and into the crowd. Three burly and grumpy farmers hoisted him roughly to his feet.

The youth brushed off his shabby overalls, and then looked towards the auctioneer, who was banging his hammer as if trying to ram in a stubborn nail.

"Get back in that ring, do you hear me?" the auctioneer stormed. "You need to sort out that cow."

Ripping off his overalls off, the youth threw the rags into the ring. "Sort the cow out yourself," he said.

"You're fired."

"Am I bothered? I mean, do I look like I am really bothered?"

Floss snorted her satisfaction at the uproar that she had created, and then she turned around. Two different men, both in white coats, had just jumped into the arena. She eyed them up. They had split up so that one was on each side of her. They were coming slowly towards her, trying to corner her. She glanced from one to the other, wondering which way to turn, and then from the corner of her left eye, she noticed that daylight had suddenly come into the barn. Doors on the other side of the arena had been opened. She spun away from the men and headed for the light.

Moments later, she was in the fresh air again, wandering along another corridor of metal-mesh fencing. It guided her into another pen, slightly larger than the one she had left. A blonde Highland cow was at the far side of it.

"Hello," said the cow. "I am Sally, and I am really pleased to see you in here. I think that we must have been bought by the same person."

"I am Floss," Floss replied. "I hope that person buys my friends too."

"So you came with friends. You are really lucky to have friends. I used to have a friend. We shared a field, but she died a while back, and I have been on my own ever since. That's probably why I was sent here."

"What is it like being alone?"

"It is not very nice, and that is why I am so pleased to have you."

"You had better not get too used to it because I won't be around for too long."

Sally lifted her head. "Why? Where are you going?"

"I don't really know."

Sally frowned. "You don't really know? I don't understand," she said.

"I am going wherever my journey takes me. The humans took my son, and I am going out into the big world to find him."

Sally's eyes saddened. "They took mine away too," she said. "And I cried many nights for him; so much, in fact, that I ran out of tears. But there is nothing that you or I can do about it. The humans have the power, and that's the way it is."

"Well, it shouldn't be the way, and I am going to do something about it."

"Hmm, good luck with that," Sally replied, her face grim. But she brightened as she looked towards the barn. "Hey, is this one of your friends? She is looking very pleased to see you."

Floss turned her head, and her eyes lit up like fireworks when she saw Prudence coming down the meshed corridor. But then she frowned. Where was Daisy? She could not see Daisy. And then she remembered how often they had been so close together that they had looked like one cow. She counted the legs coming towards her. No cow had eight of them.

"Prudence," she shouted, hurrying towards her friend. "And little Daisy too! This is good. Do you know what has happened to Bess and the others?"

"I think we are all going to be together again. The man who bought us had just started bidding for Bess as we left."

Fred Bulimer was a cow man. He had always been a cow man. Where there were cows there was money, and as he strode towards the holding pen, he was feeling pretty chuffed. The sale had been a great success, and he had managed to buy all the animals that he wanted.

The four-year-old red haired cow was first to come under his scrutiny. *Nice cow, that,* he thought to himself. She was the best of all of them, and she would breed him some good calves. His gaze then fell on the oldest cow, obviously well past her prime, as her ragged coat and tired eyes showed. What had he been thinking of bidding for that one? He had been trying to run one of his enemies up when the bidding had started, but then the bid had been dropped right on his own toes. *Oh well,* he thought. The others more than made up for the mistake, and maybe the old girl could still give him a calf or two.

He left the pen, heading for the far side of the auction field where he had parked his dilapidated pickup truck, and what a sorry sight that was. It had not seen a service in years, and there was more rust on it than paintwork. The trailer behind it was in an even worse state, with animal dung inches thick hanging from every crevice. He didn't really care though. As long as it could carry cows, he didn't intend spending any time on it. Time was money.

"There's more grass growing out of the filth in that trailer than there is in your field, Fred." The voice, which came from behind him, soon turned into a laugh. "I got you with that last cow, didn't I? It serves you right, trying to run me up like that."

Fred did not turn around. He knew the voice all too well. It was Sam Smith, his enemy at the auctions. Ignoring the other man, Fred swung the door of his pickup open and climbed inside. He cast a quick glance in his rear-view mirror. Smithy, as Fred called Sam, was walking away. Good! Fred didn't want to look at the other man's miserable face any longer than he had to.

As Fred turned the ignition key, the engine responded with the usual splutter and sluggish groan, and then it started. He smiled and patted the grimy steering wheel. No matter how badly he treated the vehicle, it had never let him down.

The trip to Fred's farm in Goole was only forty miles or so from Thirsk and it was just an hour before Fred turned off the road and onto the track to his farm. The ride became very bumpy then, so bumpy that the cows were thrown all over the place. Fred could hear them through his open window crashing about and mooing loudly as he struggled with the steering, doing his best to manoeuvre around the deep craters, but there were so many of them that he was finding it impossible. The rear wheel of his pickup struck a particularly huge lump of dried earth, throwing him violently from his seat. As Fred's head hit the roof of his pickup, his feet came off the control pedals, and the engine stalled. He groaned loudly as he turned the ignition key, expecting the engine to start, but nothing happened, not even a splutter.

Fred opened his door and climbed out. Pacing to the front of the pickup, he lifted the bonnet and stared into the dark abyss of the engine, which had not seen a service in many years. Things did not look good. There was a distinct whiff of burning oil, and black stuff seemed to have leaked out everywhere. His fingers went to the toupee on his head, and he began to scratch at it. This was not going to be a quick one to fix. In the meantime, he had seven cows to get to their field, which was a few hundred yards away. He began to work out who owed him a favour that he could call in. John sprang to mind, and a moment later, Fred was dialling John's number on his mobile phone.

"John, mate. How are you?"

"Fine, Fred, and you?"

"Well, not great at the moment. I have just brought some Highland cows from the auction in Thirsk, and the truck has let me down. I am stuck on the track, a few hundred yards from the field, and the cows are in the trailer behind me. I don't suppose you could come and give me a hand, could you, John? I would be very grateful."

"Erm …"

"It really is quite an emergency, and there's no one else I can ask."

"Oh, okay, Fred. I may be a while, though. I have just started feeding my herd, but I'll be wi' ya as soon as I can."

"Thank you, John," Fred said.

Fred tried to be patient whilst he waited for his friend to arrive. It took John a good hour to get there, but he made it at last, just as Fred had known he would. He and John's dad had been good friends, and John had always been very trustworthy as a boy. He found himself wondering how many years he had known him, *twenty years or more*, he thought. He had let the lad help out on his farm whenever he had wanted. In fact, Fred considered that a lot of John's knowledge of cattle now was down to the knowledge he had shared with him. This favour he had called in, well John was a good man who would remember such matters.

"Well then, now," John said, winding his window down as he pulled up alongside Fred and his stricken vehicle. "The old pickup's finally given up on you then!"

"Never thought it'd let me down like this," Fred said.

"Well, if you spend all your money on cows and not much on looking after everything else, what do you expect?"

"Hey, I don't need a lecture! I can get one of those from the wife."

John chuckled. Fred's grumpy wife had given them both a good dressing-down many a time. "Yeah, I suppose you can," he said, laughing. "I'll ring her later, shall I, and tell her all about it?"

"You jest, John. You jest," Fred said, also laughing. "Not even you would do that to me."

John laughed again. "So, how many cows have you got in there?"

"Six cows and a calf."

"Are they going into the near field?"

Fred nodded.

"I've brought these to help us herd them through the gate."

Fred watched John as he leaned into the open back of his truck and pulled out two stout wooden canes. He reached his hand out to take one of them. Then he made his way to the ramp of the trailer and began lowering it.

"Mmm," John said, coming up behind Fred and taking a peek. "They look like a nice lot, Fred."

"They are, John, they are," Fred said nodding. "I did well and they haven't been a bit of trouble."

He laid the ramp on the ground and stared at the first cow; the red haired Highland. "Come on then!" he yelled. "Down you come. Come on, come on."

From the back of the trailer, Floss stared out at the two men she now knew as John and Fred. Her focus then turned to her surroundings. Could she flee from these men right now, and if she did, where would she go? She looked at the track. It was between open fields and countryside, but drainage dikes lay to either side of it, and the sides were way too steep for her to descend. Even if she did get to the bottom, she would probably get stuck in the water down there, unable to ascend the other side, and that would be no good at all. There had to be a better option. Whilst she was thinking on this, John shouted at her again.

"Come on." He rattled the side of the trailer with his cane.

Knowing that she had no choice, Floss came down the ramp, and the others followed her.

Soon they were huddled together in tight group spanning the width of the track. John and Fred were behind them waving their canes, shouting all the while.

Floss turned her head towards the men and gave them an ugly scowl. She was tiring of these two humans and their commands to "get on". Prudence was next to her, and Floss looked over at her friend.

"This is it, Pru. I've had enough. I am going to escape."

Prudence looked worried, and Floss realised that escaping had not been mentioned for quite some time. Maybe Prudence had been hoping that she had forgotten all about it – but she hadn't.

"Right now?" Prudence asked, chewing the side of her mouth nervously. "But you won't be able to get across the ditches, and the men are right behind us, so you can't go that way."

"Then I will make a run for the trees up ahead," Floss said.

"But there's a house behind the trees, and houses mean humans."

"Well, it is the only way that I can go."

"But they will go after you."

"Then I will have to run faster than they do."

"But they will get in their truck, and it will be quicker, far quicker than your short legs."

"Then I will have to use my head."

Floss spoke with great determination and for a moment Prudence was silent. Floss guessed that her friend had finally acknowledged that she would not change her mind on the matter. Prudence's face then took on a thoughtful look as if she was considering saying something of great importance.

"You have something more to say, Prudence?"

"Yes, yes I do. You really are quite some cow, Floss. I only wish that I could be half the cow that you are. It was so brave of you to stand up to the humans when they took Boris and well..." She paused before continuing. "Well, I wondered if I could help you to escape."

Floss tripped and almost fell down the ditch, the shock was so great. Was this the same moaning and selfish Prudence that she had known all her life, or had some alien cow taken over her mind? For a moment, Floss was struck completely dumb.

It was at that moment that Bess came on the other side of Floss and filled the silence.

"What are you two whispering about?" Bess said.

Floss turned her head. "I am going to escape. Prudence is going to help me."

"Prudence is going to help you!" Bess raised an eyebrow.

"That's what she said."

Bess looked at Prudence and as Floss watched the expressions on both their faces, she got the impression that the older cow was expecting Prudence to back down, to retract her offer. She wondered herself, for a moment, whether it would come, but Prudence's expression did not change. The offer was genuine then. She was glad about that as she needed all the help she could get.

Bess's face suddenly softened and when she smiled at Prudence, Floss knew then that the two of them had made their peace with each other.

"Well good for you, Prudence," Bess said. "So, do you have a plan, ladies?"

Plan? What plan? Did she need one? Wasn't the plan simply to run for it?

"I am just going to run for those trees," Floss said.

"No, that's no good," Bess said. "They will come after you."

"That's what I said," muttered Prudence.

"I have an idea that may give you more time," Bess said. "My legs are too old to do it, but yours aren't, Prudence. If you make a run for it in the opposite direction to Floss, it will distract the men. They will then come after you and will not notice Floss slipping away."

Floss began nodding her head. "That's a good plan," she said. "Can you do that for me, Prudence?"

Prudence puffed her chest out proudly. "I can and I will," she said.

Meanwhile, the men of course had no idea what the cows had been planning. John was still a metre or so behind them, with Fred some ten metres further back. The gate to the field wasn't very far away, and once they went through that gate, Floss knew that her chance would be gone. She turned to Prudence.

"Pru, are you ready?"

"Ready as I will ever be," Prudence said. She then looked down at her daughter huddled next to her. "Daisy, I need you to go to Bess for a little while, sweetheart. Mummy is going to help Auntie Floss with something."

Daisy immediately tucked herself even closer to her mother, clearly determined to stay right where she was.

Prudence gave her a stern look. "Please do as you are told, Daisy."

"But I want to stay with you, Mum. I don't want to go to Bess."

Prudence carefully sidestepped her daughter. "I know today was frightening for you, but I need you to do this. Sometimes we have to do as we are told, and though it is not necessarily what we want to do, if it is asked of us by our parents, then it is usually for the best."

"But …"

Floss could see that Prudence was losing her patience, and she hoped that Daisy would do as she was told. Time was running out, and they were getting closer and closer to the field gate. She made her way over to the small calf.

"Please do this for me," she said. "Your mum is going to help me to escape and find Boris. You remember him don't you?"

The small calf nodded.

"And so you understand how important it is that you do this?"

Daisy nodded again and her expression became submissive. She slunk towards Bess who quickly offered the little calf her protection.

Floss nodded, happy that Daisy would be well looked after, and then she turned to Prudence. There was something important that she needed to say, or it would be forever left unsaid.

"Pru, I know that we have had our differences, but I want you to know that you have become a true and very dear friend to me," Floss said. "No matter how this turns out, good or bad, I am grateful to you for your help, and I will remember this forever."

At this comment, Floss noticed Prudence's eyes reddening. It was as if no one had ever spoken to her like this before. Maybe this would be a turning point for Prudence, to know how wonderful it was to put others first as Floss had always tried to do.

"No problem, Floss," Prudence said, sniffing. "Make sure that the outcome is a good one. For the thousands upon thousands of cows who have had their babies taken away from them! You go and find your Boris for all of us."

Floss watched Prudence do a U-turn around the other cows then, clearly determined to play her part in the plan. The situation was perfect. The men were still behind them all.

"Here I go, Floss," Prudence said, and Floss was sure that she could hear her friend's heart pounding. "Good luck."

Prudence scraped the ground with her right forefoot before launching into a gallop. She passed John before he had even had time to blink, and Fred, sauntering along with his cane in his right hand, seemed blissfully unaware that she was heading his way.

All of a sudden, John's hollering rang through the quiet field.

"Stop it, Fred, stop the cow! Hold out your cane, and stop it!"

Fred looked up, and there she was, three-quarters of a ton of hair and horns stampeding towards him. The ground shook beneath his feet.

John yelled again. "Put your cane out, Fred, and stop the cow!"

Fred took one look at the meagre cane in his hand and dropped it to the floor, as if it had just burst into flame. Stop a mad stampeding cow with that? He didn't think so. And then he did not know which way to run. He darted left, then right, and then when she was almost on top of him, he stepped back, but there was nothing underfoot; the ground had disappeared.

He was on his bum, sliding backwards down the side of the ditch, with his legs stuck out in front of him and his hands flailing about, trying to grasp hold of any vegetation he could, but it all came away in his hands. And then, there was nothing to stop his descent. He hit the smelly drainage water with a loud splash, and as it gushed around him like a flushed toilet, it whipped away his most treasured hairpiece.

Fred felt it leave his head, and the sight of it bobbing away downstream almost gave him a heart attack.

"My hair! My lovely hair!" he wailed.

He lifted his dripping bum from the water and began to wade after the ragged hairpiece. It was two metres away from him, and what a stroke of luck, it had become entangled in some reeds. Soon it would be back on his head, and though it would need a good shampoo and set, he was sure that it would recover from its ordeal. His fingers reached out, clutching for it, but then his luck ran out. A hungry heron had been attracted to the messy mop, and it swooped in like a hawk, grabbing it in its long beak.

"No, no, no!" Fred cried as he threw his hands into the air, clutching desperately for the bird. But all he got was a single tail feather.

Watching the man called Fred and his turmoil over the strange clump of hair, Floss understood just how important Bess's advice about humans and their hair had really been. The rather hilarious scene presented her with a once-in-a-lifetime opportunity, and she seized it for all she was worth.

"Goodbye, everyone!" Floss shouted as she ran off.

Her way was clear, and she soon passed the line of trees, heading towards the big house. When she reached the house, she paused for a moment to look over her shoulder.

Prudence and the others were scattered all over, ambling about the track like they didn't have a care in the world. The man who'd lost his hair was leaping up and down in some sort of fury, and the other was trying to calm him down.

Floss smiled as she cantered into the big field at the side of the house. This had been so very easy, and it was all thanks to Prudence.

Dripping wet and feeling pretty miserable, Fred sat himself down on the grass at the banking top. His boots were full of stinky water, and he ripped them off so that he could pour it out. John sat down next to him.

"That was my best hair," Fred said. "It cost a fortune."

John tried to console him. "You look better without it, Fred," he said. "I always say you should accept how God made you."

"Yeah, well, he originally gave me a full head of hair. So how does that work out then?"

"Hair today, gone tomorrow, I suppose," John replied, laughing.

But Fred did not laugh with his friend. There was no funny side to the loss of his valuable hair. He frowned at John whose grin quickly disappeared.

"I suppose we had better try again with the cows." John said, evidently changing the subject.

Fred lifted himself from the banking and returned his wet feet to his squelchy boots. "I suppose we had," he said glumly.

He then noticed that John was puzzling over something. He had his finger out in front of him, apparently counting.

"What's up now?"

"How many cows did you buy, Fred?"

"Six cows and the calf, so seven in all."

"That's what I thought. So, how come there are only six now, including the calf?"

"You must have miscounted, John."

"No, I don't think I did. You count them."

Fred looked towards the meandering cows, counting them for himself. One of them was definitely missing. It was the lovely red one, the best of the lot. His head turned this way and that, his eyes frantically searching. It was then that he saw her, now just a small shape speeding up the field at the rear of his house.

"Would you believe it? Just would you believe it? It's up there, John. Why on earth has it left the others and gone up there?"

John looked up towards the field and gave an audible sigh. "I suppose we had best get after it," he said, in a strained voice.

Fred cast his friend a quick glance. John looked quite drained. He could hardly blame him either. It would be dark very soon. Searching in the dark for a cow with long horns obviously did not appeal to either of them.

"I think we'll leave it where it is for tonight," Fred said. "We'll get the other cows in and leave it in that field. It's not going anywhere."

His hand went to his pocket and he brought out a large set of keys, which he dangled in front of John. "There's barbed-wire fencing all around the field. I'll close the gate and lock it, and then, first thing in the morning, I will call the vet out and have him dart the great galumphing thing with a tranquiliser. That'll teach it to mess with me."

Floss had already been around the field once, and as she cantered the perimeter for a second and then third time, she began to despair. This was not quite the open countryside that she had expected. With her sides heaving from the exertion, she came to a standstill, fighting to catch her breath. She turned her head and looked to where she had left her friends just an hour earlier, but the sky had darkened, and she could not even see the track. Just a light-blue stripe of the disappearing day remained, far on the horizon. She had never been alone at night. In fact, she had never been alone at all.

And then the blackness came, descending like a shroud across the field. Objects which had seemed so innocent in the light had taken on sinister shapes. Eerie noises came at her from everywhere, strange sounds made by animals or things that she could not see. The hedgerow behind her rustled, and her heart leaped. What on earth was that?

It took several circuits galloping around the field before she was able to calm herself, and by that time, she was exhausted. The humans had defeated her already, and she hadn't even got anywhere. She dropped her head towards the ground, so that her nose almost touched the grass, and then she started crying, tears falling in rivulets down her hairy cheeks.

"What on earth are you doing, Floss? That is not going to help one little bit."

The voice was Ned's. She lifted her head just a little bit and peered through badly swollen eyelids. How on earth had he got here? But here he was, and though his image was kind of hazy in the darkness, there could be no mistaking his mealy muzzle or the gentleness in his lovely brown eyes. She could even see the grey tufts of hair sticking out from his long carrot-shaped ears. He seemed to be scowling at her, giving her the stern expression that made his eyebrows meet in the middle. He was about to tell her off, she knew. He only ever wore that expression when he was on the verge of giving her a what-for.

"Do not give up so easily, Floss. When you fight for something you love or want, there are bound to be obstacles and setbacks. Nothing in this life comes easy. You have to pull yourself together; you have to be brave. The battle is not lost just because of a few strands of wire."

Floss began to walk towards him. "Ned," she cried. "Oh, Ned, you're here too."

But the closer she got, the weaker his image became.

"Don't go, Ned. Please don't leave me. I need you."

"Remember what I told you at the barn, Floss. You will never be alone. I will always be with you."

The image faded even more. It went wobbly at the edges, and then, just as she thought that she could touch it with her nose, it disappeared entirely.

Floss stared at the haphazard shape of the elderberry bush in front of her and shook her head. Her fear of the dark had caused some weird hallucination, a kind of a dream. And yet, she felt different now. The night wasn't as scary any more, and the strange noises, well, that's all they were – strange noises. She raised her head and looked up at the sky.

It was black, the darkest black, and black could be creepy, but tonight it seemed like a velvet blanket studded with thousands of shimmering stars that looked like diamonds. It really was quite beautiful. She let her mind wander to her dear friend, Ned. He had adored the stars, so much so that the two of them had spent many hours in Joe's meadows simply looking up at them, counting them until they fell to sleep. Ned had even told her that one very bright star could help you find your way if you were lost. If only she had listened more then, maybe that star could have helped her now. It came to her then that wherever Ned was, he would be gazing up at the same sky and thinking of her, just as she was thinking of him. She found that very comforting; it made her feel all warm inside. How true his parting words to her had been. He would indeed always be with her.

Feeling a whole lot better, Floss gave herself a hefty shake, and then she wiped the final tear from the corner of her right eye. She had done enough crying. Tomorrow was another day, and when morning came, she intended to be ready for it.

Fred threw off his duvet and stretched, yawning loudly as he picked up the clock beside his bed. It was seven forty-five; breakfast time. He swung his legs over the edge of the bed and then made his way across the bedroom to the stand where he kept his most prized possession: his toupee. Finding it missing, the nightmare of the previous day immediately returned. How on earth could he have forgotten? And now he felt tormented, tormented and anguished by the hassle that inevitably lay ahead of him.

He made his way to the corner of the bedroom and gingerly picked up the previous day's socks. They were still wet and the odour seeping from them hit him before he had even lifted them to waist height. Carrying them at arms' length, he made his way out of the bedroom and along the narrow passageway to the bathroom, where he found a slightly less offensive pair in the linen bin. He proceeded then to dress in his outdoor wear: jeans, old T-shirt, and a jumper on top. Emerging from the bathroom, he turned right and went down the staircase to the kitchen at the back of the house. All the rooms that were in use were at the back. It was just such a big old house that he simply hadn't been able to afford to renovate the rest of it.

Now where had he put his vet's phone number? He shook his head. He could not remember. There followed a frantic search of the kitchen, in every decorative cup, every nook and cranny. Finally, it revealed itself, taped to the inside door of one of the cupboards.

Fred lifted his mobile phone from the kitchen table, where he had left it charging, and dialled the number. A recording told him that the surgery didn't open till eight thirty. He looked at his watch. It was already eight thirty-five. Feeling frustrated, he began pacing the floor; up and down he went, dodging his recumbent Labrador at each turn. He redialled. This time, the recording told him to press one for appointments, two for test results, three for reception, and four for emergencies. Fred deliberated. Was it an emergency? Probably not, so he pressed number one.

"That number is not recognised. Please press one for appointments, two for test results … we only want to help."

Fred was getting very cross by now. What did the voice mean? It was number one, for goodness' sake. "You are absolutely not helping at all!" he yelled.

He felt the blood rush up to his head then, and he knew without even looking in a mirror that his face had turned purple.

"I must keep calm. I must keep calm. Doc says I must keep calm in these situations," he told himself as he rammed his finger repeatedly on the first digit. How he hated these ridiculous customer-alienating systems.

"You are fourth in the queue. We know that you are waiting. We only want to help."

"How can you possibly know that I am waiting?" Fred fumed. "You are not a 'we'. You are a computer, and you are not capable of caring how long I wait."

The voice ignored him and continued insisting on its own helpfulness. There followed a strange quietness then, which was even worse than the voice. Had he been cut off? Would he have to start this all over again?

"You are seventh in the queue. We know that you are waiting. We only want to help."

"What?" Fred exclaimed, holding the phone away from his ear so that he didn't get the full volume of the most horrendous dance music now playing over the phone system. He had an almost overwhelming desire to throw the phone to the floor and stamp on it, but he managed to control the urge. Instead, he squashed the phone up to his ear. It was very sore by the time the automated voice was replaced with a human one.

"Johnson's Veterinary Surgery. Abigail speaking." The voice was haughty and female, and it had a very high pitch.

"Good grief, a human being, a real one, and one that squeaks. Did I say squeaks? I meant *speaks*. Well, I am Fred Bulimer, and I need to speak with Ben."

"I'm afraid that Mr Blake has a client with him, so he will not be able to speak with you."

"Well, fancy that, a veterinary practice with a client! How unusual. Well, Miss High and Mighty Pants, you will just have to disturb him. This matter is very urgent."

"So is this client's case."

"Look here, you do not have to be so rude. Can you get him to call me? How hard can that be? I have a Highland cow running amok on my farm, and if something happens, I will hold you personally responsible for it. Do you hear me?"

Ben, the consultant vet, was in the room behind Abigail's desk. He was treating Mrs Carter-Primrose's cat. With or without interruptions, Mrs Carter-Primrose and her cat were never an easy consultation. He heard Abigail knocking on the door and turned his head. The interruption distracted him momentarily from the cat, and he instantly regretted the distraction, for it struck out like a fisherman casting a line, and its claws sliced into the skin of his right arm.

As Ben gave out a yell, the cat then began to howl and whilst he tried to find a plaster to cover his wound, Mrs Carter-Primrose began making a similar noise to the cat. Ben really wasn't sure which one made the worst sound. When finally he had managed to calm both of them down, he turned towards the door again.

"Yes, Abigail, what is it?"

Abigail shouted at him through the closed door. "Mr Bulimer has called, and he was in quite a temper. Says that he has a loose cow at his farm, and he needs help with it."

"Call him back, please. Tell him I'm just finishing with Mrs Primrose's cat, and then I'll set off. I know where his place is."

"The name is Carter-Primrose. Mrs Carter-Primrose." His pompous client repeated the name just as the cat made another attempt at clawing him to death.

"Mrs Carter-Primrose," Ben Blake shrieked in a very high-pitched tone, whilst holding the screaming moth-haired creature away from his person.

The woman grabbed the cat and commenced a "there, there" routine as it hissed loudly at him.

Ben spent a few moments watching the two of them in wonder. Somehow they got on well, but why on earth she had called the thing Angel, he would never know. It did not suit it at all. He leaned across the white table behind him and picked up a clean needle; the third one he had tried with.

"Now, Mrs Carter-Primrose," he said. "About dear little Angel's injections…"

Meanwhile, Fred was becoming a most unhappy man, unhappier than he had been just a couple of hours earlier and he had been pretty miserable then. It was ten thirty-five and he was still waiting for Ben to return his call. Hadn't he put plenty of business the vet's way in the past? Wasn't he owed the courtesy of a prompt visit? He had told the receptionist that the matter was urgent, and yet here he was, watching the clock and drumming his fingers on the table. Did they imagine he had nothing else to do but wait for them? He was also rather dreading ringing them up to find out why he hadn't had a response, but when the large hand of the clock moved to the eighth digit, he didn't feel like he had a choice. He certainly could not wait in all day. He had to suffer five further minutes of phone automation hell before Abigail came on the line.

"Ben set off a while since," she said.

"How long is a while since?"

"I never looked at the clock as he left so I really do not know."

Fred muttered something about rudeness and incompetence, and then he decided he should not speak with her any longer, as he might end up saying something that he would regret. She was about as much help as the automated voice – none at all. After pressing the End Call button, he put his phone on the table and flicked the kettle on. A nice cup of tea might just help to calm his nerves.

It was an hour before the knock to his door finally came.

"About time too!" he muttered as he made his way out of the back door and then around the side of the house. Ben was standing at the front door, knuckles poised to rap on it again.

"I'm here, Ben!" Fred hollered.

"Ah, there you are," Ben said sounding relieved to see him. "I was beginning to think that I had missed you."

"Yeah, well, you might have done had the matter not been so important."

"I'm sorry Fred. I got held up treating a customer's cat and then had to endure a lecture from its owner on how to treat sensitive cats."

Ben's eyes then flicked towards the red Highland in the field. "Is that the one?"

Fred nodded. "Yeah, that's the one," he said. "I bought it yesterday, along with five others and a calf. A right problem I had with them. It was like they all suddenly became possessed. I've never witnessed anything quite like it and I have had cows a long time."

"Right," Ben said. "Animals can be strange. Mind you, their owners can be even stranger."

As Ben spoke, Fred felt sure that the vet was looking right at his bald head rather than at his face. He couldn't blame him for wondering about it really. After all, he'd had a full head of hair the last time they had seen each other. Still it seemed rude of Ben to be looking at his head and so he frowned at him. It seemed to do the trick as Ben immediately looked uncomfortable with his focus shifting all over the place as if he really did not know which bit of Fred to look at.

"I didn't mean you, of course." Ben said. "I've just had a bad morning, that's all; with that other client, I mean. Right then I will get the tranquiliser out."

He left Fred and headed towards his car returning moments later with a long black case in his right hand. "Right, then," he said in a tone that indicated to Fred that he now meant business. "Let's get on with it."

The two men approached the gate together, and as they did so, the object of their intentions began to move towards the other side of it. The cow must have seen them. Fred opened the gate, and they both walked into the field. He then turned to Ben.

"So how are we going to get her then? Do we both go in after her?"

"I'll do this on my own, if you don't mind," said Ben. "It is probably best not to crowd her; it could be a long day if she keeps running around the field."

"Fine with me," Fred replied, and he closed the gate and stood back so that his bum rested against it. "I'll watch from here."

Floss had been watching the two men carefully. She recognised Fred from his exploits the previous day, but she had not seen the other man before. It was the other man who began wading through the long grass towards her. It almost seemed as if he was wading through water, the way he had to lift his legs to get through it, and she eyed him with suspicion. Feeling that she needed to conserve her energy, she did not make a move though – she would wait until the time was right to do that. Even when he had placed his case on the ground and removed his rifle, loading it, she remained where she was.

The man lifted the sight of the rifle to his eye.

"Right, my lovely. You stay right there."

Floss turned quickly and made her get away. As the rifle fired, the dart glanced across her rump and then it fell into the long grass. She did not know what it was that had hit her or what it could do but she knew that she had to get away from it. Taking herself to the corner of the field that was furthest away from the man, she looked at the sharp twists of wire that blocked her freedom – the same twists of wire that had blocked it the previous day. She turned her head. Fred had joined the man with the rifle, and now they were both walking towards her. She turned towards the wire again and touched the sharp spikes with her nose. *Ouch, that really hurt.* A drop of blood dripped to the floor. But what choice did she have? If she did not get through the wire then they would persevere and eventually they would capture her and then she would never find her son. She took a sharp intake of breath and then took five paces backwards. She must give it just enough room to hit it at full force. Kicking with her hind legs to throw her front legs forward with as much power as she could muster, she launched into a gallop.

She hit the cruel barbs with her chest first, and the momentum forced the three strands of wire out before her. They tautened against the roughly sawn posts, against which they had been strung. These posts were so rotten at their bases that they snapped in the ground, causing the loose wire to coil and entangle her legs in its razor-sharp embrace.

Blood poured from her wounds, but still she drove forward, dragging the broken debris along with her. She could see a road up ahead, just past a small coppice of trees, and she struggled towards it, but the sharp wire was tightening against her flesh; it had already opened up a gaping wound above her right knee. Desperate to rid herself of the entanglement, she leaped into the air, kicking out at the wreckage around her, somehow managing to free herself. She then staggered onto the road. It was a quiet country lane, with a thick hawthorn hedgerow running along both sides. She turned right and began hobbling down the grainy tarmac.

Seconds later she heard rubber tyres screeching against the same tarmac. She felt certain that it was the two men coming after her in their car. Only the hedgerow prevented them from seeing her, and when they rounded the next bend she knew that it would all be over. She could not outrun their car. Maybe though, just maybe she could outwit them. Her eyes scanned the road, desperately seeking a hiding place, but there was just this dense hedgerow and nothing else. She turned to look at it. Once again, she was left without a choice.

The thorns tore her eyelids open, and despite the thick hair on her face, found a way through to her skin, cutting into it, scratching and scraping. She didn't feel it, though; such was the level of adrenaline pumping through her veins. When she reached the other side of the hedgerow, she bowed her head. The car was already drawing level with her.

It slowed and came to a halt right beside her. Floss heard the sound of two car doors opening and closing, and then the men's footsteps. They were just half a metre from her nose, and if their arms had been long enough to reach out over the tall hedgerow, they could have touched her. Fred was pointing to the tarmac.

"Look! You can see blood and skid marks from her hooves just here. She must have gone down this road."

"I'm not sure. She can't be moving that fast, not with all this blood around. She must be pretty badly injured."

"Yes, that barbed wire must have made a right mess of her. She might have to be destroyed if I can't stitch her up."

"Well, that might be a blessing in disguise. I'm not that sure I want to return her to the herd after the behaviour she has shown. Imagine what the calves she produced would be like if they took on her temperament. To be honest, Ben, I am so fed up with all this, that if you asked me if you could shoot her dead, right here, right now, I would agree to it."

As she listened to their conversation, Floss had to bite her lip to stop herself from crying out, but she managed to keep her nerve, holding her breath so tight that she felt as if she might burst.

Fred suddenly swung around and stared right at the damaged hedgerow. He pulled a leaf from a broken twig and began to rub it between his fingers. "Where on earth could she have gone?" he said.

The other man, Ben, shook his head, also staring at the same hedgerow, and behind it, Floss closed her eyes, afraid that the shine in them might give her away.

"I really do not know, but I think we should go back to the house and call the police. We need to let them know that there is a Highland cow on the loose."

Fred sighed. "More trouble than it was worth, that thing," he said.

Floss listened as their footsteps moved from the hedge. The doors of the estate car opened and closed, and then there came a long and fear-instilling pause before the engine fired up. As the drone of the car's engine slowly faded from earshot, she opened her eyes and let the air out of her lungs in a long gush that seemed to go on and on. That had been so very close, but she had made it; she had escaped, and the journey to find her beloved son was finally under way.

CHAPTER FIVE

In the days that followed, Floss slowly grew weaker. She had lost a tremendous amount of blood, as it had not stopped flowing for several hours after she went through the barbed wire. Most of her injuries were superficial surface scratches, already healing, but the one above her right knee was serious. The gash was ragged and deep, and the congealed blood around it had started to fester, attracting flies to it. Hordes of them followed her every move, massing on the leg and feeding from the blood. Once again, she stamped her foot to rid herself of them, but the movement sent a shock wave of pain right through her. Within seconds, they were back again, swarming like bees around a honeypot. Desperate to escape them, she stumbled into a thick covering of elderberry bushes, where at last there was some relief. Exhausted, she closed her eyes.

Soon she had nodded off, and she dreamed that she was beneath the shade of the biggest oak tree in Joe Devlin's meadow. It was a lovely day, warm and sunny, and the sunlight sparkled through the foliage, causing bright patterns to dance around her feet. Boris and Daisy were just in front of her. They were playing, leaping in the air and dodging each other, having fun. Ned was in the meadow too, grazing not far away from the calves. There were children laughing in the dream. It was the laughter of small boys, and she drowsily opened an eye. Not quite awake, she closed it again, desperate to stay with the dream, as it was so wonderful. But the children's laughter became louder, and there was also a strange clattering sound that jolted her wide awake.

The two boys were about fifty metres away from her. They rode bicycles that appeared to be much too small for them as they came freewheeling down a grassy hill, heading straight towards her. As the boys drew closer, she pressed herself into the foliage of the elderberry bushes, hoping that they would camouflage her. The boys stopped pedalling and simultaneously dismounted, letting their bicycles fall to the ground just a few metres away from where she stood.

"Where's your den, Tom?" It was the slightly taller boy who spoke.

"Just there in the bushes."

The taller boy leaned forward towards the elderberry bushes. Floss knew that he had seen her, because a deep frown appeared on his face. The boy then cast his friend a puzzled look.

"I ... I didn't know that you had a bull."

Tom looked mystified. "Bull? I don't have a bull."

"You don't?"

"No, I don't."

"Then this is not good."

"What is not good?"

"Well, if you haven't got a bull, then who on earth does that one belong to?"

The boy called Tom looked at his friend's outstretched finger, right to the end of its dirty fingernail, and then he gulped. Both boys then started to walk backwards towards their bicycles.

"*Ru-u-u-u-n!*" they shouted to each other.

And they turned and ran so fast that it seemed as if their legs almost couldn't keep up with the momentum. Hauling their bicycles from the floor, they leaped on them, and with their heads held low between the handlebars, they pedalled feverishly up the hill, neither one daring to look behind him.

Floss waited until they had disappeared, and then she limped from her hiding place. She couldn't stay here now. If humans were anything like cows, the young boys would have bigger fathers, and they'd be sure to come to this place.

"Come on," she told herself, fighting the pain. "You must go on and find somewhere else to rest."

She forced a few stilted steps from her exhausted body, but the rest had made her limbs stiff, and her bad leg had swelled so big that it almost looked like the trunk of a tree. Soon her gait was so sluggish that she was barely moving at all. There was a cornfield up ahead, and she struggled towards it, hoping that she would reach it before she collapsed. The corn was well grown, and it should hide her well. It seemed to take forever to get to it, and every inch was agony, but she did not give up. When she finally reached the field, she dragged herself into the midst of it.

Her good knee went to the ground first. Once it had her weight, she slowly let her bad knee to the floor too, but the pain was so excruciating that it made her cry out. For several minutes afterwards, she had to bite her lip, waiting for the pulsating agony to subside. She then let her body drop sideways and lay her head on the flattened stems of corn. The seed heads of the crops rustled gently above her. The sound was soothing, and soon she felt drowsy again. Seconds later, she was sound asleep.

It was early the following afternoon when Floss woke up. She had been sleeping for almost ten hours; such was the level of her exhaustion. Very quickly, even before she had lifted her head, her thoughts turned to her leg. It didn't seem to hurt quite so much, and she certainly felt better for the long rest. The test would be to stand on it. Her left leg took her weight first, and then she brought her right one out from beneath her; but as soon as it bore just a tad of her weight, a searing pain tore through her, forcing her to abandon the attempt. Twice more she tried to stand, but each time, she failed. Defeated, she rolled onto her side and let her head flop on the flattened stems. It crossed her mind then that this would not be such a bad a place to die. The afternoon sun was warm and comforting, and her leg did not hurt so much whilst she was lying down. Her eyelids felt heavy, and as she closed them, she began to drift away.

"Don't you dare give up, Floss."

It was Ned. He was in her head again.

"I can't go on, Ned. My leg is so painful that I cannot bear it. I have given all I can. I simply cannot give any more than I have."

"Does your leg really hurt as much as your heart will hurt if you never set eyes on your son ever again? Is it really as bad as all that?"

These thoughts, almost arguments, resounded in Floss's head, torturing her and stopping her from sleeping. More alert than she had been on first waking, she opened her eyes again. She hadn't noticed the sky earlier, but it was the brightest blue, and there was a light refreshing breeze that gently feathered her coat.

Two questions came to her mind. Did she want this to be the last beautiful day that she ever saw? Did she ever want to see her son again? The answers were obvious and so she clenched her teeth tightly and threw her legs out in front of her. This time she would do it. This time she would get to her feet.

"*Arrgghh!* Watch out."

The warning as she tried to keep her balance seemed to come out of the ground. A small rabbit was standing there, staring up at her with the most indignant expression that she had ever seen. Knowing that she had almost squashed him, she looked at him awkwardly. The rabbit suddenly leaped back on his haunches, and his eyes widened. He seemed to be looking at her as if she was a monster. She smiled at him, but that seemed to make matters worse, and he turned away obviously preparing to flee.

"Please don't leave me," Floss said.

The rabbit turned halfway round. "Are you talking to me?"

"Yes, I am. Please Mr Rabbit. I need your help. Please help me."

The rabbit appeared to be intrigued, and as he inched a little closer, she hoped she was winning him around.

"Please do not be afraid. I will not hurt you," she said.

"Please don't be afraid!" repeated the rabbit sarcastically. "I will not hurt you. Well, if that is true, then you need to be careful where you are treading and who you are treading on. You almost turned me into rabbit stew with those big feet of yours."

"I didn't mean to."

"Do you know what I think?"

Floss thought this was a very strange thing to say. How could she possibly know what he was thinking? "No, I don't," she said.

"I think that you are hungry and that you want to eat me. That's what I think."

"Me, want to eat you?"

"Exactly."

Floss looked at him, horrified. "No, I definitely do not want to eat you. I eat grass and hay. I do not eat rabbits."

The rabbit cocked his head to one side, and he looked at her curiously.

"What are you?"

"I am a cow."

He laughed sarcastically. "Nah, cows are black and white. I think that you are an enormous hairy fox and that you want to eat me."

"I am definitely a cow, a Highland cow, and I definitely do not want to eat you."

He twitched his nose again and then edged a little closer, so close that if she had wanted to, Floss could have stepped on him.

"Lower your head and give me a big smile, one that shows all of your teeth."

Floss noticed that the rabbit was staring right at her mouth, and though she thought it a most strange request, she lowered her head and did as he had asked, though it was more of a grimace than a smile.

The rabbit's eyes narrowed and after a short while, he began nodding. "Mmm ... I guess that I've never seen a fox with horns or teeth like yours, so you might well be a cow after all – a very funny-looking one, mind."

"Please, can I stop smiling now? My mouth is aching, and it is hard to smile when I am in so much pain."

"I suppose you can stop," he replied, and his gaze fell onto the seeping, blood-matted fur on Floss's swollen foreleg.

"How did you do that?"

"When I escaped from some humans, I got it caught up in that awful sharp wire that some of them use around their fields."

"Yeah, well the wire is there to keep you in your field and to stop you from squashing rabbits like me. Why on earth did you want to get away from the humans? They feed you, don't they?"

"Sure, but they took something very valuable away from me."

"What?"

"They took my son."

"I see," replied the rabbit. She could tell that he was warming to her now as his voice had softened and he was looking very studious about the matter. It seemed that he was impressed.

"You are very brave to go looking for your son," he said. "I have decided that you can be my friend, and as a friend, I would like to help you out. The name is Buck by the way. Come on, follow me, and I will take you to a place where we can make your leg better."

Floss's heart lifted. She was indeed in need of a friend, and she was in even greater need of a cure for her poor leg.

As Buck hopped away, in and out of the corn, she began to hobble after him, but it was not easy. One second he was visible, and the next he was gone. This went on for a while, and then, quite suddenly, there were two rabbits hopping around.

"Meet the wife, Poppy," Buck called out jovially. "Come on … follow us … follow us."

It was just as difficult keeping tabs on two rabbits as it had been to follow one. They had left the cornfield now, and their fluffy white tails would not keep still, bobbing in and out of the summer foliage. She needn't have worried, though; unlike the rabbits, she was difficult to miss, and both of them must have kept her firmly in their sights, because she heard their voices a moment later.

"It's here! Over here, moo cow, over here," the rabbits called.

Floss looked on. The rabbits had jumped on top of a large brown rock with a flat surface. They gazed down at whatever was on the other side of it. When she reached them, she saw that it was a large pond, with bulrushes at the edges and pretty water lilies.

"Here it is," Buck said to her.

"Here is what?"

"The pond."

"Yes, I can see that, but why have you brought me here? My leg is even more painful now for coming all this way."

"Why do you think we have brought you here?" Buck asked.

He was asking her to read his thoughts again. Why did he keep on imagining that she could read his mind? "I really have no idea," she said. "But my leg isn't feeling any better from looking at your reflection. Seeing just the one of you is quite enough."

The rabbit laughed out loud. "I did not bring you here to look at me, though I must say that I do look cute today. I brought you here to so that you could get in."

"Get in what?"

"The water."

Floss frowned at him. "Why on earth would I want to do that? It's cold and wet."

"Exactly! Just what you need: cold and wet."

Floss shook her head. The rabbits were obviously having a laugh, wasting her time and her energy. She began to turn away.

"Stop! Where are you going? You need to get in. I had better explain. The water will clean up your wound, and the cold will help to control the swelling."

Floss turned to the rabbits again. "Oh?" she replied, doubt in her voice. She couldn't see how a bit of cold water could help to mend her leg.

"In you go then," Buck said. "Go on."

Feeling that she had nothing to lose, Floss slowly eased her way down the slippery bank and waded into the pond. When the water was above her knees, she waited for the cure Buck had promised. It did not materialise, and her leg not only throbbed, but it stung as well. She turned around. Both rabbits were watching her from their dry spot on the rock.

"It's not working!" she shouted. "It feels worse."

"Just stay in. You will see," Buck called back. He then pulled at a yellow dandelion head growing in a groove in the rock and began to munch on it.

Floss breathed a loud sigh. This was ridiculous, and she was feeling totally stupid. It would be dark very soon, and the water was turning even colder now that the sun had started to set.

"That's it!" she shouted. "I've had enough. My legs are so cold that I can barely feel them."

"Isn't that the point?" Buck shouted back. "Isn't that exactly the point?"

Floss wiggled her bad leg. *Good grief,* he was right. The rabbit was actually right. Her leg was so numb with cold that the pain had almost gone.

"You are very clever, Mr Rabbit," she shouted.

"I know I am," Buck replied, and to show off, he did a back flip on the rock, narrowly missing landing on his wife.

"By the way, as I told you, the name is Buck the Rabbit, and this is my wife, Poppy. What is your name or are we going to keep referring to each other formally?"

"Floss," said Floss. "My name is Floss."

"Well Floss, you can get out now if you want. I should warn you, though, when you warm up, the leg will start to hurt again, though maybe not so bad. You need to stay near the pond and keep going in and out of it for a few days – maybe a week or so. And then you should be as good as new."

Floss looked at the rabbits. She didn't really want to stay around for that long. She wanted to go on with her search for Boris; but if her leg didn't get better, she wouldn't be able to go very far. Maybe it would be better to let the leg heal, and then she would stand a better chance. After she had climbed from the water and shaken herself like a dog that had taken a dip in the sea, she began nodding her head at Buck.

"I think that I shall stay here for a little while then. That is, if I wouldn't be getting in your way. How did you know that the water would help, Buck?"

"Because we have lived by this water a long time. We have seen deer going in and out when they have swollen legs, and we've also seen how quickly it has helped them to recover. You are not used to living in the wild, are you? Out here, you need your legs to be in good working order, because if they are not, you are going to be the one left behind when Mr Fox comes along – and then you will be the one that he eats all up."

"I don't think Mr Fox will eat me," Floss said. "Even if I can't outrun him with my bad leg, I think I'm just a little bit too big for him."

"Well, what about humans and their terrible guns? You wouldn't stand a chance against them, with or without good legs."

Poppy, who had been sitting in silence, began nodding her head miserably. "We lost a baby to a human with a gun last year," she said. "It was heartbreaking."

Floss shook her head. "I am so sorry to hear that," she said, knowing only too well what it was like to lose a child. She then noticed that Poppy's belly was heavily swollen, and her eyes flicked towards Buck. She missed nothing.

"You are going to be a dad soon," Floss said. "That is so wonderful."

As he glanced at his wife's belly, Buck looked proud as punch. "I'm already a dad many times over," he boasted. "And I am a granddad and a great-granddad and a great-great-granddad and a great-great-great-granddad." He looked at Poppy then. "Was that enough greats, or have I missed one?"

Poppy smiled at him and nodded. "Yes, that was enough," she said.

"So how many children do you have then?" Floss asked, desperately trying to work out how many generations the greats added up to.

Buck began to count and recount on his little paws, whilst Floss waited and waited and waited. It was five whole minutes before the answer came.

"One hundred eighty-seven ... I think," He said at last Floss mouthed the number silently, quickly deciding not to ask about the number of grandchildren, great-grandchildren, etc.; that calculation would take all night to work out. "So," she said, changing the subject. "Where do you think I should sleep?"

The two rabbits looked at each other, and then they smiled.

"We know a great place," Buck said. "The grass next to our burrow is newly grown, and it is nice and soft. You can lie down there."

"I wouldn't want to impose on your hospitality."

"Impose away," Buck said. "So long as you watch where you are treading, we would love to have you sleep next to our burrow. You will make a great security guard. Come, we will take you there. It isn't far."

It was just two nights before Floss's skills as a security guard were put to the test. It was dusk, and the rabbits had just gone to bed. All seemed very peaceful, and so she wandered a little way from the burrow to graze longer grass. It was just as she pulled a really tasty, long seed headed stem when she heard the noise. It was a scraping kind of noise, and it seemed to be coming from the burrow. It wasn't really alarming and at first she assumed that it was the rabbits moving around but then, all of a sudden, a large clod of earth hit her square on the nose.

"What the...!" she exclaimed as she hurried towards the burrow. Some creature appeared to have its head stuck way down there. She wasn't sure what it was, not with its head missing, and so she prodded it with her nose.

"Do you mind?" she said crossly.

The unidentified creature did not seem to notice the nudge, and so she tried again, this time shoving it so hard that she practically forced it fully into the burrow. The creature could not ignore that she felt certain.

There then came a lot of shuffling as it began to edge itself backwards from the burrow. As its head popped out, Floss could see that it was a fox, and she was well aware of what foxes did to rabbits. The fox seemed oblivious to her presence, and the gums in his mouth rolled back over his teeth.

"Right then," he snarled. "Who was it that has dared to do that to me?"

"It was I," she said.

Floss noticed the fox's eyes narrow, and she got the impression that he did not know that she was standing above him. She heard him gulp as he looked up and then, all of a sudden, the gums rolled forward to cover his teeth, and he made a vain attempt to smile at her without showing his fangs.

"Are you trying to eat my rabbit friends?" Floss said.

"Rabbits? Wh-what r-rabbits would they be?" the fox stammered. "I haven't smelled or tasted … I mean … seen any rabbits today. No, definitely no rabbits, not today."

"I am talking about the rabbits in that burrow."

"Th-th-there are no rabbits in there." He was trembling like a jellyfish.

Floss glanced at the burrow. "No?"

"No," the fox replied quickly turning his attention away from the burrow and obviously trying to ignore the fact that Poppy's head had just popped up there.

Floss winked at her before returning her attention to the fox.

"So, just what exactly *were* you doing with your head in the hole then?" she asked drumming her hoof in front of his quivering nose. "Perhaps you'd like to explain, because it seems to me to be a very strange thing to want to do. I mean, I don't go around sticking my head in strange holes."

"Erm …"

The fox was visibly quaking and obviously trying to think up an excuse. Floss could not wait to hear it.

"My tail … yes, that's it … I was … erm … chasing my tail. You know foxes, we chase our tails, and then I lost it. Sure thing, I lost it, and I wondered whether it might possibly have somehow got into the burrow, the burrow that I came across most definitely, I mean, accidentally on purpose. I mean accidentally."

Floss cast her eyes towards the thick and bushy appendage firmly fastened to the fox's rear end, and she raised an eyebrow. "So you lost your tail, did you? Is that really the best that you can think of?"

The fox turned his head, gulping when he saw his tail waving, so obviously glued to his bum.

"Ah … there it is. You've found it for me. Thank you so very much. I'll be off then now that I have found it." He tucked the supposed misbehaving tail firmly between his hind legs and began to slink away.

As Floss watched him disappear into the darkness, she almost felt like chasing after him, just for the hell of it, but decided not to. Her leg wasn't fully healed yet, and she simply could not risk injuring it. Anyway, she was pretty certain that after the scare she had given him, the fox would be most unlikely to return for a very long time.

The dreadful fright the fox had given the rabbits that evening brought Poppy's babies along earlier than expected. She gave birth to a brood of six baby bunnies just a few days afterwards. She couldn't bring them out of the burrow straight away, as they were far too weak and tiny, and so she lay with them, tending to them and feeding them on her milk, whilst Buck ran around her, doing the chores and bringing food in so that she did not go hungry. Meanwhile, Floss waited and continued her vigil beside the burrow. And then, one morning four weeks later, when the time was right and the sun was shining, Poppy brought the young rabbits from the burrow and into the big world.

"Oh my goodness! They are so cute," Floss gushed as they leaped around, dashing this way and that, evidently feeling the breeze on their little faces for the first time. "You must be so very proud of them."

"We are," Poppy replied. "And I want to thank you, Floss. If it had not been for you, I doubt that they would be here. In fact, I don't think I would be here either."

Floss blushed beneath her long hair. She did not need praising for saving Poppy. Any cow would have done the same. "It was nothing," she said. "I am glad I was here to help, just as you helped me."

"You have been so very kind to us, Floss. And now we get to the part where I must tell you all of their names. The biggest one, the one who is looking right at you, he is Buck Junior.

Floss smiled. The little rabbit looked just like his father.

"And the one who has just jumped over him is Buzz, and that one there is Lucy, and then Hoppy, Fluff, and Pip."

"I wonder you can tell them apart," Floss said, smiling at the rabbits' cute little faces. "They are all so very alike."

Over the next four weeks, the little rabbits continued growing, almost as quickly as the grass and vegetation grew around them. Life was such fun for them. They had food, they had play, they had sleep, and they had love. They also had something that other baby rabbits did not have, and that was the protection of a Highland cow, and they loved Auntie Floss very much. She was always around: guarding them, chasing away any threat that came close, including feral cats that tried their luck every now and then. And Floss loved the rabbits in return, but every day that passed was a day closer to her leaving. The swelling in her leg had been gone a while, and just a small hairless scar remained where the terrible injury had been. She still had a bit of pain every now and then, just the odd twinge if she overdid playtime, but it was barely anything. So, what had stopped her from leaving days or weeks before? The six little rabbits had, as did the thought of telling them that she was going, because she knew that it would break their hearts.

Today, I'll do it, she would tell herself, but then she would not be able to bring herself to say it, and so it would move to the next day … and then the next.

This Tuesday morning, though, she had definitely made her mind up, and she called Poppy over first. It would be best to tell her before the youngsters; that way, at least their mum would be able to deal with the inevitable tears.

"Hi, Floss," Poppy said, hopping over. "It's another lovely day, isn't it?"

"It is," Floss replied pursing her lips but saying nothing further. It was hard for her to get the words out. Poppy gave her a puzzled look. She had obviously worked out that something was wrong.

"Are you unwell, Floss?"

"No, I am fine, Poppy. Well, at least my body is."

"Ah," Poppy said. "There is more than our body that has to be well. Our minds must be at ease too, and I know full well that yours is not."

Floss smiled at her. "You know," she said.

Poppy nodded. "I have been expecting it for some time," she said. "It hasn't gone unnoticed that you haven't been limping much lately."

"Gosh, Poppy," Floss said. "I didn't realise that you knew so much. What about the youngsters? Do they know?"

Poppy shook her head. "No," she said. "To be honest, they think you are going to be around forever. I have tried to hint very gently to them that you may not be, but each time I have tried, they have simply shrugged it off. And, Buck, well I haven't even thought about telling him."

"This is not going to be easy then."

"No, it isn't," Poppy replied. "Everyone is going to take it hard, but do not let their reaction make you feel guilty. You are not doing us wrong by leaving, Floss. You have a mission that you must get on with, and we knew that this day would come."

"But what if the fox returns? What if …"

Poppy quickly interrupted her. "And what if you do not get out there to look for your son? And what if you blame us for holding you back? And what if the fox comes along anyway when your back is turned?"

"What are you trying to say, Poppy?"

"I am trying to say that we cannot live our lives on what ifs, and we cannot expect you to live yours worrying each day about us. You have to let your heart decide what you must do."

"I miss my son, Poppy. I miss him so very much. Not a day goes by when he is not on my mind."

"Then your heart has already spoken, and it is telling you that you must continue your search, and you will not forgive yourself if you do not. We would not want that on our conscience, Floss. We managed without you before, and though we will miss you, we will do so again."

"Can you bring the youngsters to me, Poppy?"

Poppy nodded and turned her head, opening her mouth to call them over, but she did not need to do so. It seemed that the young rabbits had already noticed something was going on. They were peeping out from behind the pond rock, each little head atop of its sibling's. Soon they were bounding over. They sat beside Poppy, three to each side, gazing up at Floss.

"Hello, little ones," Floss said. And then, as a flood of tears came to sting her eyes, she simply added. "I am going to miss you all so very much."

A collective howl resounded amongst the young rabbits. Buck Junior and Lucy were the first to run to her. They each chose a front leg, wrapping their tiny front paws around as far as they would go, which wasn't very far.

Floss looked down at them fondly. "Please do not cry," she said. "I just cannot bear you crying. I love you all so much."

"But if you love us, why do you have to go away, Auntie Floss?" Buck Junior asked.

Floss thought for a moment before replying. "I have to go away because my son is lost in the big world somewhere, and he is waiting for me to find him."

"But what about us? Who will look after us?"

"Your mum and dad will look after you, and they love you very much."

Buck Junior glanced at the others, who shrugged their shoulders. It seemed that he had been elected as spokes-bunny, so it was up to him to come up with a response. "But our parents are not as big and strong as you are," he said.

"It doesn't matter how big they are," Floss replied. "It is what is inside that is important."

"Uh, it would matter how big they are if that fox came along like he did before we were born," Buck Junior replied. "If it hadn't been for you being here then …"

Poppy stepped in to rescue Floss. "Floss has to go, because her son needs her more than you need her."

"And how come that?"

"Because he is lost and probably very lonely, and you are not."

"But …"

"No buts."

The snivelling amongst the youngsters increased as they seemingly tried to come to terms with the now inevitable loss of their guardian. Floss found it very uncomfortable to watch them, and as they blew their tiny noses and looked at her with tears flowing from their eyes, she felt her own eyes well up. She turned away. Allowing the young rabbits to witness her crying was not going to improve this moment one little bit.

She looked towards Poppy who, seeming to notice her discomfort, called her children to attention. "Bed, you lot," she said.

"Uh," replied all six in unison.

"Now!"

Floss looked at the youngsters. Poppy's voice had been very stern and it was evident that they had worked out that a refusal to do as they were told was not an option. One by one, they filed past her, each giving her a sniff. Despite her own tears, Floss had to laugh though because as Poppy turned away from them, twelve front paws and six pairs of wet eyes returned to the entrance of the burrow, jostling for position.

"Let's go to the pond rock," Poppy said. "We can talk better there."

Floss nodded. The rock was their favourite place for a heart to heart because when Poppy was sitting up on it, they were almost at the same height. She followed Poppy to the rock and once the rabbit had leaped onto it, she began pouring out the pent up emotions that had been building up inside of her.

"I wish that I did not have to leave you all, Poppy," Floss said. "You have been such good friends to me."

She started crying a little then and had to blink to hold the tears. Her eyes were becoming very sore with all this crying.

"Oh, Floss," Poppy said, sitting upright on the rock. "Please do not cry."

"I cannot help it, Poppy. There is so much to cry about. I do not know if I will ever see my son again and if I do not then I will have left for nothing. If only I could see into the future."

"I'm not sure that it is good for us to see our futures, Floss. Being able to do so may take away our hopes and aspirations. Maybe it is better that we do not know, and that we just try to live our lives the best we know how and to try to do what is right. What is right for you at this time is to go on looking. You will know if that changes."

"I just want him by my side where he belongs. Do you think that he will know that I still love him, that I think of him every day?"

"Of course he will know, Floss. A mother's love for her son does not just go away and I am sure that you must have been such a great mum to him."

"I was … I mean, I am." Floss sobbed. "And what is really frightening now is that when I close my eyes, it is a struggle to see his little face. When I first lost him, it was easy. I could always see him, just as if he were next to me; but now, it's as though he is fading away, and I do not want him to fade away. I need to know what has happened to him. I just need to know."

"I cannot imagine what that must be like for you, Floss, and I wish I could say something that would make it better. Humans cause animals so much pain and heartache. They have such a lot to answer for."

"They certainly do."

"We will pray for you, Floss, and we will pray for your son. Maybe the strength of a rabbit family's prayers will get God to listen."

"I hope so," Floss replied. "I sure need some help."

She looked over Poppy's head then and towards the burrow, smiling as six little heads ducked. "I'll miss them," she said. "And I will miss you and Buck. Where is he, anyway? I can't leave without saying goodbye to him."

"He's gone off to the cabbage field, but I am sure that he won't be long. Somehow he always manages to drag that heavy belly of his home. You will wait for him, won't you? He wouldn't want to miss saying goodbye. I know that for sure."

Floss managed to laugh out loud. She had got to know Buck well over the weeks that she had stayed with the rabbits, and she had borne witness to his craving for cabbages. "Don't worry, Poppy," she replied. "I would not dream of leaving without saying goodbye. There is quite a lot that I need to say to him before I go, things that cannot go unsaid."

The rest of the afternoon passed by, but Buck did not return. Even as the sun left the sky, and the night drew in, there was still no sign of him. Floss paced up and down beside the burrow, each step bringing with it further anxiety. Buck never stayed out this late. After a time, she made her way to the burrow and placed her nose close to it. Poppy had taken the young bunnies down there about a half hour ago, to get them off to sleep.

"Poppy, are you there?" she whispered. She did not want to awaken the children if they were sleeping.

Poppy's head popped out. "Any sign of him yet, Floss?" she said, her voice clearly troubled.

Floss shook her head.

"This is not like him. He always returns before nightfall."

"Yes, I know."

"Something bad has happened. I can feel it."

"Don't say that, Poppy. I am sure that there is a very innocent explanation. He is a very wise rabbit, and he knows how to look after himself. He probably got so full that he had to stay behind to sleep it off." She did not sound convincing.

"Yes," Poppy replied. "Maybe that is it."

"But, just in case, and even though we both know that he's fine, I will go and have a little mosey to the cabbage field to find him and to tell him just how worried we all are."

"Oh, would you?" Poppy replied, gratefully. "I would go myself, but I can't leave the children."

"Of course I would," Floss said. "I should have gone earlier. It is the least that I can do after all you have done for me. Now remind me, how do I get to the field?"

Floss followed Poppy's directions very carefully: Right at the crooked tree, left at the broken fence post, then on for an acre, and watch out for the big hole in the hedge. Go through the hole, and then you will be in the cabbage field. The directions were very precise; that is, except for the final detail. When she arrived at the hole, it wasn't big at all, only just big enough for her to stick her head through, which she did.

The field was massive and filled with cabbages, neatly planted, with their crinkled olive leaves luminescent in the moonlight. Floss flashed her eyes back and forth across the front row, but there was no sign of Buck, and she couldn't see further into the field, as it was too dark. She pulled her head from the hedgerow and followed it along until she reached the gate which the farmer used to access the field. It was open, and so she walked into the field, calling out for Buck as she went. It was a long slog, up one row and down the next, and after about an hour, the field began running out of rows. What if she got right to the very last cabbage and still hadn't found him? What then?

Without warning, her foot suddenly struck something quite soft, and it felt very different to the soil between the cabbages. Her heart skipped a beat, and her stomach churned as she lowered her gaze. Close by her foot there was a rabbit, and it was lying on its side in a most peculiar position. Lifeless eyes stared back at her from its motionless and bloodied little face. She swallowed deeply and nudged it gently with her nose.

"Wake up, Buck," she said.

But the rabbit remained quite still, and when its eyes did not brighten, Floss knew that the life in them had been extinguished forever. Some human had shot him; some dreadful human had taken away the father of those lovely little bunnies. This was all getting just too much for her to bear, and she lifted her nose into the air and cried her pain out into the night. It was a dreadful sound that could be heard for miles around, and when she had finished making it, she lowered her head and gently closed the little rabbit's eyelids with her nose.

"Good night and God bless, Buck," she said. "Rest in peace, my dear little friend. I am so sorry that I was too late to save you."

After that, she began to sob uncontrollably, crying for the loss of her friend and crying for her son, not really knowing which she was crying about the most.

"Will you stop howling, and do something useful to get me out of here!"

The voice seemed to come from nowhere. At first, Floss thought that she had imagined it. Through heavily swollen eyelids, she looked down at her feet. The dead rabbit was still very dead. She turned away.

"Stop! Stop! Where you going?"

The voice was muffled, as if something was preventing it from reaching her ears, but there was no mistaking the bossiness. It was Buck.

"I can't see you, Buck. Please come out. This really is not funny."

"I'm not finding it funny either."

"But where are you?"

"I think that you are standing on me."

Floss leaped to one side and then nervously lifted each of her four feet in turn.

"No, I am not standing on you."

"Hurry, Floss. I cannot breathe."

Floss lowered her head towards the ground, and her ears flicked back and forth. How come she could hear him but could not see him?

"Speak to me again, Buck!" she yelled. "Speak to me, so I can find you."

She heard a scratching sound that seemed to be coming from beneath the earth. There was also a strangled kind of a cry.

"Is that you, Buck? Are you under the cabbages?"

She listened carefully. The strangled sound came again. It was Buck, she was certain of it.

Floss began to paw the ground, first with her left hoof and then with her right, casting cabbages all over the place. "Buck!" she called. "Hold on, my friend, I am coming, I am coming."

Her hoof struck something hard, and when she caught a glimpse of metal wire, she became excited, pulling at it with her teeth and pushing loosened soil away with her nose. It was some kind of cage which must have been buried in the ground. Suddenly a tiny pink nose appeared in one of the mesh squares. Floss heard Buck take in a deep breath, and then he coughed violently, as if trying to clear his airways so that he could speak to her.

"Good grief, Floss!" he croaked. "You took your time. I thought that I'd had it."

"You are not the only one," Floss said, remembering the dead rabbit. "How did you manage to get yourself into this thing?"

"Well, I was walking along the cabbages, minding my own business, well my business and the farmer's, and then I fancied doing a bit of burrowing in the lovely soil. I made some lovely holes here and there, and then I went underground for about a minute and the next minute I found that I could not move. Something cold and hard just appeared right in front of my nose, and then I heard something snap behind me and when I turned around, I found that I could not move that way either."

"It is a trap," Floss said. "It is a trap that the farmer has laid for you to stop you from eating his cabbages and making holes in his field."

"So what do we do now?"

Floss studied the cage that had imprisoned her dear friend. Though she had revealed the top of it, the remainder was still buried deep in the ground where the soil was much firmer.

"We need to work out how we can get you out before any humans come along. I guess there must be a door to the cage somewhere but I need to get it out of the ground so that I can find it."

She began to scrape at the cage again, but her efforts were fruitless. The dried earth held onto it like concrete.

"Close your eyes, Buck. I am going to try something else." She forced her right horn inside a square of mesh. "Right, here we go."

A single backward flick of her strong head sprung the trap from the ground. It somersaulted twice and landed right on top of a cabbage. Floss raced after it and pushed it off the cabbage before peering in at Buck.

He looked positively dreadful. His normally immaculate fur was covered in dirt, his mouth and feet were bleeding, and he had slugs and other creepy things crawling on him.

"Gosh, Buck, you do look a sight."

Buck lifted a paw to wipe the bugs from his face. "Do you think you can open it and get me out?"

"I don't know."

She marched around the cage, studying every detail. One end had hinges and a catch so she was certain that this was where it opened, but despite trying the catch with her teeth, she could not open it. She shook her head.

"I can't open it, Buck," she said. "It needs fingers, and I don't have any. I will have to drag it to the burrow, and maybe Poppy will be able to open it with her little paws."

At this suggestion, Buck began frantically pushing his own tiny paws through the mesh, but even Floss could see that they were not long enough.

"Think of something else, Floss," said Buck. "I don't want the children seeing me like this."

"I don't think there is any other way," Floss said. And then she paused a moment studying the cage again. "Hold on, Buck," she said. "I have an idea."

Whilst Buck looked on she took several strides backwards. "No-o-o-o-o -o!" he cried as she headed towards him.

Floss booted the cage like she was taking a penalty shot. It flew high into the air, with Buck desperately trying to cling to the sides of it, and then it came crashing down with an audible thud.

"Maybe not such a great idea that," Floss muttered.

The cage was upside down, and so was Buck. His legs were at about the place where his head should be, and his head, well, he was standing on it.

Floss hurried over.

"Are you okay?" she said, twisting her own head so that she could look at him the right way up.

"Like, do I really look okay standing on my head? Of course I'm not okay."

"Yes, right. Sorry," Floss muttered. "I thought that the door might come open if I gave it a good kick."

"And you certainly did that."

"Well, I didn't know what else to do. Do you have any better ideas?"

"It's not very easy thinking when one is balancing on one's brain."

"So what do you want me to do? Like I said, I can drag you and it to the burrow, and we can see if Poppy can open it."

"No, no, I don't want that."

"Well, what, then?"

"I suppose you are going to have to kick it again."

"Are you sure?"

"Yes, kick it again, but let me get a good grip on it first this time."

He threaded the fingers of his tiny paws through the mesh and clung on for dear life. "Right, I am ready."

"Are you sure?"

"Just do it."

Her foot struck the cage, and it toppled over and over, and Buck toppled over and over with it. It came to a slope in the field, and it just kept on toppling. Floss galloped after it, managing to overtake it, and then she put out her leg. The jolt as it hit her hoof sprung the catch on the door, and Buck tumbled out, finally coming to rest with his long ears either side of her hoof and his hind legs all the way over his head.

Floss gently peeled him from her foot, and then she did her best to straighten him out. But every time she lifted one of his ears, it flopped.

"Is anything broken?" she asked, desperately trying not to look at the dodgy ear.

"I don't think so," Buck said. "But this has been one of my worst-ever days, and I cannot wait to get home."

"We can't go home just yet," Floss said. "I need a nice sit-down first."

"What?" He had never seen her sit down ever, and what a time to want to. "Can't sitting down wait?"

"I need to sit down right away," Floss replied, and she winked at him before turning around.

She then sat her heavy bottom on top of the cage, and it creaked and groaned. She shuffled about and lifted herself up and plonked herself right back down again. And then she kept on sitting and sitting until she was sitting right on the floor.

"I bet my bum looks big on this now." She grinned before tossing the flattened remains into the cabbages. "The humans will not catch any more little rabbits in that thing ever again. Come on, Buck, jump onto my back, and I will give you a lift. You look worn out, you poor thing."

Back at the burrow, Poppy had been staring out into the darkness the whole time, when suddenly she felt a tug to her cotton-bud tail. It was Buck Junior.

"Is Daddy back yet, Mummy?"

Poppy turned around and shook her head at the sleepy-eyed young rabbit. "Not yet, son," she said softly.

Buck Junior looked solemn. He had asked the same question three times now and he was clearly not happy with getting the same answer.

"Do you think that he's okay, Mummy?"

"Of course, he is," Poppy replied, but it seemed that the young rabbit had not missed the doubt in his mother's eyes, and he looked as worried as her.

"So, can I go and look for him?"

"Of course, not," Poppy said, visibly shaken by such a suggestion. "Auntie Floss has gone to find him. Go back to your bed, Buck Junior, and when you wake up, Daddy will be home."

Buck Junior edged a little closer to his mother. "But I cannot sleep."

"Come here, son."

He went to her, and she cuddled him against her. They both stared out into the blackness, praying for Buck's safe return.

"I can see something moving out there, Mummy. Over towards the trees."

"Get back into the burrow, Buck Junior. It might be a fox."

"It's not a fox. It's bigger. I think that it's Auntie Floss, but I can't see Dad with her."

Poppy strained her eyes, trying to see across the dark field. She could just make out the large shape that Junior was talking about, and it was looming closer. "Yes, I think you are right, Junior. It must be Auntie Floss."

"But can you see Dad? Where is Dad?"

Poppy shook her head. "I can't see him, son."

She said nothing further, as she did not want to upset him, but she was thinking the worst. If Floss had not found Buck, then something awful had obviously happened to him. There could be no other explanation for him staying out so late.

And then, all of a sudden, Junior let out such a loud shriek that she almost jumped out of her skin. "Dad! Dad!"

Taking her by surprise, he then squeezed past her, running from the burrow and out into the darkness. She immediately ran after him, shouting for him to return.

It was then that Poppy saw the reason for her son's excitement. Floss was just a few metres away, and she had a strange hump on her back. It didn't take her long to realise that the hump was Buck, and he was riding as if he were a cowboy.

When Buck saw his wife and son, he leaped down and ran to them, hugging both of them so tightly that they could scarcely breathe.

"Buck, you are safe. Thank goodness," Poppy said when he finally let her go.

"Course, I'm safe," Buck boasted. "There aren't any humans clever enough to catch old Buck the Rabbit. You should know that, Poppy. You should never worry about me."

Poppy smiled at him. Apart from one of his ears being a little droopy, he seemed none the worse for whatever ordeal had befallen him. No doubt he would be telling them the tale once they got into their burrow. The three rabbits turned their heads simultaneously then looking for Buck's saviour. Floss was a little way away obviously letting them have a moment to themselves. Poppy called to her.

"Floss, are you joining us?"

When Floss got to them Poppy sat right up on her haunches and reached up and touched the young cow's nose with her paw.

"Thank you, Floss," Poppy said. "Thank you for bringing him home to us."

"It was my pleasure," Floss said smiling. "Now get in that burrow and get some decent sleep, all of you."

Poppy waited until Buck and Junior were inside the burrow, and out of earshot, before looking at Floss again. They then smiled at each other.

"Last evening then," Poppy said.

"Last evening," said Floss.

"Have you told Buck?"

"No, I thought he'd had enough excitement for one evening. Tomorrow is going to be a difficult day for everyone."

"Till tomorrow then."

"Till tomorrow, Poppy."

Floss slept relatively soundly, considering what had happened that night. She barely stirred until the first peep of the sun came through the distant trees, waking her as it sparkled through the branches, its bright light dancing against her eyelids.

She spent the next hour dozily grazing beside the burrow, waiting for the rabbits to appear. They emerged later than usual, with Poppy out first, and then pop, pop, pop – the youngsters leaped out one at a time. Buck came out last of all.

"Good morning, Floss," he said brightly. "How did you sleep?"

"Very well, thank you," Floss replied.

"Yeah, I did too, considering my headache," he said.

"Yeah," Poppy said, "considering that he wanted to keep telling the children over and over again the tale of what happened to him last night in the cabbage field. I swear he told a different story each time! Not that the children noticed, of course. He is their hero now."

"I didn't tell a different tale each time," Buck objected, and then he flashed Floss his toothy grin. "I just told them how I managed to chew a hole in the bars of the trap," he said, winking at her. "And then how you helped pull me through the hole."

"Ah," Floss said, choosing not to correct him. She knew the wink meant he hoped she wouldn't give him away.

And then Poppy turned to Buck. "Floss has something to tell you," she said. "We talked about it last night before we realised that you were missing."

Buck turned his head towards Floss. "You do?"

Floss swallowed hard. Telling Buck that she had decided to go on with her search for her son was not going to be easy, but it was something that she had to do.

"It is time for me to leave you all, Buck," she said. "I have to go looking for Boris."

Buck lowered his head for a moment, as if deep in thought, and then he lifted it again. "I was kind of hoping that you would stay with us," he said.

"If I could stay, I would," Floss replied. "But my leg is better now, and I owe it to my son to go on looking for him. It's why I escaped in the first place."

Buck remained solemn, with his head down, until Poppy nudged him. "Floss has to do it," she said.

Slowly Buck lifted his head. "So when are you going?"

"Today."

"Today!" Buck repeated loudly. "Nothing like a bit of notice."

"I have wanted to tell you for some time, but it has been hard for me."

"Yeah, well, it is hard for us too."

"Hey, don't you talk to Floss like that," Poppy said. "We all knew that she would not stay forever."

Floss heard Buck take a deep breath which he blew out loudly. She could see that he was trying hard to calm himself, and so she gave him a moment to pull himself together. He obviously needed time to come to terms with the news.

Buck drew another breath and then he smiled at her. "I'm sorry, Floss," he said. "It is just that you have become so very dear to us, like part of our family, and it has been so wonderful having you around. I cannot imagine how different our lives will be without you. I mean, you are larger than life, and some of us would not be here if it weren't for you."

Floss smiled warmly at him. "And maybe I wouldn't be around if it weren't for you, Buck," she said. "You were the one who showed me how to heal my wounded leg."

"When you find your son, you will come back so that we can meet him, won't you?" Buck said.

"I hope that one day I will be able to do that," replied Floss, blinking tears away.

"So this goodbye is only temporary," Buck said, visibly brightening. "I can live with that."

Poppy smiled at Floss. The news had been delivered and they knew that Buck was at peace in his mind with it.

Floss looked across at the six young rabbits then. They had lined themselves up beside their father, and their faces were as gloomy as his had been.

"I hope that you will be good rabbits for your mum and dad," Floss said. "And one day, I will return to see you all grown up."

Lucy began to sniffle. Buck Junior, who was next to her, nudged her gently. "We promised each other last night that we would not make this too hard for Auntie Floss," he whispered.

The sniffling promptly ceased.

Buck Junior made his way to the front of the little group. "We love you, Auntie Floss," he said. "We understand why you have to go, and we have all decided that we will be strong about it. We want you to know that we are going to miss you loads, and that we hope you find your son."

Floss's eyes began to fill up again; so much so that she was unable to stop the flow of tears, which dripped down the long hairs of her face. How suddenly young junior had grown up. It was as if he'd become an adult rabbit overnight. She blew her nose loudly. Tears seemed to come all too easily to her these days.

She turned her head to look at Buck. Theirs had been an unlikely friendship, but it had worked so well.

"So, my friend," she said. "I shall say goodbye then."

"Don't forget that we will always be here for you, Floss. You are welcome to return whenever you want. You are the nicest Highland cow that we have ever met."

Floss managed to laugh through her tears. "So you've met a lot of Highland cows?"

"You know what I mean."

Floss and Poppy then shared a wordless goodbye.

And then Floss lowered her head and gently touched each baby rabbit's nose with her own. "Goodbye, Junior; goodbye, Lucy; goodbye, Pip; goodbye, Buzz; goodbye, Fluff; goodbye Hoppy," she said to each in turn.

"Goodbye, Auntie Floss," they chorused.

She gazed at each cute little face for one last time then, seeking to imprint them in her memory. And then she turned away. "I love you all."

She broke into a canter, headed off towards the trees, and then across the cornfield beyond, not knowing that the rabbits did not stop waving their paws until she became a tiny speck on the horizon.

CHAPTER SIX

The days were long and lonely for Floss after that. There was the odd encounter with other rabbits, and even a hedgehog, but none gave her the friendship that Buck and his family had afforded her, and none returned news of her son. The long summer slowly turned into autumn, bathing the landscape in golden browns. The day of her escape seemed so long ago now, when the trees had been green, and the meadows even greener. She stopped for a moment in the middle of a ploughed field and looked out across the changing colours of the landscape. Where could her son be in this big world? Would she ever find him?

Out on the horizon, three animals were crossing in front of the setting sun. Their bodies were dainty, their legs long, and their heads bent towards the ground. *Roe deer*, Floss thought. Maybe they could have come across her son on their travels. Such an excitement came over her then that she could barely contain herself. The vibrations from the pounding of her hooves reached the deer long before she did.

It was a small family, a mother deer with her two offspring, and when she saw the tousle of russet hair and sharpened horns hurtling towards them, she let out a cry of alarm. The deer then turned around and fled, skilfully leaping over anything and everything that got in their way.

"Stop! Please stop!" Floss yelled, galloping on after them, but her short legs were no match for their agility, and they soon disappeared into the distant vegetation. She gave up the chase and came to a standstill, her sides heaving and her nostrils flared.

"What on earth did you do that for?"

Floss turned her head but could not see who – or what – had spoken.

"I'm over here."

And then she noticed a pair of brown eyes twinkling at her from behind a gorse bush. She made her way around it and found a chestnut pony, about twelve hands or so in height. He was standing behind two strands of electric tape.

"Hello," she managed to say, still panting. "I didn't see you there."

"I know you didn't," the pony replied. "But I saw you. In fact, I have been watching you for quite some time."

"You have?"

"Yes, I have, and I was wondering why you wanted to do that."

"Do what?"

"Chase the sweet little roe deer like that. Cows don't usually hunt after deer."

"I wasn't hunting them. I just wanted to stop and ask them something."

"Stop and ask them something? I thought you wanted to trample all over them, and so did they. Anyway, what did you want to ask them about? Maybe I could help."

"I wanted to ask them if they know where my son is."

"Shouldn't you know that yourself?"

"Yes, of course I should, but he was taken from me by some wicked humans, and he is only a baby. That is why I escaped; you know, so that I could find him."

"I see," the pony replied, and his face took on a very solemn expression. "Humans have made my life pretty miserable too. I was put into this tiny paddock years ago, but it just doesn't provide me with enough food to eat. The grass that comes up in springtime only lasts a month or two, and when that is gone, I go hungry. That's not all either; even worse than hunger is solitude. The loneliness drives me absolutely crazy. Sometimes I think that I might die of isolation before I starve to death, but somehow I never do."

Floss took a step backwards so that she could take a better look at the pony. His eyes, though amazingly bright and full of life, were sunken into his head, which was scabby and insect bitten. His neck was scrawny and dipped below his withers, and his ribs and backbone were so prominent that they looked as if they might pop through his skin. Burrs and sticky buds tangled up his sparse mane and tail.

"Yes, loneliness is awful," she replied. "Why did they abandon you here like this? I always thought that ponies got better care than cows."

The pony sighed. "Not all ponies are well looked after. It depends on the owners, you see. I mean, we are 'quite high maintenance', or so I have overheard them say. My owners bought me because their spoiled children decided that they wanted a pony. Well, all they wanted to do was gallop me all over the place, to within an inch of my life, pulling at my mouth all the time, until it was so sore that I couldn't chew properly. And then, all of a sudden, I was too small, and so along came this big posh showjumping horse. It bounced around here like it was crazy, pulling the children and the grown-ups all over the place, and trashing everything in sight."

"So where is this big posh horse?"

"Well, not long after its arrival, the children started talking about a new home. I was really excited. I mean, I didn't want to live the rest of my life in this dump. And so, this beautiful blue horsebox turned up, and it had their new horse's name written in fancy lettering on the side. I thought, *Oh well, maybe my name is on the other side*. But then, they just walked on past my stable as if I did not exist. Out the horse trounced, throwing itself about as usual. And what a fuss it made about going inside that beautiful horsebox! It was kicking and farting, snorting and biting all the while they were trying to drag it inside. It took them over an hour to load it, and then off they went. I am still waiting for that bright-blue horsebox to return for me."

Floss hung her head sadly as she listened to him. This was yet another horror story. This poor pony did not deserve to be treated so terribly.

"Don't they visit you?" she asked.

"If you want to call it 'visiting'! The parents turn up about once a fortnight. They run in like it's a major inconvenience, fill my trough with water – which is only to ease their guilt and make sure that I don't peg out on them – and then they leave. But just take a look at what they expect me to drink. Go on! Just take a look in my trough."

The pony nodded his head towards a rusting old metal bath that was near his gate, and Floss made her way over to it. She quickly wrinkled her nose.

"Ugh … it is green and it stinks."

"What did I tell you!" the pony replied. "I can't imagine why they can't smell it too. Somehow they imagine that I won't mind drinking it. The other day, I saw a poor black bird drop dead after taking a drink! Honest, I did. When it rains, I drink water from the puddles. Even though it tastes a bit gritty, it's still safer."

Floss lifted her head so that she could see over the pony's back. The paddock land around him was covered in horse manure; and, with the exception of hundreds of plants with yellow flowers, which stood almost as high as the pony himself, almost every stalk of vegetation had been eaten into the ground.

"It's horrible in there," she said. "There is nothing to eat except those flowers. Why haven't you eaten them?"

The pony turned his head and looked at the ugly yellow forest behind him.

"I can't eat them because they are very poisonous, and I mean deadly. Some years back, I forget how many, some other people brought a pony here, a little grey mare. Well, I told her not to eat them, but she got so hungry that she started to nibble, and the more she nibbled, the more she got used to the awful taste. Dead within a week the poor thing was; only seven years of age too. When they came to take her body away, I heard them say that it was the ragwort that had killed her. I try my best to avoid it, but there's so much of it growing that it's hard to eat the teeny bits of grass without getting some of it in my mouth. Goodness knows how long it will be before my liver has taken as much as it can."

"And I thought I was badly off!" Floss said. "But at least I haven't gone hungry. So far, there has been plenty to eat out here."

The pony lowered his head and stared longingly between the two strands of electric tape that stood between them. He could see the luscious grass at Floss's feet, but he could not reach it.

"I can see that," he said.

"Why don't you just walk through the tape," she said. "It is very flimsy, just a bit of nothing, and I am sure that it will break very easily."

The pony shook his head. "It may look weak," he said. "But don't be fooled: it has teeth, and it bites."

Floss laughed at him. "Don't be daft. It doesn't have any teeth."

"Just you try to stick your nose on it, and you will find them."

"All right, I will," Floss said.

"Don't …" his voice trailed off because Floss had already touched the tape.

Zap! The electricity pulsed and sent her leaping three feet into the air. As she came back to earth, looking decidedly sorry, the pony almost fell over laughing.

"That's the funniest thing I've seen in a long while," he said, still chuckling.

"Wow!" said Floss. "That really hurts."

"Don't worry. It will wear off very quickly. But once it has bitten you, you learn to keep your nose well away."

"That will teach me to think that I know it all, won't it? I learn something new every day. Maybe grabbing it in my mouth wasn't such a great idea."

"And now you understand why I'm stuck in here."

Floss gave a sigh and stared at the tape. "I just can't see how it can bite when it hasn't got teeth," she said. "And it hasn't left a mark on me. Maybe if I just charge at it, then it won't get the chance to bite."

"And maybe it will."

"Well, I am not going to leave you in there for the rest of your life. If I can get through a barbed-wire fence, I think that I can get you out. Stand back; here I come."

The pony watched, looking quite astounded, as she took four steps backwards. He closed his eyes, apparently unable to bring himself to witness the tape ripping her to pieces.

"So, are you coming out or what?" Floss asked.

Slowly, he opened his right eye and then his left. Floss was standing next to him, and both strands of tape were in half. She had obviously made it quite angry, though, because sparks had started flying from it, and it kept making a dreadful clicking noise. He looked at it nervously.

"Now you've upset it," he said.

"It doesn't matter how upset it is, because you can just come out. Come on, out you come! There is some lovely grass here."

"I ... I ... c-c-can't," the pony stammered. "It might follow me."

"No, it won't. It is fastened to the wooden posts."

As if to prove the point, Floss stepped right over the clicking ends of tape, and then she looked at him. "See?" she said, looking at him. "It didn't even touch me."

"I just dare not."

"Well, you will have to dare. Come on, just do it."

The pony began rocking back and forth, trying to drum up the courage to go over the tape. Floss heard him whisper, "Come on," and then, "Just do it. Do it now."

He sprang high into the air and cleared the tape by about a metre. He then skidded to a halt in front of Floss and snapped his head around. The tape had not followed him and he appeared to settle when he realised it was not going to. His mouth went down to the grass, and he feverishly pulled up the blades, chewing urgently.

"I told you that you could do it, didn't I?" Floss said.

The pony lifted his head briefly from the grass. "You must think me very rude," he said. I haven't even introduced myself or thanked you. I am Bobby. Bobby Dazzler."

"Bobby what?"

"Bobby Dazzler; you know, like a diamond."

"Oh," Floss said, trying not to sound surprised at his name.

"I guess I am not such a dazzler any longer, am I?"

Floss smiled at him warmly. "You look just fine to me," she said. "A true dazzler."

"You are very kind, but you can just call me Bobby if you like."

"And I am Floss."

"Well, Floss, there may be a way that I can repay you for getting me out of here. You say that you are looking for your son. It might be nothing, so don't get your hopes up too much, but when I was a young pony, I spent many years living in stables in a village called Gunness, which is not far away from here."

"Go on," Floss said.

"In a field just off one of the roads that I used to hack along, there was a field with cows in it. Just like you, they were not your typical cow."

"What do you mean, 'not your typical cow'?"

"They were not black-and-white ones. They were … well, hairy like you, and I hope you don't mind me saying this, but they had short legs like yours, and big, big horns."

"Just like mine?"

"Just like yours. I was thinking that maybe you are a rarer breed, and so maybe your son could have been taken to join them."

Floss's heart lifted. This was just the kind of news that she had been waiting to hear. "How far is Gunness?" she said. "I must go there at once. Please, Bobby, will you take me?"

"Oh, it's not far," he said. "And of course I will take you, but we will have to go nice and steady. My old legs aren't what they used to be."

They followed an overgrown path that led from Bobby's field, which gradually became narrower until it disappeared into a thicket of gorse and blackberry bushes. An opening to the side of this thicket took them straight into a potato field. As they crossed this field, they nibbled at the green leaves of the plants, and when occasional potatoes sprang from the soil, they nibbled at these too. When they got to the edge of the field, there was an embankment, and they scrambled up it and onto the track that ran along the top. As they walked side by side along the stone and shale, Bobby explained that the track had once carried trains.

"What are trains?"

"They are great big noisy things often full of humans."

"I don't think that I like the sound of trains."

"Well, I like them," Bobby said.

"You do? Why ever is that?"

"Because the humans are all locked away inside and can't get out; not whilst the train is moving, anyway."

Floss laughed out loud. She now liked trains also.

They continued along the disused railway track for a further mile or so, until they got to a point where it branched into two. Bobby stopped here, not making a move to go one way or the other; he just stood, looking this way and that. Floss could see that he was frowning.

"What's the matter, Bobby?" she asked, looking down the right hand track, and not really paying him attention.

She simply wanted him to decide which way they should go, and if he couldn't, then she would decide for herself.

"My feet have been bruised by the stones on the track and I am feeling very tired, Floss. If we go the wrong way then I am not sure that I will make it back to this point. That is why we must get it right first time."

But his reply went right over Floss's head. She was far too engrossed in her own plight to listen to him. They were getting closer to her son, she was certain of it and Bobby's words were simply that, just words that she did not digest.

"Come on!" she said, turning her head to look at him and failing to notice that he could barely walk. "We'll go this way."

She began trotting along the left-hand track, which led them down the embankment and onto a pathway that followed a wide canal. Bobby went after her crying out for her to slow down but a stiff breeze that had whipped up since they left his paddock carried his voice away.

It was five further minutes before Floss eased her pace. She then turned her head to look for Bobby. He was almost a hundred metres away, and she yelled to him at the top of her voice. "Come on! Hurry, Bobby. I need to get to Gunness before it gets dark so that I can at least see the cows."

By the time Bobby got to her, his sides were heaving and his nostrils were flared. Sweat was pouring off of him, running down his neck and dripping off the centre of his thin little belly. "There you are," Floss said. "Did we take the right track then? Can you tell yet?"

Bobby coughed, fighting to catch his breath, but Floss did not notice because her mind was on one thing only.

"Bobby, did we take the right track?"

"I ... I am not sure. We have been going so fast that I haven't had a chance to get my bearings. Just a moment and I will see if I recognise anything."

They were still following the canal, which looked pretty much the same as it had earlier, but on the other side of it a cottage had come into view, and at the back of the cottage, there was an enormous concrete structure with what looked like chimneys on top.

"What is that?"

"That is Keadby Power Station," Bobby said, still breathing heavily. "And it means that you chose well, Floss. We are going the right way."

"Fantastic," Floss said. "So how far is it now?"

"Only about two miles or so. We should be there in less than an hour."

Two miles? Less than an hour? If it was only two miles, they could be there in less than half that time. Certain that she was just minutes away from being reunited with her beloved son, Floss began to canter.

"Hurry, Bobby!" she called out. "We must hurry."

"Hey, Floss, wait for me. Please wait for me."

But Floss was too far in front to hear Bobby's cries, and she did not know that her feet had created a cloud of dust behind her making it difficult for him to see. Bobby blinked and coughed as he struggled through it, but it was a losing battle. Suddenly, an acute and intense pain surged through his hindquarters, and within seconds, his muscles tightened, as if they had been turned to stone. When he tried to walk, he couldn't. His legs just would not work.

"Help me!" he yelled. "Please help me." And then he fell to the ground and was silent.

Floss, still completely unaware of the events that had unfolded behind her, eventually reached a strange metal contraption that blocked her path. It was here that she turned to look for Bobby. She needed him because she did not know how to get through it. She was quite surprised when she saw all the dust and she waited a while for it to settle, expecting to see Bobby coming through it at any moment, but he didn't. What was she to do now then? Without Bobby, she would never find the Highland herd and without him, she was alone again. Realising the gravity of her mistake in not checking on him she hurriedly began to retrace her steps all the while imagining what could have happened to him. Maybe he had changed his mind about coming with her and had returned to that awful paddock of his. But then she thought of how happy he had been to get out of it, and she discounted the notion.

At first, when she saw the mound on the track, she thought that it was just a tree stump or something similar to that. But then, as she drew closer, the awful reality became all too evident. Her pace quickened, and a sickly, guilty feeling came to her. If only she hadn't been so selfish about what she wanted, this would not have happened. If only she had listened to him.

And when she reached him, never in her whole life had she seen such a sorry sight. His poor and emaciated little body was pitifully spread out on the ground, with his head outstretched and his mouth open. His nostrils were flared out, as if he had been fighting for his very last breath. Her head fell heavy with remorse. Tears rolled down her cheeks, dripping from the end of her chin and onto his body, running in little rivulets between the crevices of his ribcage. He had so wanted not to be alone, and now she had let him die thinking that no one cared about him; but she cared about him, she had just forgotten to show it. Her sobbing became hysterical, and her nose dropped so that her nostrils touched his.

"Goodbye, Bobby," she whispered. "I hope God takes better care of you in heaven than I did. I hope that the grass is green and that the sun shines brightly up there for you."

All of a sudden, she became aware of warm air around her nostrils. She pressed her nose closer to his, and when she felt the warmth again, she turned to look at his ribcage.

"He is alive!" she exclaimed, and she hurried around him in a frenzy, wondering what she should do. She looked up at the sky above her head. The light of day was fading fast, and the clouds had darkened, threatening a rainstorm. A stiff breeze started to blow from the north, and the air had taken a sudden chill to it. If Bobby was to survive the night, he needed to stay warm, but how could she do that without a blanket or straw bed? And then she used her instinct, as dear old Ned had told her to: she lay herself down and shuffled across the ground until she was almost lying on top of Bobby. After that, she prayed for his life to be spared – and she kept on praying until sleep came to her.

When Floss next opened her eyes, an early morning mist had developed in the damp air, and it hovered like a ghostly fog across the land around her. It had rained nearly all night, but it looked like the day would be fine, as she could already see the blur of the sun peeping through the mist. She arched her back, feeling for Bobby's warmth, but there was no body heat; in fact, she couldn't feel him at all.

Fearing the worst, Floss leaped to her feet, but instead of finding Bobby's cold and dead body, she found nothing. The only indication that he had been lying there was a flattened patch of grass and a big pile of poo.

An uncomfortable thought crossed her mind. The only explanation for Bobby's absence was that he had recovered and had decided that he didn't want anything to do with her any more. And who could blame him after how she had treated him? Her selfish actions could have cost him his life.

And then, quite suddenly, she heard the sound of little pony hooves moving like pistons. A loud whinny came, and a second later, Bobby appeared from behind a small coppice of trees. He trotted hell for leather towards her, skidding to a halt just before he knocked her over.

"Good morning, sleepyhead," he said. "Thank you for coming back for me last night."

Floss could scarcely believe her eyes. The change in Bobby was incredible. Last night, it had seemed that he was at death's door, but now he looked well: his belly was more rounded than she had ever seen it, and his little mouth was so full of grass that it spilled from both sides of his mouth.

"Bobby, you look … you look good today."

He managed to swallow the enormous mouthful of grass, and then he smiled at her.

"Yeah, I feel a lot better," he said. "It was an attack of azoturia. I had it before, many years ago. It happens when you work too hard after a long rest. Quite a few horses suffer from it, and it is very painful. My muscles still feel a bit sore, but as you can see, they're not stopping me from getting out and about. It's great to be free! And for the first time in years, I am not hungry."

"I'm so very sorry about yesterday, Bobby. My mind was set on one thing, and one thing only – getting to my son. I never noticed that you were struggling, though now that I think about it, the signs were obvious. I honestly thought that I'd killed you, Bobby. Will you ever be able to forgive me?"

"If humans couldn't manage to kill me by keeping me in that poisonous paddock, then I doubt that you could."

"I didn't expect you to make it; truly I did not."

"So you care about me then?"

"Of course I care about you."

"That sounds so good. Say it to me again."

"I care about you, Bobby."

Bobby took in a deep breath and smiled.

"When we find your son, we can be just like a proper family," he said.

"An unusual family," Floss replied. "What with you being a pony, and Boris and I being cows."

"It doesn't matter how different we are as long as we are all happy together, and I know that we will be."

Floss smiled at him. She could see from the expression on his face how much it meant to him to be cared about. From now on she would make sure that their coming together was the best thing that could have happened to him. Whatever lay in store for them, she would make sure that his life changed for the better.

"Are you well enough to carry on today, Bobby, or do you want us to stay and rest some more?"

"I am okay to carry on as long as we take it nice and steady. If my muscles get too sore, I will tell you."

And so they walked along the track together, side by side, two friends. Floss kept to Bobby's pace, which was slow, but they still made progress. Within just over an hour, they arrived at the metal stile that Floss had encountered the previous day.

"This is new," Bobby said, frowning as he touched the metal bars with his nose. "We are not going to be able to get through here."

The news made Floss's heart sink. She had hoped that there would be some magic button that could be pressed to open it up. How on earth would they get to Gunness and the Highland herd now?

"Hey, don't look so glum," Bobby said. "Just because we can't go through it, doesn't mean that we cannot go around it. We will have to go through marshland, though, so be warned: you are going to get your feet very wet."

"I don't mind wet feet."

She followed Bobby off the track and away from the canal. They had to pass fencing, which had been erected to stop anything from doing exactly what they were doing, and then they were in the marsh and wading through a tangle of reeds and bulrushes. Floss felt water creeping up her short legs.

"Are you okay?" Bobby shouted, turning to look at her. "I know it's a bit cold."

"Yeah, I am fine," Floss replied. "I am used to cold water. In fact, it was cold water that saved my bad leg, but that's another story."

After about ten minutes, the water began to subside again. It was no longer above Floss's knees, and she could see the track up ahead. The stile was now behind them.

"Nothing stops you, does it, Bobby?" she said.

"Only white tape with teeth," Bobby replied, grinning. "We're a good partnership you and I."

"We certainly are. We work well together, and it's a good job you knew that we could get around that fencing. I thought that it would go across the entire marsh."

"Ah … I wasn't so sure that it wouldn't, but I didn't want to tell you that. I just hoped."

"So where to now?"

"If my memory serves me well, we will come to a road very soon. It runs through an estate, and I am afraid that there is no avoiding it."

"What's an estate?"

"An estate is human territory."

"Do you mean houses and things?"

"Yes, I mean houses and things. We are lucky though. It's still very early, and most humans should be in their beds."

The thought of coming across humans made Floss feel quite uneasy. The fewer of them she came across, the better off she would be. "I hope we don't come across any," she said.

The track came to a T-junction with the road that Bobby had mentioned, where a coppice of trees and shrubs hid them from view. Bobby turned to look at Floss. "Stay here, Floss. I will see if the coast is clear before we move onto the road."

"The coast? You didn't say that we were going to see the sea. I've never seen the sea, though Ned, my old friend, used to tell me stories about it. When he was very young, just a colt, his owner used to take him onto the sands with his mother. She was a seaside donkey."

Bobby laughed out loud. "That's nice," he said. "But I am afraid that you are not going to see the sea today. When someone says 'the coast is clear', it means that no one is about. Maybe the phrase came from smugglers trying to get their ships in and out of coves without being seen. I've picked it up from some human along my life's journey."

"Oh," said Floss slightly disappointed. "You go on then and check that the coast is clear."

Except for two cars parked close to the track, the road was very quiet, and Bobby beckoned for Floss to join him. They then trotted down the tarmac, keeping close to the kerb and watching the houses carefully, in case anyone should come out.

"There it is!" Bobby suddenly shouted. "It's so long ago since I went down this road that I wondered if it would still be here, but, thank goodness, it is."

"What is?" Floss quizzed, following him nose to tail towards an overgrown privet hedge spilling out of the garden of a large detached house.

"The next track," Bobby said. "It will take us to the big river – the River Trent – and then we will not have very far to go at all."

Floss looked at the overgrown hedge. Long tendrils had grown out from it, making a kind of arch that went right across the track. Below it there was space to get through, but it was going to be a tight squeeze.

"It can't be used that much now," Bobby said ducking his head. "Otherwise, this stuff wouldn't have grown across. Come on, Floss. Follow me."

They squeezed underneath the overgrown tendrils of the privet, and after a few steps, Floss found that she could lift her head again, though she chose not to, as the grass along the track was overgrown and tasty. Both animals took a nibble or two as they walked along. After they passed the end boundary of the garden that had the overgrown hedge, the path widened into a clearing. Here, Bobby came to a standstill and turned to Floss.

"What's matter?" she asked.

"There is something that I want you to see," he said.

He nodded his head towards a metal gate to his right. Behind it there was a small paddock overgrown with grass and weeds. There was a block of stables to one side that were somewhat worse for wear, in that they had no doors and two had no roofs. These roofless sections had caved in, forming a V shape in the centre of the block. Loose grey slates lay about everywhere.

All of a sudden, Bobby let out an ear-piercing whinny that almost made Floss jump out of her skin.

"What the … ?!" she exclaimed.

Bobby was quick to apologise. "Oh, I am sorry! I startled you," he said. "Excitement got the better of me. I used to live here, you see."

"How long ago?" Floss asked, calming down.

"Oh, it was many years ago. I have lost count. But I do remember that I had four summers here, and they were the best times of my life. I had good owners then, you see. They looked after me well. I was out grazing all day; and then, at night, they would bring me in to a cosy bed of shavings and hay net, which was always plump full. I had friends here too, friends who cared about me, and that's why I whinnied. I was kind of expecting Milo and Rocky to just pop their heads up from those stables to welcome me home. I hope they fared better than I did when they were sold."

Floss noticed then that Bobby's eyes had glazed over, though he turned his head presumably to hide the tears from her.

"Anyway," he said, turning to her again. "That part of my life is in the past. It is the future that we must look forward to now – a future for you, for me, and for your son. In another mile or so, we will arrive at the river, and then it won't be long before we find out if your son is with that herd or not."

"Oh, Bobby, I hope he is. I really hope that he is."

It was shortly before two in the afternoon when they arrived on the banks of the river, and Floss could not believe her eyes when she saw the scale of it. It was so wide that it was just as she had imagined the sea would look, though she knew that it couldn't be the sea because Ned had said that the sea was blue, and this water was dirty and brown. There was a large red barge docked on the far side of it, waiting to be loaded.

"Wow!" Floss said. "It's enormous."

"It is a gateway to the sea."

"And Gunness and the Highland herd?"

"They are just over the other side."

Floss took several glances between the massive expanse of water and Bobby's face. "Did you just say that Gunness is on the other side?"

"I did."

Floss began shaking her head. "This is so not good. Why didn't you say that we would have a problem when we got to this point?"

"Is there a problem?"

"Well, there is if we don't have a boat, and I haven't seen you carrying one about lately."

"What?"

"We don't have a boat, do we?"

Bobby let out a chortle. "When did you last see a pony or a cow in a boat?"

"Well, I certainly cannot swim across."

Bobby's chortle turned into full-blown laughter, but Floss could not see the funny side at all, neither on this side of the river nor the far side. If they couldn't cross the water, then they couldn't get to Boris, and there was no comedy in that fact. She looked at Bobby sternly. "Pigs might be able to fly, but I cannot."

"Pigs don't fly, Floss," Bobby replied, laughing so much that his sides looked like they might split. "And I am certainly not expecting you to sprout wings."

"Then how?"

"Take a look over there, in the distance. Tell me what you can see."

Floss looked along the length of the river and muttered, "I can see a never-ending supply of dirty brown water."

"Look further ahead."

"Grass, a fence, some trees, and a funny thing."

"Well, that funny thing is a very important thing. It is a bridge. And do you know what they do?"

She shrugged. She hadn't heard of bridges. Even Ned had never mentioned them, and he had mentioned loads of things.

"Bridges get people across water, and this particular bridge will get us over this river."

"Oh!" she exclaimed. "This is all good then."

"Yes, this is all good. Now let's get over that bridge and see if we can find your son."

Floss's frown disappeared. She was lucky to have found Bobby. He was just so very smart, and meeting him was the very best thing that could have happened to her.

When they reached the skeletal underside of the bridge about ten minutes later, traffic was heavy, and as Floss lifted her head and looked in awe at the massive structure, the noise was deafening. It made her feel quite nervous. "It's very busy up there on the bridge," she shouted, turning towards Bobby who was just behind her.

"Yes, I think we have hit rush hour."

"Rush hour? What is that?"

"It's something quite strange. Humans do it twice a day. They get into their cars at about the same time, and then they drive them about. No one has ever been able to explain it to me."

"So how do we get on the bridge?"

Bobby nodded his head towards a steep embankment. "We have to go up there," he said. "When we get to the top, there is a pathway at the side of the road that will take us over the bridge and keep us away from the traffic. This is the most risky part of our journey, Floss. I am afraid we are likely to be seen by humans."

Floss looked horrified. "But if they see us, won't they chase us?"

"Hopefully not, Floss. There's something else about rush hour that is quite strange. It tends to make humans grumpy and selfish. When I used to go out hacking, I remember that if ever we hit rush hour, the drivers didn't used to slow down for me; not many of them, anyway. It was like they were on a mission and nothing was allowed to get in their way of it, not even a little pony and his child rider doing nothing wrong. They were really quite dangerous. It's a good job I was steady and never got frightened of anything that made me jump into the road, or they could easily have hit me and had me throw off my rider. Terrible things I saw. They would be quite prepared to risk our lives just for a few seconds' patience."

"Sounds awful, but I don't understand how that helps us now."

"It helps because if they are all in that selfish mood, then they will see us as being someone else's problem and not their own. In other words, they won't bother themselves about it. Right, then, are you ready? We need speed to get up this banking."

"Ready."

With Bobby leading the way, they broke into a gallop and began scrambling up the embankment. Bobby's hooves struggled to get a grip of the soft soil, sending loose earth and stones rolling towards Floss. She managed to dodge most of it and prayed that Bobby would keep his footing, because if he didn't, he would come crashing on top of her. Luckily, that did not happen, and soon they were both standing on the level kerbside, shielded from the traffic by a metal barrier which ran the full length of the bridge.

"Come on, Floss!" Bobby shouted. "Run!"

They cantered across the bridge, their hooves making a right clatter and causing every driver to turn his or her head. Some cars slowed as people fought to get a better look at the most unusual spectacle of a cow and a pony crossing a bridge. Not one car stopped though and when they reached the other side, Bobby slowed and turned to look at Floss.

"That was fun," he said, panting.

Floss shook her head. "No it wasn't," she said. "It was horrific."

Bobby smiled at her. "Well it's got us where we need to be. You will be pleased to know that the field with those unusual cows like you is just down the lane, over that way."

Floss's heart skipped a beat and her legs turned to jelly. "I am so excited, Bobby," she said. "It has taken me a long while to get to this point, and I just know that he is going to be there."

"I hope he is, Floss, truly I do."

When they got to the field, there was quite a large herd of Highland cows grazing at the far side of it, maybe a dozen or more. They were mainly reds like Floss, but with a few brindle and blondes dotted amongst them. Floss immediately hurried to the metal gate and began calling urgently for her son.

"Boris, Boris! It is your mum, Boris."

One by one, the Highlands lifted their heads so that they could see their visitors. Floss's eyes went from one to the other. Where was he? She couldn't see him. A few of the cows began to saunter over. One of them, a large brindle quite a lot bigger than Floss, came right up to the gate.

"There is no Boris here," she said sharply, eyeing the two of them up suspiciously. It seemed as if she did not like visitors.

Floss ignored the brindle cow, looking straight through her as she continued calling for her son. "Boris! Boris!" Her voice was even more desperate.

"Do you think that I am lying? Didn't you hear what I just said? There isn't a Boris here. You are wasting your time."

Floss began to shift about uncomfortably. Boris had to be in this field. He simply had to be. Maybe the cows were deliberately hiding him from her. She looked for Bobby. He would know how to handle this.

"Hey," Bobby said coming forward and glaring at the brindle cow. "There is no need to be rude. My friend was just hoping to find her young son here, and she has come a very long way."

"Well, then, she had better take a long way to return to where she started from, because he isn't here."

Floss stared despondently at the ill-mannered cow, tears coming to her eyes. "A-a-are you sure?" she stammered.

"Yes, I am quite sure. Can't you see? We are all adults, and we are all cows. There are no young bulls here, not one."

Bobby turned to Floss. "It looks like she is telling the truth, Floss," he said. "Look in the field. There are no calves. It was a bit of a long shot, and I am sorry but it seems that I brought you here for nothing. I really hoped ..."

She interrupted him. "You have nothing to be sorry about, Bobby. At least for a day or so, you gave me hope, and though I am devastated, this is the strongest hope that I've had so far."

"We will keep looking," Bobby said softly. "There will be other herds just like this one, and he will be with one of them. We will eventually find him."

Floss nodded and wiped her tears away. "You really are a wonderful pony, Bobby. I do not know what I'd do without you, my dear friend."

CHAPTER SEVEN

As their search went on over the coming weeks, the weather deteriorated, and food became scarce. Crops were harvested and fields ploughed, leaving acres and acres of churned-up mud. A strong and freezing wind had brought in heavy rain, and when Floss looked towards Bobby, she could see that he was shivering uncontrollably. The wind and the rain were in his face and blowing his sparse mane across his eyes. It was clear that Bobby needed to get out of the weather. She smiled at him through her wind ravaged hair.

"We need to find you some shelter," Floss said.

Bobby looked at her and smiled obviously welcoming what she had just said.

"Yes, that would be good," he said. "I am freezing."

"We should check out the old buildings over there." She pointed her nose towards a number of ramshackle structures that could just be seen through the blur of the rain. They were about a hundred metres away.

Bobby followed her gaze. "Yeah, they look quiet," he said. "But we must be careful. One of them looks like it may be a house, a cottage perhaps and that could mean humans."

Floss gave the buildings further scrutiny. One was indeed larger than the others, and Bobby was right: it could be a house, but there were no cars near it, and as far as she could see, there were no humans either. In any event, it seemed that they would have to take the risk if Bobby was not going to die of hypothermia.

"I think we should take a look," she said.

They continued wading through churned-up mud until they got to the buildings. There was a cobblestone courtyard in the centre. Apart from the noise their hooves made on the stones, and the wind whistling around them, nothing else made a sound. There were no barking dogs, no washing lines, and no hens running around – nothing to indicate that any humans lived there.

"What do you think?" said Floss, glancing nervously at her friend.

"It looks deserted," Bobby replied. "Come; let's see if we can get inside one of the buildings. This rain is getting worse."

They made their way across the courtyard and immediately noticed what appeared to be an old barn. The doorway was open and inviting. They hurried over and stuck their heads inside, but it was crammed to bursting point with bales of hay.

"No room at the inn then," Bobby said, leaning in to take a bite of the hay. "But at least we are out of the wind a bit here."

"Don't you think this is odd?" Floss said.

"Hay? What's odd about hay?" He took another bite. "It's really quite nice."

"Well, if there is hay here, then surely there must be humans too. I don't feel safe in this yard, Bobby."

"But where else can we go? I really can't face that mud again, not tonight."

Floss looked at the state of him, and sighed. "I would feel better if we got out of sight a bit," she said. "We're sticking out like sore hooves in this yard."

"What about over there then?" Bobby was looking towards the largest building in the yard, and Floss immediately shook her head.

"Are you joking?" she said. "That is the one we thought was a house! Look, Bobby, it has windows and a door. If there are humans here, they will be inside that building, and so we need to keep away from it."

"I wasn't meaning to go inside the house. If you look, there is a field at the side of it, and a brick building in the middle, which my instincts tell me is a stable. If we can get into the field, we could hide in the stable till this rain stops. It looks like it may be nice and cosy in there."

Floss still wasn't sure. "I don't think we can get to the stable," she said. "There is fencing around the field, and it is not of the white-tape variety."

"Maybe there is a gate," Bobby said.

"Okay, okay," she said, relenting. "Let's go and see."

They moved out into the yard again, and with their heads held low against the sweeping rain, they hurried past the house and towards the field. The fence was of wooden rails secured to stout wooden posts, and though there was also a wooden gate, it was closed, and the latch was secure.

"What now?" Floss said.

Bobby shook his wet head miserably. "I dunno," he said looking longingly at the stable. And then out from the dreary dampness of the field there came a sudden high pitched squeal. It was so penetrating that neither of them was certain what animal could have made it.

"What on earth was that?" Floss said, alarmed.

Bobby shook his head. "I have no idea," he said. "But I have a feeling that we are about to find out. Look."

Through the blur of the rain something was moving towards them. It made a sharp squealing sound, and then, as it neared, Bobby let out a loud whinny. "It's a little mare, Floss," he said. "It's just a little pony mare."

The pony continued towards them, and it seemed that she would reach them in less than a second, as she was galloping so fast, but then, quite suddenly, she threw her legs out in front of her, stopping so abruptly that grass curled up in front of her feet. Her eyes widened so they almost filled her small face, and she threw her head back in horror. A loud snort came next, and then she spun on her haunches and retreated even faster than she had advanced. When she reached her stable door, she turned halfway round, looked across the field, snorted once more, and disappeared inside.

"Well, what was all that about?" Floss said. "I was going to ask her if she knew anywhere we could hide."

Bobby frowned. "I think that it was my fault," he said.

"What was?"

"The fact that she ran away."

"And how do you figure that?"

"It's because I have lost it."

Floss frowned at him. "But you didn't bring anything with you."

"It's my charm, Floss. I have lost my charm."

"How awful," Floss replied. "Can you remember where you last had it?"

Bobby stared at her. "Where I last had it? What are you talking about, Floss?"

"Maybe you dropped it near the barn. I remember a strong gust of wind just as we crossed the yard."

"Oh, Floss." Bobby said. "It's not that sort of charm that I am missing. The charm I have lost is my magnetism, you know, my charisma. This is an absolute disaster."

Despite the weather, Floss began to laugh. "Ah," she said. "This is not a disaster then. And anyway, isn't it more likely that she ran from me rather than you? Remember the deer?"

A big smile suddenly crossed Bobby's face. "I hadn't thought of that," he said. "That was silly of me! So, you think that I have still got it then?"

"Yeah, I think you've still got it, and whatever it is, I just hope it isn't catching."

"She was really lovely, wasn't she?"

"I suppose."

"Maybe if you back off a bit, I can get her to come over again."

"Back off a bit?"

"Yeah, you know, so that I can get her to come over."

Floss looked at him, hurt. "But we don't need her to come over. Come on, Bobby, let's go."

"But I would like to talk to her, you know to introduce myself. It's a long time since I saw another pony, and she is so very pretty."

"So, the cold and the rain are not bothering you anymore?"

"Well, not quite so much as before. Just the sight of her warmed me up. Maybe if I shout, maybe if we both shout, she will come over."

Floss wasn't at all sure that she wanted the pony to come anywhere near her friend, but she felt obliged to join Bobby in calling out. "Please come out," she shouted. "I eat grass. I do not eat ponies, as you can well see from this one standing next to me. He has no bits missing."

The pony appeared in the open doorway of her stable, and stared at them across the field.

"Come on, Bobby, she is not coming," Floss said. "You are getting terribly wet, and we need to find you some shelter."

"Just a minute, please, Floss. We just need to give her a bit more time. Look, she's just put her hoof out of the stable."

Floss sighed loudly. If the pony carried on making such insignificant steps, it would take her till dark to reach them. A deluge of rainwater ran down her forelock, and she tossed her head. This really was becoming very frustrating. She looked across at the pony again. She had just taken two more steps towards them.

"She's coming, look," Bobby shouted excitedly.

Floss sighed again. It did indeed seem that the pony was making her way over. In fact it looked as if her confidence was growing with each stride that she took. When she eventually reached them, the pony gave Floss a quick glance, as if to reassure herself, and then she turned to Bobby.

"Hi," she said shyly.

"Wow!" Bobby whispered beneath his breath. "You are gorgeous."

Blossom's cheeks flushed, and she lifted her head over the fence and stretched her nose out. Bobby reached his nose out too and then they touched. The ponies shared an excited squeal, and soon afterwards, they were nibbling each other's necks as if they had been friends for years.

Floss cleared her throat impatiently. What did Bobby think that he was doing? Was he really that hungry? She stamped her right foot, and then she did the same with her left, but it was as if Bobby had been hypnotised; he did not even look at her. And so she marched up to him and gave him a sharp poke in his ribcage with one of her horns.

"Ouch!" He snapped his head around and stared at Floss, who, at that moment, held the sort of expression that a cow might have if it was chewing a wasp.

"Are you finished?" she said.

"Oh, sorry, Floss. I forgot myself for a moment."

"You forgot yourself? No, you didn't forget yourself, but you did forget me."

"No, I did not. I would never forget my best friend."

"Well, you just did."

"No, I did not. I was just being nice."

"Nice! Is that what you call it? That is not what I call it. I thought you were going to eat her."

"You're not jealous, are you, Floss?"

"Me? Jealous? Of course I am not."

"Yes, you are."

"No, I am not."

The pony began to shift about uncomfortably. Their argument was obviously affecting her. Floss turned her head towards her. "So, do you have a name then?"

The pony smiled at her. "Of course," she said. "It is Blossom."

"What a lovely name," Bobby said, butting in. "I love spring and you remind me of spring."

Floss was beginning to feel quite sick. Was this the charm that Bobby had spoken of before? Well, it was quite nauseating, but she supposed there was no reason to be rude to Blossom, and so she turned to the pony.

"I am Floss," she said. "And you have already eaten, I mean, met, Bobby."

Blossom smiled. "Yes, I have," she said. "And I am sorry that I ran away before. It's just that I have never seen anything like you."

"You are not the first animal to be afraid of me," Floss said. "And I am sure you will not be the last."

"So, what brings you to my field?" Blossom asked.

Bobby butted in again. "Floss's son was taken from her by some nasty humans, and I am helping her to find him. We have been on a very long journey, and it has been very dangerous."

Blossom's eyes widened with admiration. "Wow!" she said. "You are very brave, Bobby."

Floss stuck her head between the two of them before they started nibbling each other again. "So, you say you haven't seen anything like me before."

"No, I haven't. If I had, I would have remembered."

"Another dead end," Floss replied. "And so, we must apologise for disturbing you, and now we'll be on our way. Bobby, are you ready?"

But it seemed that Bobby was not listening to her at all. His eyes had a glassy stare to them, and it was as if Blossom had put him into some sort of trance. Floss glowered at him and then she looked at the pony, trying to work out what all the fuss was about. She supposed that Blossom was a pretty little thing. It was almost as if she was the product of an artist's imagination; grey dapples so neat on her coat that they could have been painted on, and a tail so silky that it looked like a waterfall behind her. She lowered her eyes to Blossom's legs. They were pretty too, pale grey to the knee, and then they turned darker, and were jet black by the time they reached her dainty little feet. Yes, she sure was a cute little thing.

Floss finished her silent assessment of Blossom's good looks, and then she turned towards Bobby. Just what was he doing now? He was puffing out his little tummy and arching his neck in a most peculiar fashion. Was he trying to make himself look taller? She wasn't sure.

"Bobby, what on earth are you doing?" she said, frowning at him. "You are standing mighty funny. Do you need a wee?"

"No, I do not."

"So do you need a poo then?"

"No, I do not need the toilet at all. Thank you for asking."

"Well, if you do not need a wee and you do not need a poo, then I really do not know why you are standing like that. It is time we left here and got on with finding shelter before nightfall. Even I am feeling cold standing around like this."

"Floss, I am way too tired to go anywhere else tonight. We should stay here."

Floss looked him up and down. He did not look overly tired, and he certainly did not look as if he would collapse again, but after what had happened before, she didn't want to take a chance and then feel guilty for having forced him.

"Okay," she said. "But we would be better off moving to the trees just over there. At least they will give us a bit of shelter."

She looked towards three small trees that were on the outside of Blossom's paddock. Their leaves were becoming sparse, as half of them had already fallen, but it was better than being out in the open so much as they were now.

"I'm okay, Floss. I am going to stay right here."

"What, right here on this spot?"

"Yes, right here."

Floss chewed the matter over quickly, concluding that she was wasting her time trying to get any sense from Bobby. She supposed that there would be no real harm if they stayed next to Blossom for the night. Little Miss Cutie Pants could share him until daybreak, and then they would leave and need never set eyes on her pretty face again.

"Okay, okay," she said. "I get the picture. We will stay here, but mind if you keep your neck bent double like that for very much longer, you best not moan to me about it hurting tomorrow."

Bobby relaxed his neck. "Thank you, Floss," he said. "And my neck will be just fine." He then turned to Blossom. "So," he said. "You know how Floss told you that my name is Bobby? Well, my full name is actually Bobby Dazzler, and do you know why?"

"No."

"Well, it is because of my trot. Would you like me to show you my extension? It really is quite remarkable."

Bobby then began trotting in front of Blossom, with his legs extending like a demented stallion, mud flying everywhere. "What do you think?" he cried. "I can moonwalk too."

"Would you please be still!" Floss shouted, trying to put herself in his way to stop him flying about. "I want to lie down and sleep, so I would really appreciate it if you could be still and quiet."

Bobby brought himself to a standstill, blowing heavily.

Good ... uh!" he said, puffing himself out as he looked at Blossom.

"Wow, you really can move well."

Floss sighed loudly. "Did you hear me, Bobby? Can I lie down without you treading all over me?"

Bobby turned to her briefly. "Yes, yes of course. Lie down if you like."

And then, just as Floss was about to sink to her knees, Blossom interrupted. "Don't take this the wrong way, but I don't think it would be a good idea for you to stay here; not right by the fence, anyway."

Floss looked at her sharply. "Why ever not? If Bobby is staying, then I am too."

"I'm sorry; I should explain. My owners live in the house over there, and they worry so much about me. If they see you here, I am pretty sure that they will call the police. Please hide in the trees, Floss. You will be so much safer there, especially now that the leaves have changed colour. They are almost the same shade as you, so they should hide you well."

Floss snorted in disgust. Same shade as the leaves! Police! Who did this little pony think she was? "Police?" she retorted. "I can just see them bringing their handcuffs out to me, a cow!"

Blossom looked at her uncomfortably. "Erm … I doubt they will bother with any type of cuffs. I think that they will just shoot you. People around here shoot all kind of things."

"I think you just want rid of me so you can have Bobby all to yourself," Floss said.

"That is not true. I am trying to help you."

"So what about Bobby's safety? Shouldn't he hide too then?"

"He doesn't need to."

"And why not?"

"Because my owners like ponies," Blossom said. "Look at my lovely stable and paddock. They treat me very well indeed."

"And what won't they like about me?"

Blossom's brown eyes gazed at Floss, at the exact level of her enormous horns. "Erm … well … those things that are growing out your head. I mean, they scared me witless when I first saw them."

Floss took several deep breaths, trying to stop exploding with temper, and then as she calmed down, she started to chew the matter over rationally. The pony was actually making sense. If she did not hide, then it was quite possible that she would be seen, and if that happened, who could tell what the consequence would be! If she did get caught, her search for Boris would be over. So why had she become so angry with Blossom and sounded off at her like that? Bobby was right. The green-eyed monster had taken a hold of her, and it had made her quite rude. She must not let it happen again.

"I am sorry," she said looking at Blossom sheepishly. "You are absolutely right about my hiding. I shall go right now."

As she turned and headed for the trees she heard a shout.

"Hey, wait for me."

It seemed that Bobby had a conscience after all, and she turned her head towards him. He was following her, but she could see that his steps were reluctant and that his face was miserable. She smiled at him, jealousy completely gone.

"I will be okay, Bobby. Don't worry about me. Stay here with Blossom. It will be good for you to have an equine friend for a few hours. Enjoy it. I will return for you in the morning. No harm done."

Bobby smiled, and his soft brown eyes looked at her warmly. "Thank you, Floss. This means a lot."

"Yeah, I know she does."

Stan James parted the long pleated curtains at his bedroom window and looked out over the rapidly darkening field that extended beyond his garden. He was an elderly gentleman, though still very active, and had just run up the flight of stairs from the kitchen to the bedroom, from where he could see almost the whole of the field. There was a pair of binoculars on the sill in front of him, and he picked them up and wiped his sleeve over the lenses. Holding them against his eyes, he moved his head from left to right, scanning the field for Blossom. He and his wife had owned her for six years now, after rescuing her at an auction market, and they loved her very dearly. Every night, just before dark, he would always check that all was well with her in the field.

It wasn't long before he caught sight of her. She was over near the fence and was easy to see, with her dapple grey coat luminescent even at dusk. Something had obviously captured her attention, as her bum was pointing towards him, and her head was over the top rail of the fence. He lifted the binoculars slightly to see what it was.

"Oh my goodness!" he exclaimed as he caught sight of a chestnut pony.

Frightened that the chestnut pony might leave before his wife had chance to see him, Stan hurried to the bedroom door and then out onto the upper hallway. When he reached the top of the staircase, he began to yell.

"Betty! Betty! Where are you, dear?"

His wife appeared at the foot of the steps wiping icing sugared hands down her pinafore.

"What is it, Stan?"

"Hurry up here, please. There is something I must show you."

He left her there at the bottom of the staircase then and rushed into the bedroom, eager to check that the chestnut pony had not disappeared. When Betty appeared in the doorway, he waved his binoculars at her. "Come and see this."

Betty sighed audibly as she made her way over, and he could see that she was forcing a smile on her face. He supposed that he could hardly blame her for being frustrated with him. He was always shouting her up their staircase to look at something he had seen. Yesterday he had brought her to the bedroom to see "a most impressive barn owl." It had not been a very exciting experience, as the bird had not moved for the whole hour he had insisted they watch it. It had taken until the next day to find out why. It was not an owl after all, but an old raincoat that he had left hanging in a peculiar position on a fence post. But, still, as she arrived at his side, she slipped her slender wrinkled hand into his, and he gripped her fingers tightly. He then let them go and pushed the binoculars into her hand.

"Over there, near the gate," he said, his index finger waggling with some urgency. This time he had not brought her up the staircase for nothing. This time he really had seen something exciting.

Betty held the binoculars to her eyes and looked towards the gate.

"Can you see him?" Stan asked pushing her arm gently. "Can you see him, Betty?"

"I can see Blossom."

"There is another pony with her, a chestnut one. Look just beyond where she is standing. He's not very big."

Betty scanned the fence line again, and then she suddenly let out a gasp. "Oh my goodness! That is no old coat."

"Pardon?"

"Oh, nothing," she replied, placing the binoculars on the windowsill and grabbing hold of her husband's hand again. "He looks so thin and very, very wet and cold."

"Yes, I know he does."

"So, what are we to do? We can't just leave him there."

"No, I know we can't. That is why I am going to go outside and bring him into the field. And then I am going to give him a nice feed and some hay. I think that he will like that."

"And what will we do with him after he has filled his belly?"

"Blossom seems to like him, so we will keep him."

A look of shock crossed Betty's face. "But, Stan! We couldn't do that. He isn't ours."

"Looking at the state of him, if he does have an owner, I very much doubt that they are going to care that he has gone. He looks as if he hasn't been loved for quite some time. I am thinking that the clever little chap has found himself a nice new home."

But Betty still looked worried. "I'm way too old to be locked up for horse theft," she said as she picked the binoculars up again to take another look at the pony.

Stan laughed gently, and his old blue eyes twinkled. "No one is going to lock you up, Betty, my love. But if you are worried, call the police while I go and get him. Tell them that we have found a pony wandering about and that we are taking him in. But I doubt anyone will claim him, and if they do, I'll ring the animal-cruelty people, and they can lock the owners up for not looking after him properly. How does that sound?"

Betty smiled and Stan could see how excited and happy she was. They had always wanted a friend for Blossom. They made their way downstairs together, and whilst Betty went to the kitchen window from where she could watch, he collected his overcoat and headed for the door.

"I won't be long," he said, closing the door behind him.

A stone path led from the house through their pretty little garden and to a field gate. Stan hurried along it, stopping halfway at the garden shed. He kept Blossom's things in there: head collars, brushes, hoof picks, and the like. Her feed was kept there too, chaff and low-sugar pony cubes, all in metal bins to keep it from the resident mice.

He lifted the lid of the first feed bin and cupped his hands to measure out the chaff, which he threw into two rubber feed buckets. A double handful of the pony cubes went in next, followed by a half dozen carrots and a cup of water. Stan stirred the mixture with a big plastic stirring stick.

"That should do it," he said as he threw Blossom's pink head collar and lead rope over his shoulder. "I hope this fits him."

He squeezed the handles of the rubber buckets together so that he could carry them, one in each hand, and then he left the shed and completed the journey to the field gate.

"Blossom, come over here, sweetheart," Stan called. "I have something for you."

He saw his little mare prick her ears, and then he heard her squeal with delight. She always did that when she saw him. Soon she was trotting over. Stan patted her as she reached him and placed one of the buckets on the ground. Blossom immediately began tucking in.

Stan then looked towards the chestnut pony watching them just a little way away. "Want some," he shouted, waving the second bucket. It was obvious that the pony did as he gave a squeal that was even louder than the one that Blossom had given. Stan laughed. "I will take that as a yes," he said.

Not wanting to spook the chestnut pony, he walked slowly across the field with the bucket of feed and then placed it on the ground, just a few metres from the gate. Carefully and quietly he opened it.

"Come on in, lad," he said softly. "In you come. There you go."

The chestnut pony came inside and Stan quickly closed the gate behind him.

"Good boy," he soothed, patting the pony's scrawny neck and fitting him with the head collar. "Don't worry; we'll soon have you good as new."

Stan then turned and looked at the house. Betty was in her bright yellow waterproofs and was on her way down the stone path. It seemed that even despite the rain, his wife had been unable to keep herself inside. She smiled when she reached him a few minutes later.

"I have called the local police," she said. "No one has reported a missing pony."

Stan grinned at her. "What did I tell you! You can stop your worrying now."

Next morning, Floss woke up just after five, and after she had hauled herself to her feet and shaken herself down to rid her coat of the unwanted dirt and insects, she looked at the sky, trying to work out what sort of day it was going to be. If it was a fine day, then, hopefully, they would be able to travel much further than they had been doing of late. The signs were positive. Though the sky was still dark, almost black, there was a cerulean strip crossing the horizon just where the sun would shortly rise, and all around her birds were singing their different songs. A bright and sunny day was about to break, a stark contrast to the terrible week it had been.

She made her way from the cover of the trees and looked towards Blossom's field, where she had left Bobby the previous evening. When she did not immediately see him, she did not panic, imagining that he must be lying down; after all, it was still very early.

She arrived at the fence, and for a moment, she was stunned into silence by his absence. Her eyebrows creased towards the middle of her forehead as she looked down at the grass. This was exactly where she had left him, as she could still see his little hoof marks in the soft turf. She stared for a moment at the single heap of manure piled up in neat balls near the gate. The sight of it made her stomach turn, not because it was poo, but because it was alone. If Bobby had been there all night, then he should have made many more piles than that. A surge of panic tore through her, and she turned around and around, scanning the yard and the buildings. Maybe he had gotten so cold that he had gone to find shelter elsewhere; but then, Blossom was nowhere to be seen either. She looked towards the stable in the centre of the field, and an uncomfortable thought crossed her mind. She tried to shake it off, but it just would not leave her, and so she began bellowing at the top of her voice.

A face appeared from around the corner of the stable door, a sleepy face. It was Bobby and he was in Blossom's stable. Blossom's face appeared next to his.

"I'm here, Floss," Bobby called as he hurried towards her.

Floss's tortured bellowing immediately ceased. "There you are," she cried. "What are you doing in there?"

She waited for him to get to the fence, and then she lifted her head over the rail, expecting him to greet her with a touch of his nose, but he didn't. "Are you all right, Bobby?"

"Yeah, I am okay," he said.

"You don't look okay," Floss replied. "I mean, you look like you have slept well, but you do not look okay. Something is on your mind."

"It's nothing."

But Floss knew him too well, and as she looked over at the stable where Blossom was peering out, she nodded her head knowingly. "So," she said. "You stayed in there all night."

Bobby nodded his head sheepishly.

"And did Blossom's owners look after you?"

He nodded again. "The man came out and fed me," he said. "And then when my belly was full, I slept all night in soft and warm straw. It was so nice, Floss. There were full nets of hay in there, and a salt lick too. Blossom says that her owners always look after her like she is a princess."

Floss looked at him, and tears filled her eyes. She was about to lose him, and she knew it. Half her heart was sad about that, but the other half was happy that he had found such a wonderful place to live out his days. Places like this were hard to find, and no matter how painful it was for her, she must not take this opportunity away from him. She must do the right thing.

"And you are a little prince, Bobby," she said. "And the little prince has found his little princess. I am so happy for you."

"What do you mean? I am not staying here. I am coming with you to look for your son."

"I will not allow you to come with me, Bobby. This is a new start for you, a new life; one that you so richly deserve. I can see that you are going to be very, very happy here. Look at Blossom. She is in tears at the thought of you leaving her. Go to her. Please go to her and love her."

Bobby turned his head. Blossom was halfway across the field, and tears were rolling down her pretty grey cheeks. Despite not having known him for long the strength of her feelings for him clearly showed.

"But what about Boris?" Bobby said turning to Floss again. "I cannot let you search for him alone."

Floss had love in her eyes as she looked at him. "Yes, you can, Bobby, and you must. I was on my own for a long time before I met you, and I will find Boris just fine on my own. I am tougher than I look."

Bobby sniffed loudly. "You are tough," he said. "You are tough and courageous, but also kind and selfless. I will never meet another animal like you."

She smiled at him. "And I will never meet one like you. Fate brought me to you, and now that same fate has brought you to Blossom. I just hope that I will get a little of that good fate for myself someday."

By now, Blossom was almost at the fence. Floss looked at her. She seemed to be walking very slowly, holding back, waiting to be invited to join them.

"It is okay, Blossom," Floss said softly. "You can join us. Bobby has something good to tell you."

Blossom joined them at the fence. "Something good?" She looked at Bobby hopefully.

"Go on," Floss said nudging him gently. "Tell her."

"I can't," Bobby said.

"Then I shall. Bobby is staying here with you," Floss said. "We have decided that it is in his best interests – oh and yours of course."

Blossom looked at Floss, her eyes disbelieving. Then her gaze crossed to Bobby, her eyes doing the talking. Bobby opened and closed his mouth like a goldfish, but nothing came out of it. It appeared that he simply could not bring himself to confirm Floss's words.

Blossom continued looking at him. "Floss must love you very much to do this for you," she said.

SUSAN JAYNE MCAULEY ──────────

Bobby found his tongue. "She's leaving me here," he mumbled.

"Yes," Blossom said. "And she is doing so because she loves you."

"I do love him," Floss said. "And I know he will be safe and happy with you here, Blossom. Look after him for me."

"I will," Blossom said.

Floss looked at Bobby then. She could see that he was very close to tears. "You do know that this is the right thing, don't you?"

Bobby nodded miserably and Floss smiled at him certain that his sadness at losing her would in the days before him turn into happiness with Blossom and his new owners. She turned her head and looked out across the farmyard. "I shall be away then," she said.

"Goodbye, Floss," Blossom said. "And thank you so much."

"No, thank you," Floss said. "It is good that Bobby has found you."

She began to walk away from them, crossing the yard and leaving the same way that she had come in with Bobby. It felt strange to be without him at her side. A shout came from behind her, and she turned her head.

"Goodbye, Floss. I love you, and I hope so much that you find him. I hope that fate leads you right to his nose."

She smiled and wiped a tear down her hairy shoulder. "Goodbye, Bobby. Goodbye, Blossom," she shouted.

"Goodbye," they called out in unison. And then she was gone.

- 146 -

CHAPTER EIGHT

Susie Clark rested her elbows on her school desk and then gazed out the window beside her. A young blackbird was dancing on the grass just down from the window ledge. It was trying to fool the worms into thinking it was raining so that they would wriggle from the soil and into its waiting beak. She watched it devour several of them before a shout from her teacher, Mr Rufus, made her turn towards the front of the classroom. Noticing that he was looking straight at her, Susie gulped, and her face reddened. She lowered her head away from his glare and stared unblinking at the test paper in front of her. But the questions were still a blur, and none of them had answers written against them. This was her new school, and she hated it. She hated the school, and she hated most of the teachers; but most of all, she hated the other children. But then, she would hate them, because none of them spoke to her yet, and two girls in particular had decided that their lives were more fun when making hers a misery.

Her thoughts turned to her former school in Castleford and her old friends – friends who cared about her, friends who would not have stood by and let her be bullied. And then her mother's face came to her mind. She had tried not to blame her mother for the misery she had found herself in, but no matter which way she looked at it, the move to this silly little village in Lincolnshire really was Mum's fault. Why hadn't she thought it through a little better before uprooting them? She simply had not given enough consideration to the impact it would have on the life of a girl thirteen and three-quarters years old.

The bullying had started with the odd snigger on Susie's first day, and a few weeks later, it had escalated into a full-scale bullying programme. Sometimes it was a kick or a thump. Other times it was her school bag that got the attention, with pages of her textbooks ripped out and thrown at her, or her packed lunch emptied out and stamped on. At one time she would not have taken this abuse: she would have fought back, and she would have given the perpetrators as much as she was getting, and more. But not now, not since the death of her father a year ago. His loss had affected her confidence and her self-esteem. Her schoolwork was suffering too. What was the point of it when she had no one to be proud of her anymore? Her father had always taken an interest in her schoolwork, and he had always glowed with pride when she had come home with strings of A grades. But Mum … well, top grades had never been as important to her as they had been to Dad.

Susie's mind switched to her two ponies, Ellie and Copper. She loved those two animals so very much, and she supposed that she could at least feel thankful that her mother had not made her sell them when they had lost her father. In fact, they had fared very well from the move to the countryside. Instead of being cooped up in livery stables, they now had permanent turnout and stables whenever they should need them. Yes, the field they had found for them in Ealand was so much better than they'd had before, and even more wonderful was the fact that she could see them from her bedroom window. In fact, if it weren't for the bullying, she could grow to like this place.

"Harrumph!"

Susie had not realised that her daydreaming had become obvious again until she heard the cough, and she quickly bowed her head, but it was too late. She had indeed been the cause of the irritation to her teacher's throat, and he was making his way over to her desk. He took a hold of her test paper, and her stomach churned as she watched him staring at it. How long would it take him to realise that it was well, very, very blank?

"Susie, are you here this Monday afternoon, or are you somewhere else?"

Susie looked up at him, trying to think of a reason as to why she hadn't written anything, but her mind was a fog of different worries, and nothing came out of her mouth. And then she heard the sound of chair legs being dragged along the hard wooden floor, accompanied by an increase in chatter. It was home time, and the other children were getting ready to leave. Her heart pounded, and she leaned towards the floor and grabbed hold of her school bag. She must get to the school gates first because if she didn't, she would face yet another confrontation with the two girls sitting just behind her – the ones who had been bullying her. After muttering a quick apology to Mr Rufus, and with his shouts for her to return ringing in her ears, she ran to the classroom door and then down the entire length of the corridor.

Her bag was heavy today, and it hurt her shoulder, so after she left the school building and fled down the concrete steps, she swapped it to the other arm before hurrying across the car park. It was only then that she dared cast a glance over her shoulder. The two girls were some way behind. They had been giving chase but had been distracted by a boy from a different class. Knowing that they both fancied him made her relax; they would be there a while, and this would be one day when she did not get a thump or a kick.

Heaving a sigh of relief, she continued walking quickly. It was a two-mile walk home, and though the danger had passed, she wanted to be there as soon as possible. At this pace, it would take her twenty-five minutes to get to the door, then a further ten minutes to change, and another five or so to get to the stables. All being well, then by four o'clock she would be out riding one of her ponies in the countryside and away from everything human.

"Mum! I'm home."

She closed the front door and threw her school bag on the sofa. Her mother was sitting there, reading a letter or something. It was instantly apparent from the stern look on her face that all was not well.

"What's up, Mum?"

"Susie, this is the vet bill. I am sorry, love, but we really need to talk about those two ponies of yours."

Susie swallowed hard.

"This is 356 pounds, Susie. We just cannot afford this."

"I'm sorry, Mum. I had to call the vet. I was worried about her."

"I know, love, but we just cannot keep paying bills like this one. Goodness knows since your dad died, it is a struggle for me to earn enough to keep a roof over our heads and food on our plates. You know how we talked about this before we came here, and how I said we would try to afford to keep them. Well, I am sorry, but we just can't. We are going to have to sell them to someone who can afford to keep them."

A scream erupted from Susie's mouth. Sell her ponies? Never! They were the only good things that still existed in her miserable life. She would rather die than sell them.

"I hate you, Mum. Truly, I really hate you."

Sobbing hysterically, she pushed past her mother, heading for the staircase. After stamping hard on every one of the eleven steps, she reached her bedroom and threw her head into her pony-emblazoned pillow. Life just wasn't fair.

After a short while she heard footsteps. They didn't come all the way up to the top of the staircase, and she knew that her mother would be sitting on the middle step. She always did that when Susie was upset. There she would sit, listening to her sobbing until she had cried it all out of her. It seemed that something was always making Susie cry these days, and her mother telling her that they would have to sell her ponies was a sure way to do that.

It took about fifteen minutes for Susie's loud wailing to calm to a soft sob. After giving a couple of hefty snuffles through her nose, she made her way to the top of the staircase. Sure enough, her mother was sitting on the middle step, head in her hands.

"Mum!"

Her mother turned her head. "Come on down, love," she said softly. "We need to talk."

Susie rubbed her sore eyes and slowly came down the steps until she reached the one where her mother was sitting. She squeezed in next to her and rested her head on her shoulder.

"I am sorry, Mum," she whispered. "I don't really hate you."

"I know that, Susie," her mother said, putting her left arm around her. "I know things have been hard for you and that our moving has made matters worse, but I had to take that secretary's job at the hospital. It was the only one with a salary that could possibly pay a mortgage. When I am settled into it and my shift hours increase like they have promised, I will buy you another pony. I promise I will."

"But I don't want another pony. I want to keep the ones I have. Anyway, I have decided what I will do. I have decided that I will get a job so that I can pay for their keep myself."

She looked at her mother waiting for her response. Would her mother see the glimmer of self-belief returning to her eyes? It hadn't been there for months, but suddenly, she felt as if she had something to fight for. Suddenly, life had a mission to it.

"Bless you, Susie," her mother said. "But you are not even fourteen years old yet. You are far too young to get a job. We will think about it when you start college in a couple of years."

"But the bills and my ponies will not wait a couple of years, Mum. You just said it yourself. You have a mortgage to pay and all the other bills too, so it is my responsibility to pay for my ponies. Anyway, I will be fourteen in just a few months and I know that some of the other kids in my class have Saturday jobs. I have heard them talking about it."

Susie saw her mother's lips crease upwards at the corners. She was getting through to her.

"Okay, Susie, you get a little job, and we'll see how we go on. I love you, do you know that?"

Susie sniffed loudly. "Yes, Mum, of course I do."

"Susie, can I ask you something else? Is everything all right at school, love? I know you miss your friends, and I was just wondering if you were making new ones at your school."

Susie chose to tell a white lie. Her mother had enough to worry about without being told of the bullying. "Yes, Mum, don't worry. I am making loads of friends," she said.

"Well, I thought you may want to bring one or two of them here for a sleep-over or something. That'd be nice."

Susie couldn't think of anything worse, so she ignored her mother's intimation and changed the subject. "Where's the local paper?" she said. "I may as well start looking for a job right now."

"I put it under the middle cushion of the sofa." Her mother waved her hand towards the living room. "But can't it wait until after tea?"

"I'll have a little look now; shout me when it's ready."

Susie gave her mother's hand a tight squeeze and then she hurried down the remaining steps and made her way through the doorway and into the living room. She took the newspaper from beneath the sofa and took it through to the kitchen, where she spread it out over their table. A small advert caught her eye almost immediately: "Wanted: Mushroom Pickers".

Mushrooms! She could pick mushrooms, and what good luck – the farm was only two miles or so down the road, just a five-minute cycle ride away. Without standing, she reached across to the drawer beneath the kitchen sink and pulled out a small pair of scissors. Soon the advertisement was a square piece of paper in her hand, and after tea, she called the number in the advert, arranged an appointment, and then pulled her bicycle from the shed and cycled down the road to the farm.

"We don't normally employ kids," Ted Smith told her as he busied himself putting new paper into the fax machine in the office. "How old are you? You did not say on the phone that you were just a kid."

"I'm nearly sixteen," Susie fibbed as she looked up at him, trying to give off the confidence that she thought a fifteen-year-old might have.

In his fifties, Ted had a mop of thick grey hair and a beard that matched. He turned away from the fax machine and studied her carefully.

"And my mum is going to sell my ponies if I can't help to pay towards their keep, so I will work hard. You will not regret it."

Susie looked straight into his eyes. Had she got through to him? The silence seemed to last much longer than the two seconds that Ted actually took to reply.

"Will I not?" he said as he looked back at her. Susie could tell from the look on his face that he still wasn't sure. She smiled at him. If he was thinking of saying 'no' then this would surely make him feel uncomfortable.

Ted pursed his lips and nodded at her very slowly as if still deliberating regardless of the fact that his head was nodding. "If I did let you work here, I could only let you work on Saturdays," he said, adding, "And we start bright and early, which is before sunrise in the winter months."

He raised a grey eyebrow, as if certain this would cause Susie a problem.

"Yeah, that's fine," Susie replied. "I'm used to being up early to feed my ponies before school."

Ted's features suddenly softened. He was warming to her; Susie could tell that by the corners of his lips creasing into a smile.

"Looks like you have a job here come Saturday, little miss," he said. "Here at 6 a.m. then. Don't let me down."

Susie grinned broadly. "I won't," she said. "And thank you so much."

She turned, shook Ted's hand, and left the office. All the way to her bicycle, she could not stop smiling. This was so very exciting. Soon she would have her own money, and she could only imagine how much independence that would bring for her. She could buy her ponies whatever they wanted, and help her mum too. The smile was still on her face when she arrived home.

"Mum! Mum, it's me, it's me!" she yelled, almost falling through the front door.

"I know it's you. Who else would it be?" Her mother dried her hands on the towel at the side of the sink and then turned to face her.

"I got it, Mum, I got it. I got the Saturday job."

Her mother came towards her and hugged her tightly. "Well done, sweetheart. That is great news. Are there other kids your age working there?"

"I dunno," Susie replied, knowing full well that there weren't any. Ted had made that quite clear, but she didn't want to get her mum talking on the subject of friends again. "I wish Dad was still around to tell about my first job."

"I wish he was too, love. He would have been so proud of his little girl. Things have been so hard lately, and you have had to grow up so very fast."

Susie knew that her mother was about to cry, the sniffing gave it away and her fingers delved into her sleeve and she pulled out a tissue and passed it over to her. Her mother blew her nose loudly.

"Thank you, love," she said.

Susie slipped her arm around her mother's waist.

"We'll get there, Mum," she said.

By Friday night, Susie had got so excited about going to work at the mushroom farm that she could barely sleep. She had managed to drop off just two hours before her alarm clock woke her up at a quarter past five. Not long after that, she was already dressed and downstairs in the kitchen.

After grabbing a quick bowl of cereal and half a cup of coffee, she stepped out of the house and into the cold November air. A freezing fog had descended during the night, and it now hung low over the fields, shrouding the landscape and clogging her senses. She reached into her pocket for her torch and turned it on, but the light bounced off the icy mist, making so little difference that she switched it off again. She would have to be very careful cycling to the farm in these conditions.

She made her way along the passageway at the side of the house and began to cross the lawn. The icy particles covering the grass crunched beneath her feet as she walked. It was so very cold. When she reached the shed which housed her bicycle, she paused and slipped her hand into her coat pocket, bringing out a key ring with three keys on it. The smallest one belonged to the shed padlock, and she opened it and pulled the door towards her. The bicycle was leaning against the side wall of the shed, and she clasped the handlebars and pushed it out.

As she wheeled the bicycle towards the house, her mother appeared at the side door. She must have got out of bed early to see her off safely.

"Good morning, sunshine," her mother said. "I am glad I caught you before you left. What time do you think you will be home?"

Susie looked up and smiled at her mother. "Good morning, Mum. I didn't expect you to get up for me. I'm not sure what time I will be home. Ted said that sometimes I will be picking mushrooms for only a few hours, and other times it will be the whole day. It depends on how the mushrooms have grown."

"Bless you, Susie. It sounds like hard work to me. Just you be careful cycling to the farm. I know the road is quiet, and there aren't many drivers that use it, but even with your high-visibility vest on, they will struggle to see you in these conditions. Try to have a good day, love. And don't worry about the ponies. They will be fine with me feeding them on my own for a change."

"Give our Copper and Ellie a big kiss from me."

"I will, love."

After giving her mother a wave, Susie continued pushing her bicycle off the edge of the kerb and onto the road, where she turned on the front and rear lights, and mounted. She then began cycling down the frosted and narrow country lane.

The tarmac glistened as she rode along it, and she was careful to watch out for any black ice. She pedalled slowly and cautiously, and when she came to the blind bend in the road, she dismounted and pushed her bicycle around it. Though she didn't expect to see any vehicles so early in the morning, she had seen cars rounding that same bend at ridiculous speeds before when she had been riding her pony, and so this seemed the sensible thing to do.

Soon she was on the straight again, and so she got back on the bicycle and pedalled for a further mile and a half. The road came to a junction then, with the track that would lead her to the mushroom farm. Here she chose to push the bicycle again, as the track was uneven, and the frozen ruts would have been very uncomfortable to cycle over. When she arrived at the gates to the mushroom farm, Ted was standing outside the office, and he waved to her.

"I'm not late, am I?" Susie asked nervously as she hurriedly pushed her bicycle up to him.

"No, you are not late," Ted replied. "I just thought I would watch out for you, with it being so dark along the track. You can leave your bicycle at the side of the house, if you like. It will be safe there, as I can see it from the office. Hurry back, and I will take you to the first mushroom tunnel and show you how to go on."

The mushrooms at the farm were grown in large wooden crates stacked to the height of the poly tunnels. The crates were laid out in rows that extended the whole length of the tunnel. A narrow passageway separated each row, and then there was a wider passageway to each side of the tunnel. Susie had never seen so many mushrooms in her life, and she gasped at the enormity of the task when she saw them crammed together like a vast sea of white pegs, fighting for space in the dark compost.

"You can take your coat off if you like," Ted said as they made their way to the first crate of mushrooms. "I bet you didn't expect it to be so warm in here."

Susie had been far too shocked by the seemingly endless growth of mushrooms to notice the temperature in the tunnel, but now that he mentioned it, she did feel quite warm. Even her frozen fingers had come back to life and had turned from icy blue to warm pink. She removed her high-visibility vest and coat, and looked at Ted, her face querying a place to leave them.

"There are some hooks behind the door," he said. "Here, I will hang your stuff up for you."

He left her briefly and returned with a small blue-handled knife.

"We use these to cut off the stalks. Watch; I will show you."

Before she'd had time to blink, he had pulled four mushrooms from a tightly knitted group, and then, chop, chop, chop, chop, the stalks fell into a plastic tray which was hanging in a cradle on the side of the wooden crate. He threw the mushroom heads into a different tray.

"I'll leave you to it then," he said.

Susie forced a smile onto her face as she looked at him, trying hard to make herself look like the happiest mushroom picker alive. And then, when she was quite sure that he could no longer see her, she screwed her face up. Where on earth had she got the idea that this would be a nice little job picking a few mushrooms? Mistake! And where was everyone else? She wouldn't be able to pick all these things in a month, let alone a day.

She took a deep breath and eased her fingers into a huddle of mushrooms, trying desperately to pick one out without damaging the others. After much poking and prising, she managed to pull one free. Pleased with the specimen, she held it aloft, admiring it a moment, and then she sliced into it with her knife. The blooming thing slipped from her fingers and landed on the muddy floor. She stared down at it in horror.

"Don't worry, love. It will get easier."

The voice made Susie jump. She had thought she was alone.

"I'm up here."

Susie looked up. There was a woman standing high above her, at the top of a pair of ladders. She had striking grey hair and piercing green eyes which shone out from her brown and weathered face.

"Good grief!" Susie exclaimed. "I never saw you up there."

"I pick the mushrooms in the upper crates. It's the only promotion you ever get in here, and it took me five years to get it! Don't worry about the one you dropped. There are plenty more where that came from. You will get quicker, and it will get easier. Who knows? In a year or two, you could be faster than I am at picking the little blighters. What is your name, love?"

The thought of picking mushrooms for that long wasn't something that Susie wished to contemplate, and she immediately determined to work harder at school, regardless of the bullying.

"I am Susie," she said. "I started today."

"Tess," the woman replied, gripping the side of the ladders with one hand so that she could lower the other to shake Susie's. "It's nice to see young people in here."

Dinner time did not arrive until Susie felt quite sure that she was turning into a mushroom, and she knew that she smelled a whole lot like one. It was Tess who made the announcement, running down the right-hand passageway like a teenager. She came into Susie's row and began ushering her towards the poly tunnel doors.

"Come on! Hurry!" she said. "We only get thirty minutes."

Susie didn't need asking twice. After hanging up her picking cradle, she quickly followed Tess outside. It was still as cold as it had been first thing, and as she hadn't thought to pick up her coat, she was forced to wrap her arms around herself to keep from freezing as she hurried after Tess. They went along a concrete pathway, passing five other poly tunnels before stopping at the door of an old and very dirty static caravan. Tess pushed the door open, and Susie followed her inside.

The former interior of the caravan had been removed to form one large room. It had a large wooden table in the centre, surrounded by about a dozen white plastic chairs.

Some of the chairs were occupied. Feeling uneasy in a caravan full of strangers, Susie kept close to Tess.

"Here, Susie, sit down," Tess said, pulling a chair up.

Susie sat down, and then she gazed at the table. There was an array of plastic bags, tubs, and bottles all over it. Her tummy rumbled then. This was everyone's lunch, and she hadn't brought any.

Tess smiled at her. "First day, and you haven't brought any sandwiches? Not to worry. Here, take one of mine. I've got plenty."

"Oh thank you, Tess. Mum and I never thought about sandwiches. I don't know why."

She took a hold of the tub and peeled back the lid. Inadvertently, she allowed a slight groan to escape her lips. The sandwiches were filled with slices of roast beef, and she could not eat any of them. Susie had been a vegetarian for five years now.

It had all come about after she had visited an agricultural show with her mother, and a small black cow had caught her attention. It was a bonny little thing, not very high, with a sweet face and gentle brown eyes. Its owner was with it, preparing it for the judging, and with the grooming, it had shone so bright that she'd thought if she got closer, she would have been able to see her face in it. The cow had been well-behaved and attentive to its young handler, just as any of her ponies were when she groomed them. The whole display had gotten her wondering why she should want to eat such beautiful animals, and in fact, why she should want to eat any animal at all. The piece of steak on her plate or at the end of her fork wasn't just food to be devoured as if it had sprung from the soil. It had been an animal that had once had a life, a life that it wanted to enjoy. It was on that day that she had made the decision that she would never eat an animal ever again.

Susie continued to stare nervously at the sandwiches, knowing that Tess was still waiting for her to take one. She began to sweat in a most unbecoming manner and felt a bead of nervous perspiration form on her brow. *Plop.* She felt quite sure that she actually heard the noise as it dripped from her face and on top of the sandwiches. With equal mortification, she and Tess stared at the affected slice.

"I hope you are going to eat that one." Tess said. She didn't look so friendly now.

Susie held the tub towards her. "I'm sorry, Tess," she said. "I can't eat them."

"Me neither," Tess said, snatching the tub. "Are they not good enough for you?"

"Oh no. I mean, yes," Susie replied, looking at Tess's scowling face. She looked about ninety now that she was screwing it up. Way beyond Botox, but Susie didn't say so. After what felt like eternity, Susie managed to say, "The sandwiches are fine."

"So why the fuss?" Tess asked.

Susie shook her head. She hadn't meant to offend Tess, and she certainly did not want to lose the one friend that she had made at the farm. "I'm really sorry," she said. "It isn't because anything is wrong that I could not eat them. It's just that I'm a vegetarian, and so I don't eat beef. I don't eat any meat."

Tess's face softened. "Are you joking with me? It is no wonder then that you are so thin and scrawny. Well, that's a first round here. It looks like you are going to go hungry then. Whatever possessed you to become one of them?"

"I believe that once an animal has been born, it deserves its life, just like we do. All animals want from life is food, water, having babies, and being loved. How people can say they are animal lovers and then sit down and happily eat one, I just do not know. Just imagine the horrors that some of them must go through to be put on a dinner plate. Instead of killing them, I think that we should take pleasure in sharing the world with them, and consider how lucky we are that humans are not alone on this planet. It would be a terrible place if we were."

Tess seemed quite taken back by Susie's speech. "Wow," she said. "You do feel strongly about it, don't you! There won't be many around these parts who would agree with you, though. This is farming country. People round here like their meat, and the animals are bred for it. But I guess it is your choice. You are new to this village, aren't you? Have come across the beast yet?"

"The beast?"

"Yes, the beast of Ealand," Tess repeated. She seemed pleased to have Susie's full attention as her eyes lit up as if excited by what she was about to reveal next. "It is a fierce bull with huge pointed horns and an evil face. It has been attacking people around here for months. Why, there are some poor folk who have been awoken at night by its terrifying cries, only to find that it has trashed their gardens and broken down their fencing. It's a wonder it hasn't killed someone yet. You want to be careful cycling here in the dark, all on your own. If it attacks you, it'll stop you wanting to be a veggie. That's if you survive, of course."

Susie smiled politely at Tess and bit her lip. It would do her no good to argue the fact that the poor creature was probably hungry and looking for food when it trashed people's gardens. Nor would it do her any good to tell her that no animal had an evil face, not in her opinion anyway.

She needed this job, and she needed to get on with the people working here, so she changed the subject.

"What time did we get here?"

"Oh good grief," Tess replied, leaping from her chair and looking at the clock on the wall. "Thirty-five minutes ago. Come on, everyone. We are late."

It was a quarter past six in the evening when all the mushrooms were finally packed away in their small plastic trays. Susie had never felt so exhausted in her whole life, and as she shuffled to the exit of the fifth poly tunnel, she ached in places that she hadn't known existed. She stretched her neck backwards in an attempt to ease the soreness in her back, but it didn't work. At least, though, she had got the first day over with, and like Tess had said, she was sure it would get better.

Ted hurried from the cabin when he saw her collecting her bicycle.

"Have you forgotten something? You don't want to be leaving without this."

Susie's tired face looked up, and when she saw the little brown envelope he held out towards her, a surge of energy coursed through her veins, enough for her to raise a vibrant smile. Her first-ever wages. Suddenly, her feet didn't feel as if they hurt quite so much. Shaking with excitement, she took the envelope and placed it safely in the back pocket of her jeans, the one with a zipper.

"Back next week then?" Ted asked.

"Sure," she said. "And thank you."

The journey home was to be in darkness, just as the journey to the farm had been, and though the fog had lifted, it had only done so because of a brisk wind coming from the north that actually made the air feel even colder. Susie's face felt quite numb as she pushed her bicycle along the track. Up ahead, she could see the tarmac of the road glinting under the moonshine, and she hurriedly pushed her bicycle over the ruts. At least when she reached the road she would be able to mount her bicycle and get moving a bit. That would surely make her feel warmer. And then, quite suddenly, she froze, just as if the icy wind had turned her to stone. Something big and dark had just crossed her path up ahead, near the trees, and it was much bigger than a cat or fox. She rubbed her eyes, wondering if they were playing tricks on her, but then she saw it again, a large and sinister shape meandering this way and that.

To her horror, she realised that she could no longer see the gleam of the tarmac surface of the road. Whatever was on the track was coming straight at her. As it slowly came closer, she saw that it was an animal, a large animal with huge horns – horns with sharpened points. She remembered Tess's words from just a few hours earlier: "It's a wonder it hasn't killed someone yet." The statement no longer seemed so exaggerated now.

Susie hauled her bicycle around and mounted it, and then she began pedalling as fast as she could over the rough ground towards the mushroom farm. She could still see the light from Ted's office. Maybe she could get to the mushroom farm before it – whatever *it* was – got to her. But then disaster struck. The bicycle's front wheel hit a frozen rut in the track, catapulting her from her seat. Her shoulder hit the ground first, and then the rest of her followed, with her bicycle ending up skewed across her legs. Bruised and shocked, she was unable to move, and as she lay there, she heard the sound of hooves pounding the frozen ground. It was going to trample all over her, and there was nothing she could do. There came an eerie silence, and then something wet and warm slurped across her right cheek. Susie gulped. She'd been holding her eyes closed tight, but now, as she twisted her head away from the ground, she opened them slowly.

The creature stuck its tongue out and licked Susie's face again. Then it lifted its head high in the air and let out an ear-piercing bellow.

Susie forced herself to look at the thing that was licking and bellowing at her, and as she stared at its large and hairy face, her heart beat like a hammer. It was surely the bull that Tess had spoken of, but what was it doing? Was it taking a lick to see what she tasted like? And then she scolded herself for being stupid. Bulls did not eat meat – at least she didn't think they did. Should she get up, or should she stay there and pretend to be dead? The animal pushed her gently on the cheek with its nose, and to Susie's surprise, it then kicked the bicycle with its foreleg, freeing it from being on top of her. It obviously knew that she wasn't dead.

Susie slowly got to her knees, and then even more slowly to her feet. And then she looked at the creature again. It did not seem quite so scary now that she was standing. Not quite as big as she had thought, but those horns! They were massive and quite alarming. And then she noticed the eyes peering at her through long and untidy forelock hair. They had to be the saddest pair of eyes Susie had ever seen. This animal was suffering. It was suffering some deep sorrow that she would probably never know the cause of. Gaining confidence now that she felt sorry for it, Susie very gently moved her hand forward and allowed her fingers to touch a few strands of its forelock.

"Hello," Susie said.

The animal replied with a moo so gentle that Susie lost all of her fear in an instant. She reached out and stroked it again.

"Don't be afraid," Susie whispered. "I am not going to hurt you."

The animal made a weird sound that almost sounded like a chuckle. Susie smiled. "Are you laughing at me?"

It made the same sound again as if it was definitely laughing. Susie managed then to laugh at herself. She must have looked very funny falling head over heels off her bicycle and sounded even funnier asking such a fearsome looking animal not to be afraid of her; a skinny five feet tall girl. Maybe it understood?

It was at this point that Susie began to examine herself. Her shoulder, which had taken much of the force of the fall, throbbed, and she was obviously going to have a very large bruise on her elbow. Her knee hurt rather a lot too, and so she reached into her pocket and pulled out a small torch, shining it towards her legs. There was a large hole in the denim on the right knee, and she could see that the skin beneath had been scrubbed off, leaving a fairly nasty graze. Other than that, she was unhurt. She lifted the torch and shone it towards the beast.

"Well, that's me taken care of," Susie said. "Now let me take a better look at you."

Susie walked all the way around the animal soon realising that it was not a bull as Tess had described, but a Highland cow, a female. She supposed though that it was an easy mistake to make, as both male and female Highlands had equally large horns. The cow's poor condition soon came to Susie's attention. Her eyes were sunken, and her body was thin and emaciated. Long and straggly hair hung down from her in matted shreds, and that which hung so low that it touched the ground was caked in clumps of manure and mud. Her feet and fetlocks were very cracked and looked extremely sore. Susie guessed that she had been digging in the soil, possibly trying to find pieces of swede or turnip that farmers had left behind during the harvest.

"You poor baby," Susie whispered. "Why is a lovely cow like you out on your own?"

The cow's ears twitched back and forth as if listening to her words and then she mooed again. Susie patted her. "You really are lovely," she said. "I can't imagine why you have been nicknamed the beast of Ealand. I really don't think that name suits you at all. Well my name is Susie and I will have to have a think about what name I shall give you."

So this young human was called Susie. Now that Floss had the name of the girl who had tumbled rather haphazardly from her bicycle, she studied her carefully. Hadn't Bess told her that humans were usually in their houses when it was dark and cold? Well, it was certainly both those things tonight, freezing in fact, even she could feel it. Susie was obviously very good-natured though and her words showed that she had a caring heart. She had a friendly face too, with soft brown eyes revealing her kind temperament, just as they would in an animal. It got her wondering. If only there was a way that she could get Susie to understand her moos then maybe Susie would help her to find Boris. After all humans had ways of doing things that she did not have. She smiled at Susie.

"Hello Susie. My name is Floss," she said. "And I really could do with your help."

"Oh, you poor darling. Whatever is matter? You sound so distressed mooing like that."

"Please, please understand me," Floss replied, her eyes pleading. "I so need you to understand so that you can help me to find my son. Some nasty humans took him away you see and..."

"Oh please, please do not cry out like that. I don't know what to do. Are you trying to tell me something? Are you in pain?"

Floss sighed. It was no use. Though she could see that Susie was trying her best, the young girl was not going to be able to understand her, certainly not enough to give her the help that she so desperately needed. She began to turn away.

"Don't go, moo cow, I want to help you," said Susie, her voice beseeching.

Floss turned her head. "I am sorry Susie," she said. "But I have to go. You travel safely now and don't go tumbling off that thing again."

She looked up the track. There were lights on at the farm building up ahead, but they did not particularly bother her. She had been past the farm before, and no one had ever given chase. As she started towards it, she could hear Susie's footsteps following on after her. She stopped a moment to let the young girl catch up.

"I know you mean me well, Susie," she said. "But you cannot follow me. I have to go on looking for my son."

Susie reached out her hand and Floss let her stroke her forelock. The girl then moved her hand so that she was rubbing the centre of her face. Floss closed her eyes for a moment to enjoy the moment. It had been a long while since a human had got so close to her; a human who cared.

"Please do not leave," Susie said. "I am worried about you. I need to think on how we can get you away from the roads and into a nice field, maybe even into my field. I'd have to get some new fencing to keep you away from my ponies though. I'm not sure what they would make of you."

"I cannot go into your field, Susie," Floss said. "I have to stay free until I have found my son. It is such a shame that I cannot get you to understand. If only all humans were like you then this world would be a much better place for all of us who share it. It was so nice to meet with you. Goodbye now."

She kicked her heels then and trotted away into the darkness, knowing that Susie's legs could not possibly keep up.

Chapter Nine

"So, you are a cowboy now, are you?"

Susie looked up. Her mother had just come into the living room where she had been for the last half hour, perched on the edge of their sofa trying to lasso the leg of an upside down kitchen chair. She sent the loop of lunge rein forward again. It missed the intended leg miserably and flopped limply, a metre short of its target.

Susie groaned and began to gather the rein up for another attempt. If she could not successfully lasso a piece of furniture, then she was very unlikely to be able to rope a wild animal. She had told her mother all about her encounter the evening before last, in fact, she had spoken of little else since then, but her mother hadn't really shown the matter as much interest as she would have liked.

"Don't laugh, Mum. This is serious," she said. "That poor animal is out there all on its own, and something awful is going to happen to it if I don't do something. You should have seen the state she was in! It was awful when she limped away and I couldn't do anything for her. I am going to keep this lasso on me when I go out riding, and then if I come across her, I will have a chance to catch her."

"You probably won't set eyes on her again."

"Tess at the mushroom farm said that she has been hanging around the villages here for quite some time. I have a feeling that the paths of our lives were intended to cross, and when they do so again, I want to be ready."

"Aren't Highland cows the ones with the big horns?"

"Yes, she did have big horns."

"Well, I am hoping that the paths of your lives do not cross again then. I mean it's got to be dangerous with horns like that, and thoughts of you trying to lasso it … crikey, I could lose sleep over it."

"I am sure that some of them can be dangerous, but not her, Mum, because she was special. I even think that she tried to talk to me."

"Well, on the subject of being kind to animals, have you seen how dark it's getting outside? Isn't it time we forgot the Highland cow and got our coats on so that we can feed the ponies?"

Susie snapped her head around and looked towards the window. "Jeez," she said, shooting off the sofa and heading for her coat and the ponies' head collars. "Just where has the time gone?"

"Well, as I recall, a lot of time went into trying to catch a chair leg, and I was wishing that the washing up got the same attention!"

"Oh, shut up, Mum," Susie replied, laughing. "I'll do the washing up when we return."

They arrived at the gate to the ponies' field, but the blackness of the winter night had beaten them to it. Susie scolded herself for not keeping a better eye on the time. It was so much harder feeding the ponies in the dark, and with almost three weeks still to go to the shortest day of the year, it was going to get even worse. She climbed over the gate first, and then turned her torch on to help her mother make the climb. The two of them then followed its narrow beam of light up the hill. When they reached the stable block, Susie pointed the torch into the field at the rear, where she had put her two ponies that morning. She saw Ellie straight away. The mare was grey, her coat lightening with each year that passed by, and she stood out in the dark.

"There's Ellie," Susie said.

"Do you want to get her then whilst I find Copper? I am guessing he must be over the far side of the field, near the bridle path."

"Go on then," Susie said. "Here's his head collar, oh and the torch too, Mum. I can manage without it."

Susie passed one of the head collars and the torch over to her mother, and after watching the beam disappearing into the darkness, she made her over to Ellie.

"Hello, girl," she said, patting the mare gently on the side of her neck. "Let's get you inside your lovely warm stable, and then we will get you your tea. There are some carrots for you both today, so it will be extra special."

As Ellie nuzzled her gently, Susie took the head collar she had brought with her, put the head piece around the back of the mare's ears, and fastened it. "There, girl," she said, clipping on the lead rope. "Off we go then."

Ellie had made just a single step with her owner when the scream came. It was short, like a yelp, and for a moment, Susie stood there not moving, mystified as to what could have made such a sound. And then she realised that it had come from the direction her mother had taken. She replayed the noise over in her head. Yes, it could have been her mother who had made the sound rather than some animal. And so, with trembling hands, she unclipped Ellie's lead rope and dropped it to the floor. She then began running across the darkened field.

"Mum! Mum, are you okay?" she yelled.

A hedgerow separated their field from the bridle path, and she noticed the glow from the torch shining along it. She hurried towards the light.

"Shush. Shush. It's me, Susie." Her mother's fingers clutched her lower arm.

"Good grief, Mum. You almost frightened the life out of me. What is the matter? Why did you yell out like that?"

"I am sorry, sweetheart. It was the shock of seeing it."

"Seeing what?"

Her mother turned the torch towards the hedgerow again. Susie could see that her hand was shaking as the beam of light was wobbling all over the place.

"The beast of Ealand," her mother said. "I...I think it is on the other side of the hedge."

Susie took a deep breath. "Fantastic," she said. "But I didn't bring the lasso. I never imagined she'd come to the back of our field. Where is she? I can't see her. Give me the torch, please."

"It or she has gone behind the big tree. Goodness I can feel my heart thumping. I just heard this rustling sound coming from near the hedge, and when I shone the torch over, there it was; this hairy creature. It almost gave me a heart attack."

Her mother handed Susie the torch, and she shone it over the hedgerow and towards the tree. She squinted and then she smiled. She could see the cow now, or some of her. Sticking out from either side of the large trunk were her massive horns. It was as if she thought that the tree was hiding the whole of her.

"OMG! I can see her now, Mum," Susie said. "This is so-o-o good. If I can just get a hold of her, I should be able to lead her around the track and into our field."

"This is not so-o-o-o good at all, Susie. You are not doing anything of the sort. We are going home to call the police. An animal with horns like that should not just be wandering around."

"No, Mum, we can't do that. If the police think that she is a risk, they may shoot her. I am going to try to get her into our field."

"Don't be so silly, Susie. I want you to keep away from her, do you hear me?"

"But I can't, Mum. She needs our help, and I know she has no intentions of hurting me. Like I told you last week, she even kicked the bicycle off me when I fell off."

"Yeah, so you said." Her mother's tone was disbelieving.

"Please, Mum, please! You know how worried I have been about her. This is the best chance that I could have of getting her to safety." Susie's eyes were pleading, beseeching her mother to relent to her will.

"Come on, love, it is way too cold to argue about this. Let's get the ponies in, and then we'll go home."

"Well, then, we'll both have to freeze, because I'm not going home – not until I've at least *tried* to get her. Perhaps I could use a lead rope or something? If I stay here and keep an eye on her, will you get one for me? Please, Mum!"

Her mother sighed audibly, quite obviously wishing that she had not yelled so loudly and then Susie would have been none the wiser to the cow's presence. It was too late now though. Susie's mind was set on getting the cow safe. Her mother would know that there would be no persuading her to leave the cow alone.

"Look, Susie," her mother said. "I'll make a compromise. If I go and get you a lead rope, do you promise to stay here and not to go anywhere near that beast until I return? We will go and see it together, right?"

Just as she thought, her mother was relenting. "Yes, Mum," she said.

The sigh came again. Her mother still seemed uncertain about leaving her there. Susie would have to convince her again.

"Mum, I promise. Please get the lead rope."

This time her efforts worked and her mother headed away. Susie stood in silence until she was quite certain that her mother was well on her way across the field. Then she began to walk along the hedgerow. She was sure that she had seen a gap in it a few months back, and recalled thinking that they needed to put some extra fencing there. She stopped at what looked to be a space, and then she pulled the rotten undergrowth apart.

"There," she muttered to herself. "I knew there was a gap."

She sank to her knees, pulled more dead weeds out, and dragged some twigs and small branches out of her way. This was definitely the place, though the gap was not quite as wide as she had imagined it would be. Grimacing as the dampness soaked through her jeans, she moved the torch to her mouth so that she could free both of her hands, and then she squeezed her shoulders together to make herself as small as possible. She then began to inch her way through the hedgerow. Small twigs scratched her face, and she was forced to close her eyes. How far had she gone? When she felt a thorn push into her right eyelid, she guessed not far enough. Keeping her eyes closed, she crawled a little further. When she could no longer feel anything scratching her face, she slowly opened her eyes.

"Jeez," she said, for a moment startled by the sight of the unruly red hair. The cow's face was just inches away from hers. Susie scrambled to her feet.

"Hello, girl," she said. "I didn't realise that I had crawled quite so far."

The cow had its head cocked to one side as if it had been quite baffled by what had been about to emerge from the hedgerow. Susie brushed herself down and reached her hand out.

"I bet you didn't expect to see me coming through here uh!"

The cow seemed pleased to see her as it gave a soft moo and then she felt the usual slurp to her cheek. She laughed loudly and a cheery smile crossed her face. "It's so lovely to see you again," she said. "Mum is with me today, and she has gone to get a rope so that we can get you into our field. You see, you can't stay out here because you have been frightening people, and people who are afraid or do not understand sometimes do nasty things, especially to animals."

Susie smiled as she listened to the continuing bellows. They no longer sounded quite so painful, more like the animal was trying to communicate with her in the only way it could.

"I can't understand what you are trying to tell me, but what I do know and can see for myself is that you are very lonely and very sad. Well, you don't have to be lonely any more. I am in need of a friend, and it looks like you could do with one too. We'll get you into my field, and then get you some hay and some water, and then tomorrow we will work out what we are to do. That sounds good uh!"

The cow seemed to be shaking her head. Was she disagreeing with the statement she had just made? Was she actually answering her? Susie looked astounded by what she was witnessing. She must ask the cow something else, check if it was coincidence.

"Susie, Susie. Where are you?"

Talk about a wrong moment! Susie thought, because on hearing the sound of her mother's sharp voice, the cow's eyes widened with alarm, and she began to back away.

"It's only Mum," Susie said soothingly, moving forward to reduce the gap that had been created between them. "She is here to help you too."

The fear remained etched in the cow's eyes, and she turned and began limping away. Susie was mortified. She had been so close to catching her, and this chance may never happen again, not as near to the field as they were now. She chased after the cow, as fast as her legs would take her, but the quicker she ran, the more the cow accelerated. Even trotting lame it was much faster than her. Soon it was putting distance between them. Her mother's yelling rang again in Susie's ears. Goodness she was loud, even fifty metres away, her mother's voice was loud.

"Susie, where are you? Are you with that beast? Didn't I ask you not to go near it?"

Susie stopped running and with her hands on her knees she took a moment to catch her breath. She had lost sight of the Highland cow anyway.

"I'm here, Mum," she shouted. "And I'm fine."

"Susie, I am going to call the police if you don't get back into this field right now."

"Okay, Mum. I am on my way."

She took a last lingering look along the path. It was no use trying to find the cow when she could barely see more than six feet in front of her. Even the light from her torch was fading. The batteries were obviously wearing down. She might as well earn some good behaviour points with her mother now and use them up another day. She turned around and hurried up the path. Then using what was left of the light from the torch, she found the gap in the hedgerow again and made her way through. Her mother was waiting for her and grabbed a hold of her hand, helping to pull her free of the hedgerow.

"Didn't I tell you …?"

Susie quickly interrupted with her apology. "I am really sorry, Mum," she said. "I lost sight of her, so I just went through to see where she had gone."

"And did you see her?"

"Yes, I did, and she was in an even worse state than she was the last time I saw her. She was limping pretty badly. I was so close to catching her though, Mum."

"Lucky you didn't then, Susie. You know that we cannot keep her in our field. Think of the ponies and her horns and how bad you would feel if she hurt either of them. Besides, maybe she doesn't want to be caught. Consider why she ended up out in the countryside on her own in the first place. Maybe she wants to stay wild."

"But she is starving. I cannot just let her starve, can I?"

"Well, why don't you put some hay out for her on the bridle path? She knows where you are now, so she will probably come back, and when she does, she will find something to eat."

Susie's face brightened. "Actually, Mum, that's not a bad idea," she said. "If I can get her to trust me, then, eventually, she may just follow me right into the field."

Susie heard her mother sigh. Clearly this was not what she'd had in mind when she had made the suggestion. Such a good idea was not going to go to waste though, and Susie intended to make certain of it.

Every late afternoon from that point forward, Susie began leaving large piles of hay dotted about the bridle path. It became quite the ritual: feed the ponies and then feed the Highland cow. Some evenings they saw each other, and the cow would greet Susie with a loud bellow. Susie would then run to her and pet her, even managing to take some lovely photographs. Other times they missed each other.

As the days wore on, Susie worried less about trying to capture the animal. Her new friend had put on some weight and looked lots better, so Susie saw no reason to spoil their relationship by trying to force her into the field against her will. But then, right in the middle of a very cold January night, matters suddenly took a turn. Susie had been sleeping quite soundly for about four hours when something disturbed her, waking her with a start. As she sat bolt upright in bed, she could feel her heart racing and her whole body dripped with sweat. Yet, all seemed quiet in her room. Had she just been in the middle of a nightmare? If she had, she could not recall any of it.

Bleary-eyed, she reached her hand out to the bedside cabinet, her fingers seeking her alarm clock. It was just three o'clock. Exhausted, she gave her pillow a good shake and then sank her head back into the new softness of it, but sleep would not come to her, and she tossed and turned, all the while trying to rid herself of the terrible feeling of dread that seemed to be lingering on her mind. Eventually, she gave up trying to sleep, and she pushed the bedclothes off her and looked towards the single large window of her bedroom. The curtains had not been properly drawn across, and the street lamp from outside was shining through the gap. Branches from the large oak tree opposite the house were swaying and casting weird dancing shadows all over the ceiling. Maybe it was these eerie shapes that had disturbed her.

Slipping from her bed, she walked barefoot across the wooden floor to the window, where she pulled the curtains apart. She could see her stable block on the crest of the incline of her ponies' field, silhouetted against the backdrop of the lights of Scunthorpe town. Usually, the view was much the same; but, tonight, something unusual caught her attention. There were two strange lights to the back of the stables. Susie frowned and rubbed her tired eyes, but the lights did not disappear. It seemed to her that they were headlights from some vehicle or other, and that it was most probably on the bridle path. But what could it be doing there at such an hour? Her mind worked on the reasons, and when no innocent or plausible cause for it being there came, she knew that she would not be able to rest easy until she had investigated.

Her thoughts turned to her mother sleeping in the bedroom next door. The sensible thing to do would be to wake her and alert her to the problem. But then she considered her mother's most likely response, which would be that she should go back to sleep and ignore it. And then her mother would be awake, and any attempt that she should make to go down the stairs alone would be thwarted. There was only one thing for it then: she would have to check it all out on her own.

Susie got onto her knees and stretched her right arm beneath the bed. They were there somewhere – the pair of black leggings that had been crawling around the floor for weeks – they were there somewhere. Her fingers touched fabric, and she pulled them out. There was no time to find a decent jumper, and so she left her pyjama top on, tucking the ends of it into the waistband of the leggings. A pair of thick woolly socks, drawn up to her knees, followed, and then, finally, her winter coat. Quiet as she could, she turned the handle of her bedroom door and began to pull it towards her. Knowing that it always creaked at the halfway point, she slipped through the gap before it got there, and then she gently closed it behind her. The door to her mother's bedroom was just along the hallway on the opposite side, and she tiptoed towards it. It was ajar; she would have to be careful. And then as she crept past, her foot stepped on a wonky floorboard, and a loud creak suddenly filled the silence. Her hand went to her mouth to stifle the gasp that came out. For a moment, she did not dare move again, not until the sound of her mother's gentle snoring reached her ears, and then she continued along the rest of the hall and down the staircase.

Outside, the wind was fierce and icy, and Susie shivered as she hurried along the road, clutching the collar of her coat against her neck. It took her four minutes to reach the gate to the field, and she instinctively grabbed the top rail, but the crystals of ice that had formed there burned her fingers, gluing them to the aluminium. She pulled them free and rubbed them together before pulling her coat sleeves over them. She clasped the top rail again, this time hauling herself over the gate.

Standing alone in the gloomy and darkened field, Susie looked nervously towards the stable block. The headlights were still there, only they were brighter now that she was closer, and she felt a chill that was not from the cold run down her spine. She had hoped that they would have disappeared by now. A thought crossed her mind then. She could turn around and return to the safety of her bed. But what if her ponies were being stolen right underneath her very nose, and she did nothing about it? That was a risk she could not take.

She jogged the rest of the way to the stables, and when she reached them, she paused at the gable side a moment to catch her breath. Two loud neighs broke the silence. Her ponies had recognised her footsteps.

"Shh!" Susie whispered, hurrying to the stable doors, where she gave each pony a quick rub down its nose. "I don't want them to know I am here."

She left the stables and began to cross the rear field, heading for the bridle path. As she neared the hedgerow, she began to crouch down low, making sure that her head was below the height of the thicket. Creeping stealthily, she made her way to the gap that she had been using to get to the Highland cow. When she found the gap, she knelt down and thrust her face into the space, trying to see what was going on.

Two enormous lights mounted up on the rear of a pickup truck illuminated the track as if it were daytime. She could see the shapes of three men – at least she thought they were all men – standing against the wing of it. They were smoking, and the stench of nicotine and burning tobacco drifted across her nostrils. She wafted her hand at her freezing nose to show her disapproval, and then she turned her head so that her right ear was closest to the hedge, trying to hear what was being said. Their voices were low, though, and the engine noise from the pickup prevented her from being able to make anything out. Undaunted, she straightened her back and lifted her head so that it was just above the hedge. And then, quite unexpectedly, the glare suddenly swung towards her, lighting up her entire field. She gasped and sank to her knees again. Had they seen her? The sound of their voices returned to her ears. Surely, if they had seen her, they would have shouted out and let her know it. She remained stock-still. It looked as if she had got away with it, but no matter how hard she tried, she could not pick up any gist of their conversation, just the odd word here and there. There was only one thing for it then: she would have to get closer, and to do that, she would have to get onto the bridle path.

The manoeuvre through the hedge was much trickier without the use of a torch, and though she had brought it with her, she dared not use it. *A few more feet should do it,* she thought, inching along, and she kept her eyes closed as she pushed her way through the twigs. When the scraping to her face stopped, she opened her eyes. Something was right in front of her, blocking her vision. It was the large booted foot of one of the men. She began crawling backwards towards the hedge, seeking the gap, but it was as if it had closed up. And then, suddenly, the most excruciating pain shot through her left hand. The boot had just stepped on her fingers. She tried to stifle the resulting scream, but the pain was too great, and a squeal escaped.

"What the hell was that?"

"Stop worrying, Kev. God, you're on edge tonight. It was just a bird in the hedgerow or something. How long is your mate going to be with that gun?"

"Strange bird, that. It sounded like a girl's voice to me."

"I wouldn't think there are any girls out here tonight. Chance would be a fine thing, uh!"

Susie heard the man called Kev laugh as she tried to free her fingers. She managed to do so, and held them in her other hand, hoping for the throbbing to subside quickly.

"Do you think we'll be able to get the body in then?"

Susie's eyes opened wide as saucers. Body! The situation was even worse than she had imagined. They were not out to thieve, they were out to dispose of a body. And what would they do if they realised that they had a witness? There would then be two bodies. Heart thumping wildly, she tried desperately to find the gap in the hedge, but she still could not find it. And then a contingency plan came to her. She would phone for help. She would phone 999 and tell the police that there had been a murder. And then, as she felt around in her pocket, her heart sank. There was only a long cylindrical object in there, and it was her torch. In her hurry to get out of the house and investigate, she had left her phone on the kitchen table.

"Yeah, the winch should get it in no bother. That's if Pete gets here with his gun before it disappears. Prime bit of beef, that, and all for nothing."

For a moment, Susie sighed with relief, but the reprieve from worry did not last long. So there wasn't a human body after all. These horrible men were poachers, and they were after her beloved Highland cow. She had thought that she had been doing a good thing feeding her, but, in fact, what she had done was to lead the men right to where they could easily kill her. They had obviously seen where her cow was eating and recognised her as an easy target. What could she, Susie, do to stop them? She cast her mind back to half an hour earlier, when she could so easily have turned around and alerted her mother, but it was all too late now.

Another set of headlights appeared on the bridle path, and shortly afterwards, a second truck pulled up. A fourth man got out of it and made his way to the others. All four of them then stood in front of the truck, staring down the track to the place where Susie had left hay for the cow. The man who had arrived in the second vehicle made a move down the path, and he lifted something from his shoulder and began to mess around with it. She squinted against the glare of the lights. It was a rifle; he loaded it, and now he was raising it to his shoulder.

"*No-o-o-o-o!*"

Had she really screamed that out loud? Looking towards the men, she knew that she must have done, because all four of them had turned their attention towards her. The hair at the back of her neck prickled, and then she felt herself being hauled roughly to her feet.

"Nice evening," she said meekly, looking into the face of the man who had a grip of her right arm. It was the same man who had stepped on her fingers, the one called Kev. He had a gaunt and sinister face, with emotionless eyes, and he stank of body odour. Certainly he did not look like the sort of person a young girl would like to meet or smell when she was on her own on a bridle path in the dead of night. She cast a glance towards the other three men crowding behind him, but her hope of seeing a friendly face amongst them was soon dashed.

"I told you that it was a girl I heard. Didn't I tell you?"

"Well, I'll be darned. You were right, Kev. But where on earth has she come from?"

Susie opened her mouth to speak, to demand that he let go of her, but she was so frightened by now that nothing came out.

"So," Kev said. "Never mind 'nice evening', what are you doing out here, child?"

Susie cleared her throat and coughed. Nerves were making it very dry.

"Did you hear me, or has a cat got hold of your tongue? This isn't a place for a little girl. This is a hunt, and you are spoiling it. This is the sixth time we have been up here, and it's time we had our reward."

Susie felt tears come to her eyes, and she fought hard to hold them back. She must not let these thugs know how afraid she was, because she still had work to do – and that work was to save her beloved cow. Kev shook her then, as if trying to force an answer, but she remained silent, planning in her mind what she should do. She obviously wasn't strong enough to fight him off. What would a cornered animal do in such a circumstance? It would use whatever natural defences God had given to it. And so, she opened her mouth, and she bit the hand that was holding her arm as hard as she possibly could; so hard, in fact, that she thought her teeth might break.

"*Arrgghh!*" Kev cried, pushing her violently away from him.

As he clutched his bleeding hand, she seized her opportunity. She threw herself between the other men, pushing them to one side, and then she ran down the bridle path, screaming and yelling like a banshee.

Even in the dark, Susie could see her beloved cow. She was contentedly eating the pile of hay that had been left on the bridle path some hours earlier. Susie ran to her.

"Go on shoo," she yelled at the top of her voice and waving wildly. "Get out of here and never come back. Do you hear me? Go on then shoo."

The cow lifted her head, and it broke Susie's heart to witness the betrayal in her eyes. But, she had no choice. She had to make the cow leave because if she didn't, then the men would kill her.

"Didn't you hear me? Get out of here."

Susie looked down at the track and picked up a piece of broken timber from an old bit of fencing. Without force or intent to hurt her, she then threw it at the cow. "For goodness sake, go away."

Instead of leaving, the cow remained right where she was. It was as if she was waiting for Susie to change back into the Susie that she had known before. Susie turned her head.

Dark human shapes were looming down the track towards them. Soon it would all be over.

"Please," she begged in a desperate tone. "See behind me; those men mean you harm. You must leave here now and you must not return.

This time, the cow suddenly seemed to take notice. She then began to bellow in a most disturbing fashion.

"You understand now don't you," Susie whispered.

And to Susie's amazement the cow nodded her head. She then leaned forward and gave Susie a slurp across her cheek with her long tongue. Susie had become quite accustomed to this display of affection, and she smiled duly convinced that the cow understood everything that she said to it.

"Go on, hurry," she said.

The Highland cow turned away from Susie and immediately broke into a canter. It was only when she had disappeared from sight that Susie's mind turned to her own safety. The men were bound to be very disagreeable now that their dinner had done a runner. She spun to face them, but the track had turned to darkness. The big lights from the back of the truck were no longer shining, and the only light was coming from the half-moon, and it wasn't much, as it kept dipping in and out of the clouds. She noticed a dark shape looming in front of her, and then something touched her left shoulder. It felt like fingers. Shrieking loudly, she clenched her fingers tightly into a fist and then launched it with all the power that she could muster. Her knuckles struck something surprisingly hard, and it grazed her skin. She pulled her sore hand back, preparing to launch her fist again, but found that she could not move her arm. Something seemed to have gotten a hold of it. Struggling like a wild cat, she desperately tried to break herself free, but it seemed to be wrapping itself around her. And then, as she fought with it, she tripped and fell to the ground. Lying there and breathing heavily, she felt about in the undergrowth, and her fingers managed to grab hold of a broken tree branch. Standing quickly, she lifted it above her head, and then she swung it with a brutal force that she did not even know she had in her. It hit her target, and she felt bits of something fall onto her face and hands. Confident that her attacker had been felled, she dropped the branch and stooped towards the ground. Her fingers touched what she could only imagine was his bare leg, but it was cold and rigid, and she could feel gnarls in it like hardened veins. Had she killed him? Her heart raced. If she had killed him, the police might say that it was murder. She was far too young to be locked up for life. Her thoughts turned to the courtroom dramas she had watched on television. Self-defence. Could she really claim self-defence?

And then, quite suddenly, the track became bright again. The two trucks were heading down the track towards her, and they had their full-beam headlights on. Maybe they were coming to pick up their recently deceased chum. She looked down at her feet to see what a dead person looked like, and then she frowned. There was no body. In the panic and mayhem, she had in fact been attacking an elderberry bush.

The relief was short-lived. The trucks were still heading her way. She looked about her, and seeing a dark area close to the hedgerow that was outside the beam of their lights, she stepped into the shadows. She did not move from her hiding place until they had passed her, and their red tail lights had disappeared into the distance.

CHAPTER TEN

A freezing rain battered the bleak countryside of North Lincolnshire on and off throughout the week that followed, and Floss shivered uncomfortably as she shuffled her bottom against the trunk of a tree. In the bleakness of the ploughed fields around her, it was the only tree she had been able to find, but it had long since lost its leaves, and so it offered little protection from the elements. Dirty rainwater poured down her forelock, running into her eyes. She wiped them across her mud-ridden legs, but that only made matters worse. When would this bad weather give her a break? Not any time soon, if the dark clouds above her were anything to go by.

She stood the pounding rain for a further hour before realising that she had no choice but to move on and look for some better shelter – somewhere. With her head held low, she moved away from the tree, heading south so that at least the strong wind was behind her. It was difficult going. Everything around her was mud, and she slipped and slid in it. At times the slurry was so deep that it came up to her belly, and it was all she could do to find the strength to trudge through it.

After an arduous half-hour of endurance, the mud finally came to an end at a country lane. Though she would normally fear anything that resembled the presence of humans, the tarmac was a welcome sight, and she stepped onto it, shaking herself wildly to free herself of some of the heavy mud. She then tried to make her mind up which way she should go next.

The downpour seemed to be coming at her from all directions, with the wind howling first from the south and then from the north. It seemed that rain would be in her face whichever route she chose. She could hear several dogs barking in the distance, and they sounded like large dogs. It would be a wise choice to go in the opposite direction to them, and so, listening carefully for the source of the sound, she turned right.

Shortly after turning, she came to a bend in the road. On the inside of the bend, a grassed slope led away from the road in a gentle curve. Her gaze went up the hillside, falling on an object that was right at the top. Rubbing her eyes to clear them of rainwater, she took another look. It was a metal arc, the kind of arc that Joe Devlin had used as shelter for his pigs. It looked like it might be bigger than the ones that Joe had used, though, and she imagined that if she could get inside it, she would then have an excellent refuge from the wind and rain.

She made her way slowly towards the arc and poked her nose inside. As she had thought, it was quite a lot bigger than Joe Devlin's pig arcs, and it was certainly large enough for her to walk into, but she hesitated. It was dark and gloomy, and she could not see to the end of it. For all she knew, it was already home to some creature or other which might not take so kindly to her invading its privacy. And then, as she rocked back and forth, trying to pluck up the courage to go in, she got the eerie sense that she was being watched.

She spun around but couldn't see very much, as the rain had got so heavy that it was almost like fog. And so she decided that she had imagined it, and she turned to the arc again, this time placing her right foot over the threshold. There was an odour of dampness and mildew, but as far as her nose could tell her, nothing sinister. To be on the safe side, she bellowed loudly and then listened to echoes of her own voice returning to her. Nothing else made a sound – that is, until the snapping noise. It came from behind her, and it was loud and sharp, immediately followed by the feeling that something had just slapped her on the bum. She backed out of the shelter and threw her head around to look at her rump. Something strange, green, and luminescent had landed there. The weird noise came whistling through the air again, and then another patch of green stuff appeared on her coat. To her horror, she heard the sound of human footsteps coming up the hillside.

A peculiarly dressed little man came running through the mist, heading straight for her. His face was weird in that it had black stripes marked across the cheeks and forehead. His green coat and trousers were daubed in dark marks similar to those that were on his face. In fact, to all intents and purposes, it was as if he had tried to dress himself up as a tree. But it wasn't his strange dress sense that bothered her; it was the rifle slung over his shoulder. Her heart rate quickened, and her mind went into turmoil. What should she do? Should she run into the arc and hide, or should she make a break for it? All of a sudden, the funny little man fell onto his belly and brought the butt of the rifle to his shoulder.

Floss spun around and plunged herself into the darkness of the arc, continuing until her nose touched the cold metal at the end of it. She turned and looked towards the semicircle of light at the entrance. At least if the man did come in after her, she would see him.

Five minutes passed, and he still did not come into the arc. She was certain that he had seen her, though, and so she tried to stay awake so that she could watch for him. But the patter of the rain on the metal roof above her was hypnotic, and as the minutes went by, her head began to loll towards the floor. Her eyelids almost closed, and she scolded herself as she forced them open again. But, seconds later, they did the same again, only this time they did not reopen.

The sleep did not last long, just a minute or so, and then a loud noise suddenly jolted her awake. Something was being dragged across the metal ripples outside the arc. The noise stopped as abruptly as it had started, and a dark human figure crossed the light in front of her. He returned then, only to stand in the centre, hands on hips. Though she could not see any of his features, his frame told her that it was the same man she had seen earlier, the one dressed like a tree.

There was a flash, and then a bright spotlight came into the arc. As it flashed from side to side, it was blinding, causing spots in front of her eyes. The man had come into the arc. The funny snapping sounded again, and she felt something wet and sticky trickle down her face.

"Gotcha."

Floss retreated, pressing her bottom against the rear of the shelter.

"Did you hear me? I have got you, and you are both out of the game. I got you earlier too, and you should have been out then, but I guess as no one was looking, you thought you could get away with it. Anyway, your Highland cow costume is absolutely terrific. It's added a touch of real class to this paintballing session. It's been just like the Wild West. How many of you are inside it then? Two? Usually there are two: one for the front legs and one for the back legs."

Floss snorted. What on earth was this funny little man talking about? She must try to frighten him away.

"*Moooooooo! Moooooooooo! Moooooooooo!*"

She gave three of her loudest-ever bellows, and then she shook her horns so wildly that she thought her head might fall off.

"Hey, that is so real! You could win an award for that. But come on, lads, the game's up. Out of the gear."

Gear? What gear? What on earth was he on? She lowered her head and shook her horns even more fiercely, giving another loud bellow.

"Well, if you refuse to die, then I may as well just hide in here with you out of the rain. I've brought a picnic. If you get out of the costume, you can share it. Do either of you fancy a sandwich and a beer? I've brought plenty."

The man turned and walked towards the entrance. He then pulled an old milk crate away from the side and sat his bum down, right in the middle of the gangway. He turned briefly, and his hands reached backwards towards a hump on his back. It was his rucksack. Soon he was bringing all sorts of things out of it and laying them on the floor in front of him. Floss heard a strange fizzing sound and then a *glug, glug, glug,* followed by a loud burp.

"Well, do you want a sandwich and a beer, or what?"

Floss watched, mesmerised, as he put the first sandwich to his lips, and her tummy began to rumble. She remembered the taste of bread. Every so often, Joe Devlin had brought half-eaten loaves into the barn to share amongst the animals, and that bread had been such a tasty treat. She began to edge slowly towards the man, and when the aroma of freshly baked granary bread reached her nostrils, she simply could not resist it. A pool of saliva came to her mouth and drooled in a long sticky line from her hairy chin. In a single snatch and one gulp, the sandwich was gone.

"What the ... ?!"

The man leaped to his feet, staring nonplussed at his empty hands, which were positioned as if they still held the sandwich. She'd left some saliva on his fingers, and he rubbed them together before bringing them to his nose. His face turned crimson first, and then it quickly darkened to purple. Obviously, cow saliva did not appeal.

"OMG! It's a real one!"

The rucksack flew towards Floss, and then the man fled the arc. His screams went on for three whole minutes as he ran slipping and sliding down the boggy hillside.

Floss's attention turned to what had been left behind, and what a feast there was. She had seen some of these things before when Joe Devlin's family had come to the farm and had a picnic, but she had never had the opportunity to taste them. Now was her chance. The remaining sandwiches went down first, and then she turned her attention to the little plastic packets which had what appeared to be dried slices of potato inside. They were nice. Her eyes moved to the big slice of cake, all wrapped up nicely in tissue. She remembered cake. Humans had cake when they had a birthday party. She had heard Betty Devlin talking of it one day when she had returned from shopping with this huge box. She had passed her in the field and showed her what had been inside it. The cake that the man had left was not quite as fancy as that but it tasted like a slice of heaven. She licked her sticky lips and then looked at the only items that remained – the cans that had liquid inside them. She stood on them one by one so that they burst, and then she sipped the liquid that came out. It tasted strange, but she was thirsty and so she drank the lot.

"Urp! Hic! Hic! Urp!" Burps and hiccups emerged from her mouth, and she felt really funny.

Her belly began to blow up. She could see it expanding behind her, getting bigger and bigger and bigger, and then, just when she thought that she would explode, the gas came out of her bum in a great long burst of flatulence. It almost propelled her from the arc. Wow! Her tummy felt much better for that, but her head did not. It felt really weird, as if it were spinning. She tried to walk, but her legs wobbled like jelly on a plate.

"Come on," she said to herself. "Pull yourself together. You must get away from this place before that man brings more humans up here."

But she couldn't pull herself together, and after wobbling from side to side for a time, she eventually fell to the floor. She lay there then with her head still spinning and a mist over her eyes.

It was exactly one hour later when Fred Bulimer received the most unexpected phone call ever. It came from Ben Blake.

"Are you quite certain that it is my cow?" Fred asked. "I was told a month or two ago that it had been shot."

"Well, I think you were told wrong," Ben said. "I can't imagine that two Highland cows have been on the loose."

"But it's been so many months, Ben. I just can't see that it could be mine."

"When we get her, we can check the ear tags, but I'm pretty certain that she must be the one you lost, Fred. She's quite some cow, isn't she?"

Fred moved the phone from his face so that he could groan without Ben hearing him. Quite some cow! He didn't think she was quite some cow. He thought that his day was busy enough already, and to be told that he now had a captured cow to deal with did not make him very happy at all. He returned the phone to his ear.

"I still can't believe it. As if she didn't cause me enough hassle when she escaped! So, go on, tell me where she is."

"The call I got said that she was captured at some outdoor activity centre in a village called Ealand."

"Ealand? Where on earth is Ealand?"

"It's a village in the Isle of Axholme. It's about sixteen miles away from your farm."

"I can't believe that I haven't heard of it if it's only sixteen miles away."

"It's only a tiny village. It's next to Crowle."

"Ah, I've been to Crowle. It's got a nice little pub in it. So ..." he paused.

"So?"

"So what do *we* do about her now?" he said, emphasising the "we".

"The owner of the centre says that they have her trapped in one of the bunkers they use as a hideout. Apparently, she is lying on the floor and not looking too well. I am not sure what has happened to her. Anyway, he says he has sealed the entrance to keep her where she is until we can collect her. You do still have your trailer, don't you?"

Fred shook his head. His trailer had disintegrated into a mess of metal and rotten wood weeks before.

"I don't have it any longer, Ben. I can ask my friend John if I can borrow his trailer, but he's in Leeds today and doesn't return until the evening."

"Well, we can't leave her at the activity centre all day, Fred. They want her out of their way, and I can hardly blame them."

"If I haven't got a trailer, then I haven't got a trailer."

"Look, I'll make some calls and see what I can do. I may be able to get someone to help out, but I can't promise anything."

"I would appreciate anything you can come up with."

"Okay, I will try."

A half hour later and Fred's phone rang again. It was Ben.

"Lucky you," he said. "I've managed to get in touch with a lady called Tracey who has some cattle in Crowle. She will let us use her trailer for a few hours until we get something sorted. I am to meet her at the activity centre in an hour's time, and she will bring it with her."

"That's great, Ben. I really appreciate it," Fred said thinking that maybe he could just leave the two of them to it. His hopes for that though were dashed by Ben's next words.

"You'll have to come as well, Fred. She is your cow, and you need to be there to help me load her up. I can't expect Tracey to help so much with that. I only asked to borrow her trailer, and you know what a problem the cow was last time."

Fred sighed. "Could I ever forget?" he said. "I'll be there, but as soon as we have her loaded, I will have to leave again. I have an auction to go to later today and bags of other stuff to do. I've already called John, and he will come through for her when he's finished in Leeds. He's says it'll be about teatime, whatever time that is. Will Tracey be okay to hold her for us till then?"

"Yeah. I told her it may be early evening before anyone can get out."

"So how much is this all going to cost me, Ben?"

"I can't say. It depends how long it takes, and you'll have to give Tracey a bit for her time."

Fred sighed again. "Well, if it takes as long as last time, it's going to be expensive then."

"Nothing could take as long as last time, Fred. And at least you'll be getting your cow back. She's got to be worth a bit."

"Yeah, she has and in more ways than one, but we'll talk more about that when I see you."

The rain had reduced to light drizzle as Ben Blake pulled up on the narrow road beside the activity centre driveway. The house and office of the centre were at the top of the drive, and he could see one car parked in front. It was a small yellow car, and it looked so clean that he could not imagine it belonged to Fred. As it seemed that he was the first to arrive, he decided to wait at the roadside so that when Fred and Tracey turned up, they would recognise his estate car and know where to pull in. He checked his rear-view mirror. There was no sign of either of them yet, and so he passed the time listening to the radio, singing along to anything that he knew.

About ten minutes passed by before Ben caught sight of Fred's familiar pickup truck in his mirror. He lowered his window just so much as to not let the rain in. The pickup truck slowed and stopped beside his car. Fred leaned across the passenger seat and wound his window down.

"Nasty day for catching a cow," said Fred.

Ben looked through his windscreen at the black clouds. "Yeah, it is pretty awful."

"Has Tracey arrived yet?"

"No, not yet, but I am sure that she will not be long. Do you want to go up to the house now so we can talk to the chap who found her?"

"It's up to you."

"Well, I don't want to keep him waiting too long, and I've already been here a good fifteen minutes. It might be best if you leave your pickup on the road, though. I am not sure how much room there is up there for Tracey's trailer."

Fred tipped his head forward to gesture his agreement and drove his pickup to the front of Ben's car. He then climbed out and hurried along the road, head bowed against the rain. Ben could see deluges of water pouring from the hem of his long coat. Fred hitched the leather fabric up before opening the door and sitting himself down.

"Right then," Fred said, turning his head to Ben. "Let's go. Time is money *my* money!"

They drove up to the house. It was quite a pretty house, with white stone walls and big Georgian windows on two floors. The roof was of terracotta pan tiles, and there were two doors to the front, both painted postbox red. One of them had an office sign on it, and as they got out of the car, the office door opened. A short grey-haired man of about sixty years stood in the doorway, looking as miserable as sin.

"You'll find it in the bunker up the hill." He waved his arm towards the metal arc.

"Right, thank you. You must be Jim," Ben replied, and in an attempt to break the ice, he held his hand out for the man to shake.

Jim glanced at Ben's hand and then at the veterinary logo printed on the side of the estate car.

"Are you the vet then?"

"I am, and this is Fred, the owner of the cow."

Jim did not shake Ben's hand. He simply nodded in acknowledgement of the gesture and then his eyes turned to Fred. "So, you will be the one responsible for paying compensation for the customers who refused to pay for their paintballing session today then. It's nice of you to come by and cough up."

Fred cleared his throat. "Erm, I don't know about that."

Ben quickly changed the subject. "You did well to catch the cow, and we really can't thank you enough for getting in touch."

"Mmm," Jim replied. "It's been a right hassle, and if this episode puts my corporate clients off booking their paintballing experiences with us again – well, then the bill is just going to get bigger and bigger."

Jim glared again at Fred, who lowered his eyes from the stare.

"So what happened?" Ben asked. "How did you come to catch her?"

"It was earlier this morning," Jim said. "I was busy in the office, doing the accounts, when one of my customers burst through the door, claiming that he had been attacked by a wild bull. Well, to start with, I thought that he had hit his head or something, because it certainly sounded like a load of old bull to me. But, after I gave him and his friends their money back, I went up to the bunker, and there it was, just lying there on the floor, with its eyes sort of staring. It was as if it was on another planet. I don't even think it noticed me, which is a good thing, considering the size of its horns. Well, anyway, I sealed it in with some old wooden boards, and I haven't been up there since."

"It seems unusual that the cow didn't notice you. She doesn't sound very well to me," Ben replied. "I hope I don't have to put her to sleep." He looked at Fred as he spoke, but the older man showed no emotion, and so Ben continued. "So, shall we go and take a look?"

"I hope you are going to do more than just look – I want it gone. And where is the trailer that you are going to put it in?"

"On its way as we speak."

"Thank goodness for that. Right, I will leave you both to it then. The weather is awful, and I have some paperwork to get on with."

"No worries," Ben said. "When Tracey arrives with the trailer, can you tell her to bring it up to the bunker?"

"I will, and don't forget to call for my bill before you leave."

The men drove up the hill in Ben's estate car and when they arrived at the bunker, they climbed out and started removing the wooden pallets. They cast the first to one side and had just lifted up the second pallet when Ben turned his head to look down the hillside. Tracey's little red jeep was pulling up at the house.

"Tracey's here," he said, turning to Fred.

"Good," Fred replied. "I hope she can get up the hillside. It's getting muddier by the second.

Tracey suddenly looked up the hillside. She had obviously spotted them as she waved and then returned to the jeep. Moments later and it started up the hillside with the trailer in tow.

"There, well done, Tracey," Ben said. "She's passed the worst bit. Here she is."

Tracey climbed out and smiled at the two men. "Hello Ben," she said.

"Hello, Tracey," Ben said, also with a smile. He hadn't seen her in a while, not since he'd vaccinated her cattle. He tried to remember how long ago it had been, probably at least six months. She was looking well, even if her long hair looked like it needed a good brush, but then he had always thought that.

"You're a real star for helping out like this," he said.

"So how is the fugitive?"

"The fugitive is looking pretty rough. She got off the floor as we arrived but I can't examine her properly in this weather. I'm going to dart her so she doesn't get away like she did last time and then give her a quick look over before we load her up. Have you got a winch in your trailer?"

Tracey nodded. "I have."

"Fabulous. I was hoping that you would say that. It makes our lives a lot easier. When she's out cold, we will winch her into your trailer then."

"How long has she been loose? I've been hearing quite a few stories about a Highland cow running around the villages, but I wasn't sure till now if they were true."

"Oh, they were true, all right. How long has it been?" Ben looked at Fred.

"Nine months? Something like that."

"Wow! A long time then," Tracey said. She then looked at Fred. "What are you going to do with her? She'll be a bit of a handful now that she's been wild for so long."

"Actually, that's brought me on to something I wanted to ask you, Ben." – Fred turned to look at the vet – "It's a bit awkward."

"Spit it out, Fred."

"Well, the thing is, I don't really want to return her to my other Highlands now that she has gone wild. And what with all the bills that are coming in because of her, I could do with some money back – and quickly."

"So what are you saying?"

"It's more of a question, really. If we were to... you know... have her slaughtered, will the meat still be okay for humans to eat after she's had the tranquilliser stuff in her?"

CHAPTER ELEVEN

Susie Clark dropped the handles of her wheelbarrow and straightened up as she looked down the field towards the road at the bottom. She had been in the field an hour having returned early from an unusually short shift at the mushroom farm. A jeep was coming along the road with a cattle trailer behind it. It was the rattling of the trailer that had alerted her to its presence. She frowned and pursed her lips. What was a cattle trailer doing down a road where there were no cattle kept? The same sinking feeling came to her gut that she had suffered on the night that the poachers had been on the bridle path. There could be only one explanation – it had her Highland cow in it. Someone had caught her.

Susie's mother had just brought some barrels of water to the gate and had not driven off yet, so Susie began running towards the car.

"Mum!" she yelled, waving her arms wildly hoping to catch her attention. "Mum, don't drive off!"

Her mother stopped the car at the side of the road and climbed out. "What on earth is matter, Susie?" she asked.

"Quick, Mum, after it!" Susie said, panting.

"After what?

"My cow! I think they have her in that trailer."

Her mother looked down the road at the rear of the disappearing trailer. "There could be any number of reasons for it being here, Susie."

"No there couldn't. They have my cow, Mum. I know it."

Her mother gave a resigned sigh. "Okay," she said. "Get in."

Susie did not need asking a second time, and she wrenched open the car door and practically fell into the passenger seat. "Hurry, hurry," she yelled.

"Seat belt, Susie."

Susie hauled the seat belt across her chest. "Right! Come on, Mum."

They set off down the road, but the trailer was nowhere to be seen. Even when they reached the junction opposite the village church, it could not be seen in either direction. Susie's stomach did a turn.

"Where is it?" she yelled. "Mum, where is it?"

"I don't know, Susie, but I would imagine it will be going to the main road."

"Yes, the main road, of course – hurry up, Mum. Get your foot down."

Her mother cast a stern look in Susie's direction, and Susie awaited a reprimand for her remark, but it seemed that her mother had decided to let it go as she made no comment. She turned the car left, and they headed past the village Post Office and towards the main road. When they reached the junction opposite Seven Lakes Caravan Park, Susie turned her head this way and that. There was no sign of the trailer.

"Which way now?" her mother asked. "Hurry – there's a car coming up behind us."

Susie despaired. How did she know which way to go? If they turned left, they would be heading for Scunthorpe or Thorne – right would take them to Crowle. She would just have to choose and if she got it wrong then she felt certain that her beloved cow would be gone for good. It was a big decision.

"Head for Crowle, Mum."

They turned onto the main road with the car behind right at their bumper. They passed Susie's school and then as they reached the main part of the village, the traffic lights were red. The trailer had been held up there.

Oh, thank you God," Susie said, clasping her hands to her chest and looking skyward. "Now all we need to do is follow it."

They pursued the trailer all the way through the village, off High Street and onto the narrow road that led to Crowle Moors. The landscape became bleak and lonely, with nothing around but fields and more fields. And then, in the distance Susie caught sight of a barn, just off the road. She turned to look at her mother.

"Do you think that's where it is going?"

Her mother shrugged. "I don't know, Susie," she said. "I imagine that it may well be as there doesn't seem to be much around here other than boggy land and birds."

"There's a bit more than that here, Mum. Crowle Moors is a nature reserve. Didn't you see the sign as we turned off from the village? We've talked about the moors at school. Crowle and Hatfield Moors have some of the richest lowland peat vegetation in the north of England, attracting lots of rare birds and other wildlife."

"Wow!" her mother said. "So you do learn at school then. Hey, look, the trailer brake lights have come on. *It* is going to the barn."

The jeep pulled in front of the gates to the barn and a woman got out. Susie's mother flicked on the indicator of her car and pulled onto the grass verge at the side of the road about fifty metres back.

"So what now," she said turning to Susie.

"We go and ask to look in her trailer."

"And she might tell us to keep our noses out of her business."

"I don't care what she says. If my cow is in there, I want to know what is happening to her. Come on, Mum. Drive up to the gate."

With a look of doubt on her face, Susie's mother did as Susie had asked. By the time they got to the gate, the woman had pulled her jeep and trailer into the yard, and was closing the gate behind her. She looked up as they approached and paused with her hand on the top rail. Susie and her mother climbed out of their car.

"Can we come in?" Susie asked, blurting, "We want to look in your trailer."

The woman looked at the two of them. "Look inside my trailer?"

"Yes, thank you! We will."

"Hey, hold on, what are you doing?"

But Susie did not hold on; she ran into the yard and to the trailer. The moment she placed her hands on it, she knew that her Highland cow was inside. Lifting one of the air vents, she held her eyes to it. The poor animal was on her knees on the cold metal floor. Her breathing seemed shallow, and she was making a strange noise down her nose, as if struggling to get air inside her. Susie let out an anguished yell when she saw the state of her.

"OMG! What have you done to her?" She turned and glowered at the woman, who by now had come up beside her.

Her mother quickly reached Susie's side as well.

The woman gazed between the two of them. "I haven't done anything to her. I was just asked to pick her up and to keep her here until someone comes to collect her. It was the vet who drugged her up. And anyway, can I ask why you are here and what she is to you?"

Susie's mother, who had been silent until now, answered the question. "My daughter has been looking after her for quite some time. Her name is Susie, by the way, and mine is Janet. Susie has been feeding her hay and watching out for her. They have formed quite a bond, and that is why we followed you. Susie guessed that the cow was inside your trailer, and it seems she was right."

The woman's eyes softened as she turned her gaze to Susie. "I see," she said. "It was nice of you to take care of her, Susie. I am Tracey, and I am pleased to meet you."

"Yes, well, Tracey, I think you must get the vet to come back. Quite obviously, she is ill. I think that she is dying," Susie said.

"It might be for the best if she does, Susie."

Susie again glowered at Tracey. "What on earth do you mean?" she stormed. "How can it be for the best?"

Tracey cleared her throat anxiously.

"I asked what you meant by that."

Tracey glanced at Susie's mother, then at the ground, and then at Susie. It seemed to Susie that she was uncomfortable with telling the truth. She must get it out of her.

"Come on spill! I deserve to know."

Tracey sighed and shook her head. "Look I am sorry to have to tell you this as you obviously have a great deal of affection for this Highland cow, but when the owner, Fred, came to claim her, he said that because she is feral he won't be able to return her to the herd."

"Is he going to kill her?"

Tracey averted her eyes from Susie's piercing stare and looked at the ground again. "I am afraid so," she said. "I wish I could tell you different, but I cannot."

Just then a loud noise came from the trailer, making all three of them jump. There came a further thump and then a clatter.

Susie hurried to the air vent again and lifted it. A soft pink nose immediately appeared, and a warm wet tongue stuck out, slurping her face.

"She's on her feet!" Susie rejoiced. "Oh thank goodness! She's on her feet."

She then began to caress the cow's nose with the tips of her fingers. "Hello, sweetheart," she murmured. "What on earth has been happening to you this last week or two?"

The cow gave Susie a soft moo. It seemed all she had the strength to manage. Susie turned briefly to look at her mother and Tracey. "She's going to be okay," she said. "I think that Floss is going to be okay."

Tracey moved next to her and put an arm around Susie's shoulder. "That's sweet," she said.

"What is?" Susie answered, pulling away from the arm.

"That you have given her a name."

Susie looked at Tracey and frowned. "I haven't given her a name," she said.

"You just called her Floss."

"Yes, I did, didn't I?"

"So, if you didn't name her, who did?"

Where had the name come from? Susie frowned. She couldn't recall using it before, and yet it had suddenly just come to her.

"You're not going to believe this, but I think Floss told me herself, long ago. At the time, I just didn't understand her."

"Talking cows," Tracey replied. "Well, I suppose I have heard everything now."

Susie turned to her mother then, her face solemn. "We must do something to save Floss, Mum," she said.

Her mother immediately looked uncomfortable. "Sweetheart, she doesn't belong to us, so what happens to her is the owner's decision, not ours – however hard that is to take."

Susie shook her head. "But, Mum, we cannot just let this Fred person kill her. She is so very special, and after all she has been through, she deserves better than to have her life ended at a slaughter house."

"We have no choice, Susie."

Susie glared at her mother and began nervously curling the hairs of her fringe around her index finger as she tried to think of some way she could save Floss. And then she heard the rattle of a trailer. When she looked up, she felt quite sick. A pickup was heading their way, and it had a trailer in tow. It was coming to take Floss to her execution, and no one but Susie seemed prepared to do anything about it. The pickup pulled up in front of the gates and a slim man with dark hair and a greying beard wound down his window.

"Good evening ladies. I am John. Fred has sent me to collect his Highland cow. I am guessing she is in there." He pointed to Tracey's trailer.

Tracey hurried over to him. "Yes, she's here. Pull inside, John."

John did so, and then he climbed from his pickup. "Well, at least it has stopped raining," he said, looking from one to the other of the three of them. No one answered. Susie was not in the mood for pleasant conversation and the atmosphere was distinctly frosty.

"I'll get on with transferring her then shall I?"

John looked at the only face that had any hint of pleasantness about it, Tracey's. "Thank you for the use of your trailer," he said.

Tracey smiled and nodded. John then turned to Susie who scowled at him. "Hi there," he said, in a very friendly tone. "Have you been helping too?"

Susie's icy scowl did not waiver. Why was he talking to her like she was a child? She no longer felt like a child. "You can't take her," she said. "I simply will not let you take her."

John looked confounded. Clearly, he had not been expecting any trouble.

"And why ever not," he said.

"Because," Susie replied, and she sniffed loudly. Tears were welling up in her eyes. She must not cry. She simply must not. She took a piece of ragged tissue from up her sleeve and blew her nose loudly.

"Hey, I am not here to upset you," John said. "It has been a long journey from Leeds. I am here doing a friend a favour, and then I want to go home."

"Well, you are not doing me any favours, so you may as well take a long journey back with your empty trailer. Go on! You are not required here."

Susie saw John cast her mother a quick glance. He was obviously trying to get her mother on his side. She hoped that her mother would not take the bait, but unfortunately she did.

"Susie," her mother said quite sharply. "Stop that, please. He is only doing his job."

Susie gave her mother an evil stare, and then she ran to Tracey's trailer, and, with her back to it and her legs akimbo, she spread her arms out across it.

"You are not taking her!" she screamed. "And that is final."

John looked towards Susie's mother. "This is getting a little ridiculous," he said. "Please, will you remove your daughter, Janet, so that I can open the ramp and get that cow away before it gets dark?"

Susie saw that her mother was making her way over. "Go away, mum," she screamed.

Her mother took her lightly by the arm. "Come on, love," she said pulling it gently. "You are making a fool of yourself. This gentleman has come a long way, and you have to let him take the cow."

"He's no gentleman. He can't be a gentleman if he's going to take Floss to be killed."

"Ah," John said. "So now we are getting to it. Sweetheart, the cow isn't a pet. She is a farm animal, and farm animals …" He stopped. Tracey had put a finger to her mouth. He appeared to heed the warning, saying only, "Farm animals are not pets."

Susie blinked rapidly but her tears overwhelmed her eyelids and fell uncontrollably down her cheeks. "Please have some mercy. I love her so much. Please do not take her."

Clearly affected by Susie's pleas for clemency for the cow, John pursed his lips as if thinking about something. Then he gave a loud sigh.

"Look here, please don't cry," he said. "Maybe I have a solution. You buy her, or at least your mum does, and then you can do as you wish with her. Fred will not mind where the money comes from as long as he gets it."

Susie looked at her mother who opened her mouth to protest, but Susie's loud voice drowned out anything she had to say.

"How much is she?" she asked, turning to John again.

"He paid 450 pounds for her at the auction, so I imagine that he'd accept that."

Susie's eyes brightened and she looked at her mother again.

"Susie, you know that we don't have that kind of money, and even if we did, we have nowhere that we could keep her. You already know that. We have spoken about it."

"But, Mother ..."

"Susie, please do not address me like that."

"I will if you don't do something to help my cow."

And then her mother appeared to lose her patience. It was rare for Susie to witness her mum throwing a tantrum which was behaviour usually reserved for her – Susie, but her mother opened up her handbag and emptied the contents all over the ground.

"Look, Susie. Do I have to prove to you that I do not have the money? You already know how badly we are struggling."

Susie bent down and poked at the items on the gravel with her index finger. There were two pound coins and sixty-two pence in small change, three old receipts, one of which blew away as she touched it, a small hairbrush, and a pink lipstick. She raised her eyes towards John.

"Can we owe you the rest?"

John lifted a single eyebrow. "I don't think that is quite my colour. Come on, we have to be serious here. I've thrown the only lifeline that I can."

Just then, a heart-rending moo came from the trailer. Susie immediately turned to it and lifted the air vent again.

"Oh, Floss," she snivelled. "I will save you! I promise I will. I will not give up."

Floss gave her another moo, this time a brighter one.

"I know, girl. I know," Susie murmured, pressing her forehead against the trailer's side. "This must be so awful for you."

And then she felt an arm around her shoulder.

"I am sorry, Susie. I know this is hard, and I didn't mean to empty my handbag out like that. It is just that there is simply nothing we can do now. We have to let the man get on with his business."

"But please, Mum. We can't just let him take her when we know what …"

Her mother interrupted her. "We have to let her go, love. At least you have been kind to her. You really did all you could, and I feel sure that she will know that."

Susie's eyes were so full of tears now that she could barely see. Through the blur she looked towards Tracey. Tracey was her last hope.

"I am so sorry," Tracey said. "I haven't got the money either and even if I did, I couldn't keep her with my short horned cattle."

Susie took several rapid breaths, fighting the rising bawl that was about to burst out. She simply couldn't bear this a moment longer. She could break down right there in front of them all, or she could run away and do it. For a moment, she stared at each of the three of them, and then she fled, running across the yard and towards the open barn. Her blurry eyes scanned the interior. To the left was a large pen where a dozen or so cows were contentedly munching hay. To the right was a stack of rectangular hay bales that almost reached the roof. A ladder leaned at the side of them. She ran to it and began to climb. When she was about halfway to the top, she heard a trailer rattling, and soon after that came the sound of rubber tread turning on loose gravel chippings. That awful man was taking Floss, and there was nothing she could do to stop him. She ran up the remaining rungs and threw herself onto the hay, beating it with her fists and howling hysterically. It was five minutes before she heard her mother calling for her.

"Susie, are you up there? I need you to come down, sweetheart. She has gone, and we need to get you home."

Susie crawled to the edge of the hay bales and looked down. Her mother and Tracey were at the foot of the ladder.

"Thank you both for your support," she sobbed.

"Susie, please don't be like that. We all tried."

"No, we did not all try. I tried; you didn't. I will never get over this, and I will never forgive you."

"Come down, love."

Susie watched as her mother turned to look at Tracey.

"I'm sorry I brought my daughter here," her mother said. "We should never have followed you."

"I just feel sorry for Susie. To be as upset as she is, she must really love that animal, and I wish that I could have helped. After all its efforts to survive, it really is a shame that they are going to slaughter the poor thing."

Susie slowly came down the ladder making them jump as she leaped from the third rung.

"Oh Susie! Thank goodness you are down," her mother said, holding her hand to her heart. "I was worried about you so high up there. Come here and give me a cuddle."

Susie ran to her, and her mother put her arms around her and hugged her close. Then she gently pushed Susie away and looked at her face. A slight upward crease appeared at the corners of Susie's lips.

"That's better," her mother said, softly. "I knew there was a smile in there somewhere."

Susie cleared her throat. It was sore with all the sobbing she had been doing. Whilst up on the hay bales she had not just been crying though, she had been thinking too – thinking on a scheme to save Floss. Her mother was not going to like what was coming next.

"I have an idea how we can still save her," she said.

"Oh, Susie, please let it go."

But Susie was not about to let it go, and she looked now into Tracey's eyes, trying to figure her out. Had this woman who had her own cows been affected by the misery that had transpired that day, or did she not care a hoot? To Susie's relief, her eyes had compassion in them – she could see that. It was enough compassion for her to ask Tracey the question that had been running through her mind.

"I overheard you saying that you wish that you could have helped. Did you mean that? Will you help me, Tracey?"

For a moment, Tracey looked taken aback as if wondering what there was to help now that the cow was gone and then she said, "If I can then I will."

"First of all, I need to know that you have that man's number," Susie said.

"You mean John's? Yes of course I do."

"Please, will you text it to me?"

Her mother began to shake her head. "Don't give her it," she said. "This has to end."

"Please, Tracey."

Tracey looked awkwardly at Susie and then at her mother, clearly unsure what to say. Susie turned towards her mother.

"I am not going to ring him to abuse him, Mum," she said. "What I have in mind will not affect anyone and it will not cost us or Tracey a thing. It may, however, save Floss's life."

"Are you sure about that?"

"Yes. I am sure. All I am going to do is ring John and ask him to keep Floss safe for a little while; just till I can get to work on raising funds to buy her with."

"Raise funds? But you've never done any fundraising."

"Well now is the time for me to start."

"And if you do somehow manage to raise that large amount of money, where is she going to go? We cannot have her and Tracey says she can't have her either."

"That's why I've asked Tracey to help me. Whilst I am fundraising, I want her to find a sanctuary – you know, one of those places that takes animals in."

"I've never heard of any sanctuary that takes farm animals in," Tracey said.

Susie took a deep breath. This was so not helping. "Will you help me or not?" she said, sharply.

Tracey looked taken aback by Susie's abruptness and she lowered her head and nodded. "Yes, yes, of course I will," she said. "But what if John refuses to hold onto her? People who raise cattle don't have your sense of kindness, Susie. It is business to them. I should know. I have cattle myself."

"Oh, don't you worry about him. He will not refuse, not when I tell him that I am going to the newspapers, the radio stations and the television about Floss's plight. In fact, I am going to tell everyone that will listen. I will make that special animal such a celebrity that he will not dare to harm a hair on her head."

Tracey seemed impressed and she turned to Susie's mother. "So can I give her the number then, before it's too late?"

Susie's mother nodded and Tracey immediately hit the keypad with her thumb.

"And so it begins," Susie said. "Operation Floss begins."

CHAPTER TWELVE

John pulled into the lay-by at the side of the road and slowly let his head sink into his hands. He had just spoken to Susie on his hands-free phone, and now his mind was in turmoil. Would she really go to the press? And even if she did, would anyone listen to a teenager? What sort of bad publicity would it bring down on his head if people did listen to her? Good grief! He was getting an even worse headache than he'd had the last time he crossed paths with the darned cow that was now in the trailer behind him. It was as if the thing was cursed. After a while, he lifted his head from his hands and stared up into the roof space of his truck, trying to collect his thoughts. At the very least, he was going to have to ring Fred and tell him what was going on. John simply did not feel that he could take the cow to the slaughterhouse with all this on his mind.

"Fred, it is John."

"Hey, John. Did you pick the cow up okay? Have you dropped it off at the abattoir?"

"Erm … no, not yet."

"Not yet? Why not? Where are you?"

"I am about ten miles away from the abattoir, but … I am sorry, Fred …I can't take her."

"What do you mean? Why can't you take her? What's going on?"

"She says she's going to the press."

"What are you talking about?"

"I am talking about the cow."

"The cow is going to the press? John, have you been drinking?"

"No, I have not."

"So who is going to the press?"

John's account of the happenings of the afternoon took ten minutes to tell, and when he had finished, he sat back in the driver's seat, waiting for Fred to digest it all.

"Jeez, that cow," Fred said. "It was sent here from hell. I am sure of that."

"I don't want my family thinking that I am the bad guy in all this, Fred. And I have to say, though the girl is a nuisance, she really is just a nice kid trying to do right."

"It'll just blow over, John. You know what young girls are like. They obsess with one thing one minute and then something else the next. She's hardly going to be able to raise that kind of money anyway. She'll realise that she can't do it, and then we will never hear from her again. That cow has cost me a lot, and I need the money urgently, so I say take it to the abattoir now."

"You didn't meet the kid, Fred. I think she is very serious. She will not just go away, so if you want this cow slaughtered, you'll have to take her yourself, and then you can be the one to tell Susie. I don't want to be the one to do it."

Fred blew a loud sigh down the phone. "Okay, okay," he said. "If you feel that strongly about it, we'll give it a reprieve for a few days to see what happens. But if we don't hear anything else, will you take it for me then?"

"If we don't hear anything else, yes, I suppose so."

"Do you have anywhere to keep it for me?"

"I've still got my old barn in Leeds. I could put her in there for a few days. Last summer's hay crop is inside, so at least she will not have to starve."

"That's great, John. I really appreciate your help."

"You owe me for this one, Fred."

An hour later, John was at his barn. It had no acreage to it; houses had been built on the land decades ago, and now it was simply an old barn with a yard in front of it. John used it as temporary accommodation for cattle in the winter, and also for hay and fodder storage. He parked the pickup and trailer in the yard and then opened up the barn and looked around. He could not just let the cow loose inside yet. There was too much valuable equipment about, not to mention the hay. If he let her loose, she would rip it out all over the place. His eyes fell on a pile of old wooden pallets that had been rotting in the corner the last few months. They had come in with a delivery of fertiliser. One by one, John began dragging the best of the pallets from the pile. He then began hammering and cursing, hammering and cursing; the cursing happening each time he missed a nail with the hammer. After about a half-hour, he had constructed a crude pen. He placed his hands on his hips to admire his work. Not bad for the short time it had taken him, and it should hold the cow in whilst her fate was decided. It was time to drive her into the barn and let her out.

From the confines of the trailer, Floss had been listening to the banging and hammering, wondering what was going on. Where had Susie disappeared to? Since the trailer moved off, she hadn't heard her at all and she couldn't see very much through the gaps in the trailer sides. She turned her head towards the ramp, but it made no noise – it seemed that no one was coming to open it up yet. She heard footsteps come past her and then the engine of the truck in front of the trailer started up. They were on the move again. The journey was very short, though, and it was just seconds before the engine fell silent and the vibrations ceased. The familiar chinking sound came to her ears. At last, the ramp was about to open. She turned her head towards it. Slowly, it came down, and Floss peered out. They were inside a barn, and a man was standing close to the foot of the ramp. She stared at him, a look of puzzlement on her face. She knew him. He was one of the men who had been there the day that she had first escaped – John was the name she recalled. But where was Susie? She turned her head this way and that. Susie had promised to save her and yet only this man – a man she did not particularly like – was here. Susie was nowhere to be seen.

John brought a stick from the rear of his pickup and gently rapped the side of the trailer with it. "Come on! Come on!"

As Floss came to terms with the fact that Susie had not made the journey with her, she began feeling anxious. What was this place that John had brought her to? Her eyes widened and she scrutinised the inside of the barn. It was very gloomy, and the artificial light was barely adequate. There were no other animals there either; in fact, there was nothing to make her feel at ease at all. She became quite distressed, mooing repeatedly at the top of her voice.

John waved the stick at her again, and then he leaned inside the trailer and lightly prodded her with it. "No trouble, do you hear? I've had enough trouble from you." He then moved closer to the ramp. "Come on then!" he shouted. "Out you get. I need to be away. I have my own cattle to see to yet."

Recalling Bess's words from many months before – that one way or another, humans would make you get off the trailer – Floss determined that despite her fears, she had no choice. She placed her left front hoof on the ramp and began the short descent, but the mixture of alcohol and tranquiliser still floating about her system impaired her senses, and her legs wobbled all over the place. She tried to right herself, but the lean had gone too far, and she tumbled off the edge of the ramp, landing heavily on her side. The fall knocked the wind right out of her, and as she struggled on the ground, trying to get up, she felt a presence. John was standing over her. As she waited for his stick to come down on her, she gazed at him fearfully through her mop of hair, her eyes begging for his mercy.

"Come on let's have you up," John said, but this time he did not shout and his words were spoken softly.

The sudden change in John took Floss by surprise. She looked up from the floor, straight into his blue-grey eyes, and noticed something in them that she had not seen before – compassion. It seemed that he had been moved by her plight. As if to prove Floss's thoughts, John suddenly threw his stick to one side and knelt beside her.

"Oh sweetheart – you poor thing – Can you try to get up for me? You can't stay on the floor like that."

Floss struggled to her feet and as she looked at John again, wondering if the humaneness would last, her tummy rumbled loudly.

"You hungry?" John said.

She watched him then almost disbelieving as he closed the makeshift gate he had made and crossed to the other side of the barn. He pulled on one of the hay bales there and it fell at his feet. Shortly afterwards he returned to her pen and tossed three sections of hay towards her.

"I expect that you will be thirsty too," he said.

He left her again then returning moments later with a large black bucket which he placed in the corner of her pen. Still mistrusting, Floss kept her eye on him but she was thirsty and so she was thankful for the gesture. She made her way over to the bucket and sank her nose into it. The water was cold, freezing, but it had been a long time since she'd had fresh clean water to drink, and she gulped it down.

John watched her absorbedly. "I can't believe that I am saying this," he said. "But I am kind of hoping that you do not end up at the slaughterhouse, as it really would be quite some shame."

He smiled at Floss before getting in his pickup and leaving. The light in the barn went out soon afterwards, leaving her alone with only her thoughts for company – and they were terrible thoughts. John's parting words to her about the slaughterhouse had not gone unheard, and as she considered her life, she felt cruelly betrayed. It had been so very short, and then there was her son, her beautiful son; despite everything she had suffered, it looked as if she would never see him again – not in this life, anyway. Maybe it was time to let the humans win, to give up the fight and let them put a stop to her suffering. She was tired of running, tired of being hungry, and tired of fighting. Her tummy rumbled again, and her eyes cast towards the hay that John had left for her. There was no need for it to go to waste. There was no need for her to die hungry, and so she made her way over to it and tossed it with her nose.

"Moo ... ow!"

The excruciating pain that tore through her left nostril caused her to fling her head into the air. But the pain did not stop. It went on and on, and when she looked towards the end of her nose, she saw the cause of it: a small piece of fluff that had somehow attached itself to her nostril. She flung her head wildly to one side, and the fluff left her nose and flew across the barn. A sound like *splat* followed, and then there was a louder sound, more like *squeak*. Floss watched as the fluff slid unceremoniously down the woodwork of the barn. It then sprouted what she could only think were the smallest legs ever, and it scurried into the depths of the straw.

When little Gnaw arrived at his nest, his heart was beating wildly. The beast from hell had almost killed him. He rushed to his wife, who was chewing an ear of corn, and flung his arms around her.

"Nibble!" he cried, pulling the corn away from her. "Nibble, we have to leave. We have to leave our home now and get out of this barn right away; now even."

Nibble shook him off and reached out to retrieve her corn. "Get off me!" she yelled. "I was enjoying that."

There followed a tug of war over the ear of corn, and his wife won. As she settled to enjoy her treat once more, Gnaw made another attempt to get her attention.

"Nibble, please listen! This is serious, deadly serious. It almost cost me my life."

He heard his wife give a loud sigh and imagined what she was thinking. Yes, he was always the drama queen, but this time it was real and serious. This time it wasn't just a drama, it was a crisis. He pulled Nibble towards him, and after spitting out the tiny piece of the beast's nostril that had been sticking between his sharp little front teeth, he took in a deep breath. Even speaking of the beast terrified him, as if the whole incident were happening all over again.

"Go on," Nibble said.

Gnaw looked to either side of him, and then he swallowed. "A monster has come to live in the barn. It is big and it is bad, and it has great swords sticking out of its head. I think it is the devil."

"There is no such thing as monsters."

"Yes, there is. I have just seen one."

"Did you try talking to it?"

"Did I try talking to it? Of course I didn't. Why would I want to try to talk to a monster? And, anyway, I think I made it quite cross when I bit a piece of its nose off."

"You met a monster with swords on its head, and you bit a piece of its nose off? Well, in the scheme of stupid things to do that ranks pretty high up the list. What did you go and do something like that for?"

"What was I supposed to do when it poked its ugly nose into my gut, say hi to it? I thought it was a big hairy cat, and so I bit it."

"Mmm," replied Nibble. "I think that I will go and see this monster of yours, and try to undo the damage you have done to our relations. After all, if we have to share our home, we need to get on with it."

"Undo the damage to our relations! What on earth do you mean, Mrs Mouse? It definitely does not look like any relation of mine, not even big Aunt Sylvia, the rat, and she was very scary."

"Sometimes I wonder about you, Gnaw. I don't mean that sort of a relation."

"So what relation do you mean?"

Nibble shook her head. "It doesn't matter, Gnaw," she said. "Anyway, I am going to take a look at it. Are you coming with me?"

Gnaw shivered nervously, staring at his wife as if she had just grown two heads. "I saw enough of it last time," he said. "Be my guest if you want to go take a look, but I warn you, it is the most terrifying thing that you will ever set eyes on."

A skilled climber, Nibble clambered like a gymnast through the many layers of slippery stalks of straw. When she reached the surface, her keen eyes scanned the barn, immediately falling on the new occupant. Remaining unseen and hidden, she studied it a while. So it was a cow then, this creature that her husband had described, and though it was no monster, even she had to admit that it was the strangest cow she had ever seen – so hairy, so very hairy. She looked at its horns. Even though they weren't actual swords, they were certainly quite fearsome. She took a deep breath. If she and her husband were to share the barn with it, then she was going to have to go and talk to it, whatever the size of its horns.

She scurried across the barn towards the cow, and when she was close enough for her to imagine that the beast would be able to hear her, she began to squeak.

The cow immediately took a step backwards. It was obvious from its quick reaction that the cow had heard the noise before, probably when Gnaw bit its nose. Maybe then, despite its size, it had become rather wary of tiny mice. Nibble decided that she must try to reassure it and so she moved a little closer.

"I'm not going to hurt you," she said. "My dear husband, Gnaw, didn't mean to hurt you either. He only bit you because he was frightened, that's all."

The cow looked down and at first Nibble wasn't sure whether she had been seen. And then the cow began to lower its head towards her, very slowly, and as it did so,

Nibble noticed the wound on its nose from where Gnaw had bit it. Then the cow began to lift its foot. Nibble swallowed hard. If she couldn't convince the animal that she was not going to bite then it looked as if the foot would be dropping right on her tiny head.

"Hello there," Nibble said, in her loudest possible voice whilst her heart thudding against her chest like a tiny hammer. The cow's face was down near the straw, so close to her that it could swallow her up in one gulp if it wanted. She tried to stay calm. It seemed to be studying her and she noticed its focus shift to her tail.

A booming voice rang out. "So what type of worm are you then?"

"Me?" Nibble answered indignantly. She suddenly forgot that she was afraid and her tiny paws moved to her hips. "I am no worm."

"Yes, you are. I have seen many worms in the fields, so I know what one looks like and you are a worm, a very unusual worm and watch that you do not bite me again worm or you will be a very flat worm and not the round one that you are now."

Nibble laughed as she turned and looked at her tail. "This is no worm," she said. "I am a mouse, and my name is Nibble. This here is my tail. It is a very useful thing to have."

"Mmm, well my name is Floss. I think that I have heard of mouses."

"Pleased to meet you, Floss," Nibble said. "But the word is mice. More than one mouse is mice."

"Ah, mices. Yes, then, I have heard of mices. Thank you for explaining that."

Choosing not to correct Floss's grasp of the correct grammar, Nibble instead changed the subject. "So what brings you to our barn?" she said.

"I don't really know. I didn't come here by choice. A man called John brought me here against my will."

"Ah, John," Nibble said. "He comes here often. It is strange that he brought you on your own, though. He has brought cows to the barn before, but they have never been on their own. There have always been a few of them, never just one."

Nibble noticed Floss's bottom lip drop, as if she had said something to upset her. In fact, the cow looked as if she might burst into tears at any moment. Nibble shifted about uncomfortably. "Hey," she said. "Whatever is the matter?"

"It's just when you mentioned about being on my own. It made me realise how long it has been since I had company. You see, I am a fugitive. I have been a fugitive since my son was taken from me by some humans. I escaped from them, and I have been looking for him ever since. At times, it has been an incredibly lonely existence."

"Wow!" Nibble said. "So how come you got caught?"

"I was foolish. I let my guard down and ventured into human territory for some shelter when I should have known better. Then I found myself here."

"What do the humans plan to do with you now?"

"Oh, I think the humans plan to make me into burgers."

Nibble's face dropped. "That is horrible!" she said. "We cannot let that happen. You must escape again and go on looking for your son."

Floss shook her head. "I haven't the strength to go on any longer," she said. "When they do it, I will be glad. This world is no place for me now. I am tired of the heartache that never leaves me. I am ready to go sleep forever, and then at least I will no longer feel this hole left so painfully in my heart."

"Is your son dead? Do you know that he is dead?"

Floss shook her head again. "I do not know."

"Then you must not give up. How terrible would it be if you were to get to heaven and he was left down here? Life here on earth is a precious thing, and mice know that more than any animal. We do not live very long, you see. Three years if we are lucky; so we pack as much into our little lives as we possibly can."

"But I can't find him," Floss said. "Even if he is alive I can't find him."

"Tell me about him."

Floss's eyes brightened, and Nibble could see that just talking about her son had cheered her up. She must continue encouraging her to talk. Then she would forget all about being made into burgers.

"Oh," Floss said. "He was such a handsome boy, just like his father. He could be cheeky at times, but he was so very cute too. He was just like a woolly bear the last time I saw him." She took in a deep breath then. "He will be much bigger now," she added. "And I guess not quite so woolly."

"So where have you been looking for him? Tell me all about it."

"There is a so much to tell," Floss replied. "A lot has happened while I have been free."

"I have loads of time," Nibble replied.

"You may well have the time, little Nibble, but I am getting quite a stiff neck talking to you way down there."

"I have an idea. If I get on your head, then you will be able to talk to me so much better, and without getting a sore neck."

Floss laughed loudly. "You are very brave for such a tiny little thing, Nibble," she said. "Okay then, up you come."

Nibble watched Floss lower her head till her nose touched the floor, and then she scurried up the centre of her face, climbed into her forelock, and scrambled between her ears.

"Are you comfortable, Nibble?"

Nibble, settling down in the comfort of Floss's long hair, peered out and nodded. "Very."

"Right, then," Floss said. "I shall begin ..."

When his wife first left, Gnaw had not been worried. He had expected that she would look at the monster, agree with him that it was the devil, and then return immediately. He had also imagined Nibble proceeding to pack up their things so that they could leave as quickly as possible. But, when half an hour had passed, and then three-quarters, he began to fret. Chewing urgently on a piece of broken timber, trying to steady his nerves, his mind worked overtime on what might have happened to Nibble. The monster could have eaten her, swallowing her up in one mouthful; or maybe it had stamped on her, squashing her like a tomato. And then his thoughts turned to the swords on its head. It had probably speared her like a piece of kebab meat. Yes, that was what had happened. Nibble had intended to make a friend of it. *Yeah, and then let it eat you – brilliant idea!*

His mind then became saturated with feelings of guilt. He should not have let her go to see the monster on her own. He should have stopped her from going, or he should have gone with her. Timidly, he peered out through the twisted stalks of their nest, and his little legs turned to jelly. The very thought that he should now venture out to see what remained of Nibble was making him very nervous indeed. In a vain effort to drum up some courage, he flexed his tiny muscles, but that didn't help at all. He felt his heart skip a beat, and he banged hard on his chest to make sure that it didn't stop. "Go on," he said out loud to himself. "Go out and find her."

Gnaw crept from the nest and nervously made his way through the straw. When he was close to the surface, he poked his little nose through to the barn, his little whiskers twitching in time with his speeding heart. He could see the hairy monster with the swords on its head. It remained close to where it had been when he first saw it, but his wife was nowhere in sight. The corners of his mouth curled downwards. Just as he thought, the monster had eaten of her up, and he would never see her again.

Salty tears came to sting his tiny eyes, and in the darkness, he glowered at the beast. How dare this ugly monster with the weird lump on its head eat his wife! How dare it! Wait a minute – what was that weird lump? His focus turned to the lump, and he noticed that it was moving. He then saw a worm-like tail dangling through the strands of the beast's long hair. Gnaw rubbed his eyes, in case he was imaging it, but when he looked again, he could see that his wife was definitely on the monster's head. And goodness, she was waving at him. He slunk into the straw. Nibble waved at him again.

"For goodness' sake!" he exclaimed, peeping out. "Don't let it know where I am."

"Hey, Gnaw. I'm up here. Look at me, Gnaw."

Was she mad? Didn't she realise that it was about to toss her up into the air and devour her? "Quick! Jump!" Gnaw yelled, suddenly feeling brave and running towards the monster. "Jump, Nibble, and I will catch you."

And then a booming voice rang around his ears, almost deafening him.

"Hello, Gnaw," the monster said.

Gnaw cowered, lifting his nose just as the monster lowered its own.

"I said, 'Hello, Gnaw.'"

The beast's breath almost blew him over, and he stared up at it and then at the tooth marks that were so very visible on its left nostril.

"Erm … hello," he said with a squeak.

"I am sorry, but I cannot hear your apology all the way down there," the beast said, its voice still booming. "Climb on my head and sit with Nibble. Then I might be able to hear you."

Climb onto its head to apologise?! And what if it didn't want to accept his apology? He shuddered to think what it would do to him.

"I really would love to climb on your head – yes, I would love to – but I am afraid that I am very busy today. There is a lot of mouse work to do in the nest, and so I really must be going. Goodbye. Nibble, I will see you when you get home."

"Did you hear me, little worm … erm … I mean mouse?"

"Gnaw, get up here now." It was Nibble. "And do not tell me you have mouse work to do; I have never seen you lift a paw to do any mouse work, ever."

Gnaw trembled. He so wanted to run away, but Nibble was reaching through the monster's hair and holding out her paw. He closed his eyes as he grabbed it, and then he felt a rush of air as she hauled him up.

"Oh my giddy oats! Oh my giddy oats! I so hate heights," he squealed, and when Floss lifted her head, he flung his arms around Nibble.

"Stop it, will you? Just stop it," Nibble said, pushing him away with an angry squeak.

"Are you two okay there?" Floss said, her eyes crossing as she tried to look at them where they sat atop the middle of her head.

"We are fine," Nibble replied. "Gnaw is just getting himself nice and calm. Aren't you, Gnaw?"

Gnaw, his body trembling and his teeth chattering, forced a nod.

Nibble turned to him. "This is Floss the Cow. Some terrible humans took her son away from her, and so she escaped to find him. But now, they have captured her again. She has been telling me all about it."

Nibble may as well have spoken gobbledegook. Gnaw was far too nervous to take in a word that she said.

She nudged him gently. "Did you hear me, Gnaw?"

"What?"

"Did you hear me telling you about what has been happening to poor Floss?"

"Poor Floss? What about poor me?"

"Poor you? There is nothing wrong with you."

"There wasn't until I got up here."

"Oh, stop babbling like a baby mouse, Gnaw. Floss, can you start your story again so that Gnaw can catch up? And don't forget the part where you met the rabbit family. I liked that part."

As Floss repeated her story, Gnaw's rapid heart rate slowly began returning to normal. Maybe it wasn't so bad up here after all, almost like a nest with underfloor heating. In fact, it was so cosy that by the time Floss reached the part of her story where he had taken a chunk out of her nose, Gnaw had dropped to sleep.

"Gnaw, you aren't asleep, are you?"

"What? Who? When?"

He felt something move over his mouth. Nibble had placed her left paw over it. "Shush. Floss is just getting to the part of the story about her nose. I thought you should know."

"The noise? What noise?"

"Not noise, *nose*. The one you bit – hers, remember?!"

"Oh the nose! OMG, not the nose."

Gnaw felt his throat go dry. He must not let Floss recall him biting her nose, or she might well decide that she didn't want him on her head after all, and that she would much prefer to eat him. He determined that it might be best at this point in time to distract her and get her to change the subject. He hurried to her right ear flap and lifted it up. "So, where do you think your son is then? Are you going to escape again?"

Floss's right eye crossed towards her forehead.

"My poor baby is probably in a supermarket by now; and, no, I am not going to escape again. My last hope was with Susie, but she abandoned me. And so I am going to let those humans do with me as they want, and then at least my heartache will go away."

Gnaw looked puzzled. Why on earth would Floss's son be in a supermarket? He had never seen a cow pushing a trolley, ever. He moved over to his wife again so that he could whisper in her ear. "I didn't know that cows went shopping."

"What?"

"I did not know that they let cows into supermarkets. I just cannot see how they would be able to push those trolleys around, you know with not having any hands and all."

Nibble shook her head at him. "Are you serious?"

"Well, Floss did say that her baby is probably in a supermarket."

"Floss doesn't mean that he has gone shopping, silly. She thinks that he has been made into beefburgers. It is the *burgers* that are in the supermarket, not her son."

"Oh, I see," Gnaw said, feeling rather silly now that Nibble had explained it to him. "I am glad that humans don't make burgers out of mice."

Nibble turned her back on him, and he watched her go over to Floss's left ear.

"Please don't give up," Nibble said. "Don't let the humans turn you into burgers."

"I have no choice, Nibble. I am just so weary. When I escaped all that time ago, I thought that the world ended at the horizon – the horizon that I could see from the barn. But when I got to that horizon, there was another horizon beyond it, and then another and another. It is time that I joined my son in the great horizon in the sky. I was a fool to ever think that I could actually find him in this life."

"I don't think you are a fool. I think you are very brave indeed. And you say that the young girl, Susie, has abandoned you, well you do not know that for sure. Maybe she is doing something to try to save you right at this very minute. From what you have told us of her, she sounds pretty persistent."

Floss gave a half smile. Thinking of Susie had clearly raised her spirits just a little. "Ah," she said. "She was so lovely, a bit eccentric, but the nicest and kindest human I have ever met. She tried to help, she certainly did, but I am afraid that it must have got to be too much for her. I have lost a lot of friends on my journey."

"We are your friends," Nibble said. "In fact, we are such good friends that we are going to chew a way out of this barn for you, and then you will not be made into burgers."

On hearing this comment, Gnaw turned and scowled at his wife. What was she thinking of, saying that? Couldn't she see that it would take them their whole lifetimes to chew a hole big enough for the cow's bear-sized head to fit through, and then a second lifetime to make it big enough for the rest of her immense body?

Nibble returned his scowl. "What's up with your face?" she asked.

"Not half as much is up with my face as is the matter with your brain," he scoffed. "How on earth do you suppose that we could chew a hole that big?"

"We could try."

Floss coughed then, and it was such a forced cough that it silenced both mice.

"I am really tired now," she said. "I could do with a good night's sleep and some peace and quiet so that I can be prepared for what lies ahead for me. I am going to lower my head so that you can both get down. Thank you so much for listening to me. It has made me feel a tiny bit better for getting it all off my chest."

Gnaw slid down Floss's forelock first, and then he turned to see his wife coming down the same lock of hair. "Glad that's over with," he muttered under his breath, feeling thankful that he was still breathing. He looked up just as Floss gazed down on them both.

"We will see you in the morning then," Nibble said.

"I imagine that you will," Floss replied.

"And we will talk some more about how we will help you to escape."

Floss gave a weak smile. "We will see," she said. "Now off you go."

Nibble did not sleep well at all that night. She spent the dark hours tossing and turning in the nest, thinking of ways they could get Floss out of the barn. She just could not switch her mind off. No plan would be any good without Floss's participation, and as she ran this fact through her head, she determined that her first course of action must be to engage the young cow in wanting to be free. When this had been achieved, she would plan Floss's escape and then maybe she – Nibble – would be able to sleep properly again.

The next two days swept by without any success in devising a plan. No matter what she said to Floss or which way she presented it, her new friend seemed determined to accept her demise from the world. Nibble despaired. She could not force Floss to participate in any freedom scheme if she refused to co-operate.

Tuesday came by. Tuesday was dustbin day in the streets near to the barn, and dustbin day was the favourite day of the week for the mice. Hours before the wagons came by, the humans would drag their bins out to the roadside, and then along would come a stray dog, or a good gust of wind, and some would be knocked over. Out-of-date bread, biscuits, and bits of cooked vegetables made for tasty treats for hungry little mouths. Often there would be so much food that they would carry some to their nest to stock up their larder – the larder that was currently empty.

Gnaw's little belly was empty as well, it seemed. "Come on," he said, pulling at Nibble's tiny paw. "We must get out of here and find some food. It will be a whole week before we get another chance, and we have nothing left – only a piece of green-coloured bread, and I have left that for you."

"Yes, I noticed it! But we cannot leave Floss on her own. If we do, they may come for her, and we won't be able to help her if we are not in the barn."

"And what do you think two little mice could do if they came for her anyway?"

"I don't know, but I want to be here for her, and so we will just have to make do nibbling hay."

"But they may not come for her for days, weeks even and I am hungry. I cannot manage with hay alone for all that time."

Nibble looked at him contemplatively. For once, her husband was squeaking some sense. They could hardly help Floss if they were weakened through lack of nourishment.

"If we go to the bins, we must only do the first street," she said. "The one from which we can still keep our eyes on the barn."

Gnaw nodded his head, clearly happy with this as a compromise. "Okay, he said. "The first street is usually the best anyway. The lady at number 36 always throws out lots of waste and last time I got some lovely green peas and a piece of cooked carrot. Delicious as I recall."

Nibble made her way to Floss. The thought of leaving her alone was still weighing heavy on her mind. She must let her new friend know that they would not be gone long.

Floss looked down at her. "You can be as long as you like," she said, coolly. "I am past caring in this world."

"When are you going to snap out of this, Floss?" Nibble said. "Don't leave it till it is too late to do anything."

"But it is too late," Floss said. "It was always too late. I should have done more to prevent Boris being taken from me in the first place. The fact that I didn't – well, that's why I am here now and Boris is not."

Gnaw came over at that point. "Are you ready?" he said, tugging at Nibble. "If we don't get there soon, we will end up in the dust bin wagons along with the rubbish."

"Okay, okay," Nibble said, shaking him off her. She looked at Floss. "We can see the barn from where we are going, Floss," she said. "If we see any sign of a trailer coming for you, then we will be back in a squeak; if we don't see one, we will only be a half-hour anyway."

Floss gave her a half smile. "That's fine," she said with a long sigh as if she didn't care much whether it was a minute or an hour. "I'll see you soon then."

The first house, number 36, was just fifty metres or so away from the barn. It was an end terraced house with a garden to the side of it and a garage, unlike the rest of the houses which were all attached to each other. They hurried to the blue box belonging to it, which was at the side of the kerb. Blue boxes were the recycling boxes, and they did not need to be tipped over for the mice to be able to get inside them. Jam jars and tin cans were the prizes to be found in these boxes, and if they were lucky, the tops would have been removed, and the jars or tins would not have been rinsed out.

"You go in first," Nibble said as they leaped onto the rim of the box. "I'll stay here and keep an eye on the barn. I will take my turn once you've had your fill."

It seemed that Gnaw didn't need any further encouragement. He dived into the box and Nibble watched as he disappeared inside a cereal carton. She could hear crunching and munching as he ate whatever remains were inside it. He emerged a minute or so later only to vanish again, this time into a baked-bean tin.

Nibble's tummy rumbled noisily as she saw him emerge with a large baked bean. "Are you done?" she called out.

"For now," Gnaw mumbled through his full mouth. "I am saving this for my supper. I should be able to carry a bit more, but you can take a turn if you like."

Nibble stared down into the box, planning on where she would go first. Gnaw would have no doubt emptied the baked bean tin. There was a glass jar over near the corner, sitting on top of a half-folded newspaper. It looked to have some foodstuff or other left inside it. She would try that first. And then, just as she was about to leap down, the folded newspaper caught her eye again. There was an image on it – an image of something she recognised.

It was as if Gnaw had been struck by lightening when Nibble's very excited but ear piercing squeak left her mouth. He leaped so high into the air that he overtook the sides of the box and then came crashing down onto the rim of it where he began running around like his tail was on fire. Nibble noticed with dismay that he had lost his bean. She imagined that he would not be very happy about that. He came skidding into her rear end, almost pushing her off the box.

"What are you doing?" she said sternly, turning to look at him, her eyes piercing his.

"I should be asking you the same question. Why on earth did you squeak like that? I have lost my bean – my big and beautiful, shiny bean."

"I squeaked because there is something very exciting in the box."

"Something exciting? In the rubbish box? Maybe you saw my bean – my big and beautiful, shiny bean."

"Will you forget the bean for just a minute? I didn't see your bean, Gnaw. I saw Floss. Look, inside the box."

Gnaw frowned, and his tiny whiskers twitched as if he could not believe his ears. "My dear wife," he said triumphantly. "There is not a cow alive that could possibly fit inside this box."

He looked at her smugly, and she could see that he was feeling very pleased with himself, probably because he thought he was going to be right. He would soon find out differently.

"I didn't say that she was in the box. I just said that I had seen her."

"No, you said that you had seen Floss and that she was inside the box. I know what I heard, Nibble. But she cannot be in the box, because quite obviously, she just wouldn't fit into it."

"Well, she is definitely in the box; loosely speaking, I mean."

Gnaw's scowl deepened. "Loosely speaking? What is that supposed to mean? How can you loosely speak? Is your tongue dropping off, Nibble? Either Floss is in the box or she isn't, and I say that she isn't."

"Look at the newspaper in the corner. Her picture is right on the front of it."

"Huh?" Gnaw leaned over the edge of the box and eyeballed the image on the folded newspaper. A perplexed look crossed his face. "Don't Highland cows all look like that?"

"I doubt it. I am certain that it is a picture of Floss. Haven't you noticed the special look she has about her? The look that no other animal could possible have? Well it's staring right out of that newspaper sheet. Come on Gnaw, enough of the chit chat, get down in the box and help me with it."

Nibble jumped inside the box and began to tug at the newspaper.

"Can you see my bean anywhere?"

"Good grief! Forget the bean. We need to get this newspaper to Floss. It may just be the boost she needs to lift her spirits and give her the will to fight on."

"But I don't see how it will help."

"It will help because it will show her that someone cares enough about her to put her picture in the newspaper. Remember the young girl she told us about, the one who tried to help her? She obviously did not abandon Floss after all. Yes, you can bet your life that this is Susie's work."

"Can we bet your life instead of mine?"

"Whatever," Nibble said. "Now get in here quick and help me. If the dustbin people come to get the box, it will be gone for good, and maybe us along with it."

Gnaw jumped inside the box.

"Right," Nibble said as he joined her. "You get hold of this side of the page, and I will run over and get the other."

A large chunk of paper immediately came away in Gnaw's teeth. "That's torn it," he muttered, looking woefully at the damage. Sheepishly, he then looked Nibble's way - clearly expecting her rebuke.

"Oh, do be careful, Gnaw," she snapped.

He retaliated. "I am being careful, but it is just too heavy for us to pull. If we keep on, then it will eventually be torn to shreds."

Nibble closed her eyes and took a long and laboured breath. With much regret, she had to admit that Gnaw was right. With the newspaper having all of its pages and being folded the way it was, they were not going to be able to move it – not unless they could separate the page with Floss's image from the others. An idea began forming in her mind, and then her eyes glinted with wicked excitement.

"I have an idea," she said.

Gnaw's face took on a sick look, like he was about to have a bad bout of the runs. Nibble remembered that some of her past ideas had not always turned out well for him. This one though was a corker, in her mind anyway.

"Go on," Gnaw said, his voice trembling.

"Do you see those dirty old boots and training shoes over near the green dustbin?"

Gnaw cast a worried look towards the neighbouring dustbin and nodded.

"Can you get the laces for me, please?"

"The laces?"

"That's what I said."

"But what do you want them for?"

"All in good time, Gnaw, all in good time. Whilst you get those, I am going to do a little investigating. I won't be long."

Nibble watched him a moment, making sure that he was doing as she had asked. If this plan of hers was to succeed, then they both had work to do. She smiled when she saw him chewing and pulling at the laces. Now she could get on with her own venture. She turned around and made her way to the house next door. Lifting herself up onto her hind legs, she took a peek though the metal rails of the gate. Sure enough the next part of the plan was there, sleeping next to his kennel. "Excellent!" Nibble whispered.

She hurriedly returned to the blue rubbish box where Gnaw was waiting. He seemed quite pleased with his haul and laid the laces he had recovered at her feet.

"Fabulous," Nibble said as she placed them in a long line. "I am delighted to say that my investigating went very well. He is in perfect position."

Gnaw looked nervous and began to fidget with his whiskers. "He?" he spluttered.

"All in good time, Gnaw, all in good time," Nibble said. "Now we need to tie these together. You get hold of the end of that one and cross my path with it."

Gnaw did as she instructed him, though she could hear his teeth chattering all the while that he was doing it. "That's it," she said, keen for him to stay focussed. "And again – now pull harder. That's it. Now grab the end of that one, and do the same again."

When they had finished the task, Gnaw stared down at the three-metre length of twine that they had made, and then he looked up at Nibble. She could tell that he was daring himself to ask her what it was for. Well, now she was ready to tell him. Any sooner and she felt certain that he would have refused to assist.

"N-n-now wh-wh-what?" he stammered.

"Now we tie one end to the handle at the side of the box."

They did so.

"And now what?"

"And now," Nibble said. "Now comes the most exciting bit."

"Wh-wh-what is the most exciting bit?"

"Well," Nibble said. "You know Diesel, don't you?"

She could see that every part of Gnaw was trembling like a jellyfish. She knew all too well that her husband knew Diesel. Goodness the dog had barked at them often enough, but they had never dared to go into his yard – not ever. Even the postman would not go into that yard, choosing instead to leave any mail in a metal box on the outside of the gate. Gnaw very slowly nodded his head at her.

"Diesel is going to tip the box over for us," Nibble said triumphantly.

"And why would he do that?"

"Because we are going to tie this rope to his tail."

Gnaw gave the most frightened squeak that she had ever heard leave his lips and she had heard plenty.

"No! I mean, absolutely not, not ever, there isn't any way. It is a hare-brained idea."

"No, it is not hare-brained, it is mouse-brained, and it is the only way we are going to get the newspaper out of the box."

"That's it. I am dead. I am a dead mouse walking."

"You are not dead and you are not yet walking, but you will be soon. Come on, we must be quick. I hate leaving Floss all of this time."

"But Diesel will eat me," Gnaw protested.

"No, he won't. Diesel is next to his kennel, and he is asleep. I have checked. That's where I was whilst you were getting the laces. Now get a hold of our rope, and follow me. We have to work together."

With a queasy expression, Gnaw reluctantly got a hold of the rope and helped Nibble to pull it along the pavement and through the gate. There was Diesel, lying next to his kennel, with his head on the floor and his drooling tongue hanging between the fangs of his wide-open jaw.

Gnaw grabbed a hold of his wife and pulled her to him. "We can't do this," he said. "It is suicide."

"It will be homicide if you don't," Nibble said. "I can't tie this alone."

"I have a bad feeling."

"You have a bad feeling about most things. We just need to keep our heads."

"My thoughts exactly."

"Look, the sooner we get it done, the sooner we can get away."

Gnaw took a deep breath and swallowed. "Okay, okay," he said.

Hauling their rope with them, they crept cautiously towards Diesel. He was snoring loudly, every now and then giving a tiny woof that made him sound more like a tiny terrier than the mammoth creature that he was.

"What now?" Gnaw whispered nervously whilst trying not to look at the dog's enormous mouth.

"Crawl under his tail and hold it up. I need to get our rope underneath."

"You've got to be joking. You are not joking, are you?"

"Do I look like I am laughing out loud, Gnaw?"

She noticed Gnaw's eyes flick over her face as if to check whether she was joking. Her face held stern. He needed to know how serious she was, and now it all came down to which he feared the most, her wrath if he didn't do as he was told, or the dog. Seconds later and he was holding Diesel's tail above his head.

"Hurry," Gnaw said, panting. "It is really heavy."

Diesel grunted twice, and his tongue moved unconsciously across his fangs. Nibble heard Gnaw take in a breath and hold it as she ran the rope beneath the dog's tail.

"Right," she whispered. "Put it down again. Now cross paths like we did earlier. Pull, Gnaw."

Nibble gave the rope a gentle tug. "It's tight," she said. "Now run to the gate. Hurry up! I will be right behind you. Poor Diesel is about to get a rather rude awakening."

When Gnaw was halfway to the gate, Nibble opened her tiny mouth as wide as she could, and then she sank her sharp front teeth deep into Diesel's fleshy tail.

"*Hoooo-wee-hoooo-woooo!*"

Poor Diesel didn't know what had happened to him, and as Nibble made a dash for the gate, he leaped a whole metre up into the air and ran towards the safety of his kennel. The rope pulled taut against the knot the mice had tied to the box, slamming it against the gate. Nibble whooped with delight as it toppled over. The newspaper was out and on the pavement.

"I told you that we could do it, I told you," she grinned as she slipped through the metal bars of the gate to join her husband. "Just because we are small doesn't mean that we cannot get things done – we just have to use our brains to think them through."

There was a stiff breeze, and the newspaper sheets had already separated, gusting about the pavement. The mice ran to them.

"It's this one," Nibble yelled, sitting on the page she had found. "Hurry and help me."

They lifted it up, one mouse to each end, and then they hauled it above their heads and started walking, Nibble in front and Gnaw behind. It was very awkward keeping a hold of the sheet of newspaper, especially as the wind kept coming from under it. Several times they were lifted off their tiny feet, often going sideways instead of straight ahead.

"Nearly there," Nibble said, panting as she took a look from beneath the sheet.

They had reached the entrance of the yard belonging to the barn.

"Oh good," Gnaw said with a puff, also out of breath. "I can't keep a hold of it much longer."

They went a little further, and then Nibble peeped out from beneath the sheet again. "Okay, we are here," she said. "You can put it down, Gnaw."

Gnaw immediately dropped the page, taking a moment to catch his breath before turning to look at his wife, who was sitting proudly on the newspaper sheet.

"You really are quite something," he said. "I never thought we'd be able to do that."

Nibble beamed at him. "You of so little faith," she said, and then she suddenly scrunched her eyes up and pursed her tiny lips. She had forgotten about the hole – the weenie, tiny hole.

"Whatever is the matter?" Gnaw asked her. "We have done really well getting this today."

"Yes, but we have forgotten something very important."

"Look, about the bean – don't worry! I could always go back for it."

"It is not about the bean, Gnaw."

"What then?"

"We may have got the newspaper page here, but how on earth do we get it into the barn through that?"

They both gaped at the small crack which was at the bottom of the doors they used to come and go from the barn. Nibble shook her head at it. Even if they spent a few hours making it bigger, they were not going to get the newspaper sheet through without tearing it to pieces.

"It won't fit through there," Gnaw said.

"I know it won't."

"So what do we do?"

"Just be quiet a minute. I need time to think." And then an idea came to her. "I have a plan," she said.

"It doesn't involve dogs does it?"

"No dogs."

"So how do we do it then?"

"We will hide with the paper and wait until John returns to the barn to feed Floss. Then, when he opens the doors, we can slip inside with the newspaper. The best-laid schemes of mice and men, uh!!"

Gnaw screwed his little face up. "Won't he think it mighty odd when he sees a sheet of newspaper walking into the barn with him? And then we are definitely dead mice walking, dead mice walking with a newspaper on our heads."

"Will you stop saying that awful thing?"

"Dead mice walking, dead mice walking, dead mice walking with a newspaper on our heads."

From their hiding place under a pile of old wood, the two mice watched out for John arriving. He turned up about an hour later, parked his pickup in the yard, and then made his way towards the barn doors. Before placing the key into the lock, he looked around, almost as if he knew that he was being watched. Nibble ducked down underneath the old wood and placed her hand on Gnaw's head to make him do the same.

"As soon as he opens the doors we must make our move," she whispered. "We will only get one chance at this. Grab hold of the newspaper, Gnaw, and on my command, run with it."

Nibble's whiskers twitched apprehensively and then as the barn doors swung open she nudged her husband. "Quick!" she said. "We need to go now."

Once more, they lifted the newspaper page above their heads, and their tiny legs motored beneath it. And then, quite suddenly, Nibble felt the ground disappearing from beneath her feet.

"What on earth have we here?"

John hoisted them into the air, and Nibble could feel his eyes on her as he dangled her in front of him. Then, she heard her husband squeaking with fright. He was dangling too. "Hold on," she yelled.

"Vermin!" John roared, dropping the page.

As Nibble felt herself falling she looked across at her husband. He was clinging tightly to the page which was acting like a parachute. Nibble landed softly on top of the straw, and she quickly shot a glance at Gnaw. He seemed none the worse for his fall either. Then a dark shadow suddenly loomed above her head. At first, she thought that it was the newspaper page about to fall on top of her, but it wasn't the newspaper. It was John's very large and booted foot. She grabbed Gnaw's paw. "Quick, run."

The foot came down but by the time it did, the mice had managed to scurry out of harms way. And then Nibble heard a whirring sound pass her by. John had taken the boot from his foot and he had lobbed it after them. She pulled Gnaw into the relative safety of a big heap of straw, not far away from Floss's pen.

"That was a bit close for comfort," she said.

"Close for comfort!" Gnaw exclaimed, rubbing the ear that the boot had just skimmed. "You can say that again. I knew this idea was a bad one."

"It was the only way we could get the newspaper into the barn, Gnaw. Come, let's take a look. We need to get it again."

Nibble made her way to the edges of the straw and let her nose peep out through the strands. John was right where the newspaper page was. He was rubbing his socked foot with his hands as if the straw had irritated it. And then, to her horror, she noticed his eyes fall onto the sheet of newspaper – her prized sheet of newspaper.

"What have we here?"

John picked the page up, and his eyes seemed to settle on the image on the front of it. Then they flicked between the sheet of paper and Floss.

Nibble gasped and turned to Gnaw who was just behind her. "He's recognised her," she said. "How do we get the paper from him now?"

She watched John as he made his way towards Floss's pen where he began waving the sheet at Floss.

"Can you believe this?" he said. "The National newspaper! Can you honestly believe this?"

As John plonked himself down on a bale of old straw, seemingly to read the story on the page, Nibble turned to her husband.

"We must get it from him," she whispered. "Floss must see it."

"He has just waved it at her, surely she already has."

"Look at her, Gnaw. She is bemused by it. She does not realise how important that sheet of newspaper is. We must lay it out in front of her and explain what it means – that Susie has not abandoned her after all."

"You can't be certain that it is that girl, Susie. And anyway, John seems quite engaged with it. I don't think he will be leaving it here."

"I don't either. I think he will keep it if we don't do something to get it from him."

"You don't have another plan, do you? I can't keep surviving all these plans. I don't have enough lives."

"Yes, I have a plan, but do not worry your chattering little front teeth, Gnaw. It is a plan that I can carry out on my own."

Without even giving her husband time to blink, Nibble scurried from their hiding place, crossed the straw, and then scaled one of the posts of Floss's pen. After running across the top rail, she stopped when she was level with John, who was far too enthralled in reading the newspaper to notice her there. Casting a glance towards her husband, who was peering at her through the straw, she put her little thumb up.

"Don't do it!" he yelled.

But Nibble had her mind set on completing the task, and she never took much notice of her husband anyway. Launching herself from the rail like a winged bat, and with her tiny arms and legs outstretched, she aimed herself at the newspaper where she landed with a splat in the centre crease. From there she spun around. It seemed that she had taken John by surprise as he simply stared at her with ever widening eyes. Quickly, she jumped again, belly flopping on top of his nose with her legs splayed to either side of it.

Visibly horrified by the sudden arrival of a mouse right in the centre of his face, John let out a blood curdling and ear-piercing scream, and then, as he dropped the newspaper, Nibble felt his fingers clasp around her tiny body. She couldn't breathe. He was squeezing the life out of her, and if she didn't act fast, she knew that she would die. Managing to free her head, she opened her tiny mouth and bit down on his hand as hard as she could.

"Arrgghh!"

The tightness gripping Nibble's body ceased, and she began free-falling to the floor. Coughing and choking as she tried to recover her breath, she did not see the shadow of John's foot hovering above her. And then she felt herself being pushed out of the way. It was Gnaw. It seemed that he had seen everything and had come to her rescue just in time.

"Ye-o-o-o-ow!"

Instead of landing on a squidgy rodent, John's foot – the one wearing just a sock – came down on a sharp nail that had been left sticking out of a lump of wood. There was a lot of yelling and blaspheming as he pulled the nail out, followed by a hopping dance of elaborate proportions.

"Unlucky," Nibble yelled, laughing. She turned to her husband. "I think you just saved my life, Gnaw."

Gnaw smiled. "Thought you needed my help," he said.

John seemed to have lost all interest in the newspaper now that he was so preoccupied with his foot and so the mice hurried over to where he had dropped it. It was looking somewhat worse for wear having landed in a rather large cow pat.

"Uggh!" Gnaw visibly grimaced as he looked at his wife. "Are you sure about this?"

"Just get a hold of it, Gnaw. Right, pull it under the rail so that Floss can see it."

Floss made her way over to them. "You two have been a while," she said. "I thought you were only going to be a half hour. And what have you been doing to that man, John? He's making a lot of noise."

Nibble smiled at her. "I bit him," she said proudly.

"Why did you do that?"

"Because he had this sheet of newspaper – It is a present for you, and it took some getting here."

Floss looked down at them sitting by the side of their shabby sheet of paper and they smiled at her expectantly. She raised an eyebrow at them.

"A present for me?" she asked, scrunching up her nose.

"Yes," Nibble said proudly. "Do you like it?"

Floss's eyes widened as she stared at the rather smelly cow-pat-afflicted sheet of paper.

"It is … erm … really nice," she said. "Thank you."

"So, what do you think of it?"

"What do I think?"

"Yeah."

Floss stared at the smeared sheet again, and Nibble noticed that she was frowning. Gnaw appeared to see the frown too, and he made a move towards his wife's ear.

"She doesn't know why we have brought it. I mean, look at the state of it."

"I think that you can still see the picture."

"Little guys," Floss said. "I am really quite flattered that you have brought me this sheet of paper as a present, but I am not sure why I need it."

Nibble lifted herself up onto her hind legs.

"Floss," she said. "Please look at the paper closely. It has something very recognisable on it."

"Yes, my poo," Floss replied. "I see it every day – far too much of it actually."

"Look beneath the poo, Floss. There is a picture of you. We think that Susie did not abandon you after all; in fact, it seems she is still trying to save you."

"A piece of paper with my picture on it is hardly going to save my life, and it certainly is not going to help me to find Boris."

"But being famous might, Floss. And you are very famous now that you have your picture in the paper. We have never met a famous animal before, have we, Gnaw?"

Gnaw shook his head.

"But how will my being famous help?"

"Because I don't think that humans eat animals that are famous."

"Oh," Floss said. "Do you think that being famous will help me to find Boris?"

"I think that it may do."

Floss's eyes brightened – a glimmer of hope at last for Nibble – she seized the moment.

"So are you going to start fighting for your life again, Floss? Are you going to let us help you?"

Floss stared again at the crumpled sheet of paper and then at the two mice who had risked their lives to bring it to her. Slowly, she nodded her head, and then she smiled.

"Thank you for bringing me this," she said. "It was very brave of both of you. Maybe I do not want to be made into burgers after all. Maybe I would much prefer to try to find Boris."

Nibble beamed her biggest smile ever. "It is about time you said that, Floss," she said. "This is all good."

John was far too distracted with the pain his foot to notice the mice talking to Floss. He had managed to retrieve his boot and had put his wounded foot inside it, but the pain had been so agonising that he hadn't been able to walk without a frightful limp. Keen to get home and look at his foot properly, he hobbled out of the barn and to his pickup truck. After opening the door, he slumped sideways in the driver's seat and gingerly lifted his affected foot inside. Slowly, he brought his other leg in, and then he pressed his wounded foot down on the clutch pedal, but the resulting agony made his eyes water so much that he had to lift it off again. He felt sick, almost as if he could vomit at any moment. He stared blankly at the dashboard, waiting for the pulsating throb to ease. It was then that his eyes fell onto the radio. Maybe a little music would help ease the pain. He turned it on.

"So where is Floss now?"

Floss? Wasn't that what Susie had called the cow – the same cow that was now in his barn?

"They're holding on to her, somewhere in Leeds, but if we do not get her from them soon, I think they are going to eat her."

John's eyes widened, and he stared at his radio in disbelief.

"So, what made you want to raise money to save her?"

"Because she is special, and I love her."

"What is the full story then, and how can our listeners help?"

"Well, I think it all started when she escaped from a market …"

By now, John had his head in his hands. Not only had Susie managed to get the story into the National newspapers, but she was on the radio too. He was pretty sure that a television appearance would follow. He had just lifted his head up again when he felt his mobile phone vibrating against his thigh. He took the phone out of his pocket and held it to his ear.

"Hello."

"It's me."

"Who's me?"

"Susie, the cow girl."

Speaking to Susie was definitely one thing he could well do without right now. She would have him talking for ages, and all he wanted to do was to go home and nurse his foot. He dropped the phone into his lap.

"Are you there? Hello, are you there?"

John watched the phone buzzing away in his lap, with the squeaky voice emitting from it. If he didn't answer her, what would she do? She certainly would not go away. Reluctantly, he lifted the phone to his ear again, holding it about an inch away so that the volume of her voice didn't burst his eardrum.

"Oh good, you're back," Susie said. "For a minute there, I thought I'd lost the signal. I've just been on the radio. In fact, I've been on three stations today. Floss has really got the media going. They think her story is great, and they want to help her."

"Yeah, I just heard you tell everyone how I was going to eat her."

"Well, you were going to."

"No, I wasn't – well, not me personally, anyway."

"So how is she then?"

John cast a glance towards the barn, and even though he couldn't see Floss through the walls, he imagined her happily tucking into her hay. His thoughts then turned to the kooky teenager on the other end of the phone. She really was quite something to have taken all this on and to have run with it like she had. He certainly could not help but admire her. Goodness! Both the cow and the girl were getting to him now. He raised a smile.

"She's doing fine," he said. "In fact, I think she's put a little weight on these last few days."

"Really? Oh, that is fabulous. You are obviously feeding her well then. She needed feeding up. She looked so thin and …"

John interrupted. "So how is the fundraising going? I really can't keep her much longer, Susie. It really is getting quite painful having her at the barn."

"Painful?"

John wiggled his wounded foot. "Yeah, painful," he said.

"Well, if it is that painful for you, you will be pleased to hear that the collection we started in the local villages is going well. In fact, we almost have all the money together. The people in Ealand, Crowle, Belton, and Epworth have been marvellous. The shopkeepers have put collection tins in their shops, and the local paper has been getting donations in too. We have got over 300 pounds already. I even asked the butcher's shop to put a collection tin in, though you can imagine that they politely declined."

"You never asked the butcher."

"I did," Susie said. "The biggest surprise, though, has come from my school."

"Have you managed to raise money there too?"

"Yes, I have. Even two girls who were bullying me have put in."

"Bullying you? I wouldn't have thought that anyone would bully you."

"Yeah, I don't know how I let it happen, but I haven't been myself since Mum moved us to the village. Anyway, the two girls caught me off my guard yesterday, and I thought they were going to have a go, but instead they each pushed a two-pound coin into my hand and said it was for my cow. They were nice to me all day after that too."

"No one should have to put up with bullying. I hate bullies. Did you not tell your mum?"

"No, she has enough on her plate as it is. She thinks I have been making friends, and I didn't want her to worry."

"What about the teachers?"

"No. I just thought I could deal with it."

"Well you should have told someone."

"Yeah, maybe I should, but I am pretty sure that it's done with now. I have become quite the celebrity at school. I suddenly have loads of friends."

"That's good to hear. All bullies are just cowards, really."

"I know they are, but when there are two of them and one of you, it is hard to stand up to them, especially if you are small."

"You may be small in height, Susie, but let me tell you that you make up for it with your guts and determination. In fact, I have never come across anyone quite like you, adult or otherwise."

"Really?"

"Really. So what about a new home for the cow? Have you got one yet?"

The phone went silent, and John knew that for Susie to be silent, something was obviously wrong. "You haven't got anywhere for her, have you?"

"Not yet, no, but we will soon."

John sighed. This was not the news he wanted to hear. Looking after Floss was proving to be more of a pain than he had imagined, and in more ways than one. Fred had been losing his patience too over the last few days; he wanted the cow gone and the money in his hands. John was going to have to tell Susie that she needed to get matters finalised, and soon.

"I'm sorry to hear that," John said. "Listen, Susie. This is not easy for me to tell you, but Fred has been having a go at me over the cow. He has a hefty vet bill to pay, and he wants to use the money from selling her to pay it. He doesn't really care so much where the money comes from, if you get my meaning."

"Tracey and I, we really are doing our best, John."

"Yes, I know that. I have just heard you on the radio, but I am not Fred. He doesn't have my level of sympathy, and she is his cow, not mine, Susie. You know that."

Susie did not answer him, and John was sure he could hear her sniffling. He began wishing that he hadn't said anything, but he'd really had no choice. It was better she know now whilst she could do something about it than when it was too late.

"Don't cry, Susie," he said. "Look, I will ask Fred if he'll give you another week, and that should satisfy him. It should also give you time to get a home for her."

"A week!"

John heard Susie blow her nose. He knew how short a week must sound when her beloved cow was at risk and hoped that he had explained enough for her to realise that this was not his fault. "Yeah, a week," he said. "To be honest, Susie, if you haven't found a new home for her after that time, then...well then I guess that you never will."

"Okay, a week," Susie said. "We will have the money and a home for her by this time next week."

John smiled to himself. In the days following their first meeting at Tracey's barn, he had warmed to Susie – though sometimes difficult, she was also endearing, and he felt certain that she would succeed in whatever she set her heart on. She simply wasn't the sort of person to fail, and he had a strange feeling that he was about to become part of something good. It was a feeling that he was not used to having where animals were concerned, and it was a feeling that he liked. He wiggled his injured foot – it didn't feel quite as bad as it had earlier either. Yes – he was definitely feeling positive about things right now. Soon the cow would be gone and he would have his life back.

"Right, then," he said. "We are agreed. I imagine that you will be calling me to check on the cow tomorrow, so we will speak again then."

"We will speak again then, John. Goodbye."

CHAPTER THIRTEEN

With a deadline now to be met, Susie and Tracey spent the next four days frantically scouring the Internet at every spare moment, seeking sanctuary for Floss. But, it seemed that the answer was always going to be the same: no, we don't take in farm animals. Or, perhaps with a slight variation: no, we only take in cats and dogs. Susie sighed as she put the phone down on yet another wasted call, and then she stared blankly at the search engine on her computer screen. What else could she try? She was all out of ideas, and Floss would soon be all out of time. Susie's chest heaved as she fought back tears, and then she felt a comforting arm fall around her shoulders.

"Found anything yet, love?"

Susie turned her head. "No, Mum."

"Do you want a cuddle?"

She rose from her chair and hurried to her mother, who squeezed her tightly and then held her face in her hands to look at her properly. "You'll do it, Susie," her mum told her. "For some reason, life brought that animal to you, and I think that you were destined to save her."

"But, I thought that you wanted me to keep away from her."

"That was then, and this is now. I have watched how hard you have fought to save her, and I have also watched how she has brought your confidence back. You were such a cheerful and bright person before your dad died. Losing him really hit you hard, but since you met Floss ... well, I can see my daughter returning to how she used to be. I mean, a year ago, I couldn't imagine you just walking into a strange shop with a collection box and asking if they would mind having it on their counter, and I certainly couldn't imagine you having a conversation on the radio."

"No, me neither."

"And so, I want you to know how very proud I am that you have not given in. You will find a home for Floss. Something will turn up. I am certain of it."

It was just as her mother had finished praising her that Susie's favourite tune rang out from her mobile. She immediately hoped that the call would be from Tracey, who had been trolling the Internet all day too. She hurried to the kitchen table and picked up the phone. It was Tracey, all right. Susie swallowed nervously before answering, praying for good news.

"Hello." Her voice was tense.

Tracey got right to the point. "I am real sorry, Susie. I have tried my very best, but I haven't found a place. No one wants to know. They are either full or do not take in farm animals."

Susie's stomach did a turn, and she gave a heavy and audible sigh. "I've had no luck either," she said, her voice breaking. "What are we going to do, Tracey?"

"I don't think there is anything we can do ... not any more. You can't say we haven't tried, though, Susie."

"Please don't say that, Tracey. We simply cannot give up. We just about have all the money for her; at the moment, she is safe and she is well, and that is what matters."

"But if we cannot find a home for her then ..."

"We will find one. Please, Tracey, don't tell me you are backing out of helping me."

"Oh, Susie, darling! Of course, I am not backing out. But, well, I guess what I am saying is that you need to prepare yourself for the worst."

"But we simply must find somewhere."

Thinking that it may help her cause, Susie then sniffed extremely loudly. It was vital that Tracey knew how upset she was. The plan seemed to work.

"Hey," Tracey suddenly said. "I have one more number to try, which I couldn't get through to earlier. It is for a Shire horse sanctuary down in Norfolk. I wasn't holding out much hope for it, though, with it being a horse sanctuary. But you never know. Maybe this is the one."

"Try it now. Please, try it now. I have a good feeling about it."

"Okay, give me a minute, and I will call you back."

The minute turned to ten minutes, and then to fifteen. As the seconds ticked by, they seemed to be the longest of Susie's young life. The phone never left her hand, and when it finally rang again, she answered it on the first vibration.

"So?" she said, her heart racing.

"So ... you are not going to believe this, Susie."

Susie felt her heart lift, though she dared not hope too much – not yet, anyway. "Go on, for goodness' sake! Tell me."

"You know that feeling of yours?"

"Yes."

"Well, a woman at the horse sanctuary answered, and as it turns out, they don't just have a sanctuary for horses."

"No? So what else do they have?"

"It's amazing, this; truly it is."

"Hurry! Tell me!"

"They have a sanctuary for farm animals too. She gave me the telephone number, and so I called them. It was the founder, Wendy, who answered. Well, we had a really long conversation, and she told me how much she loves animals and went on about the fantastic campaigning the sanctuary does against cruelty in the farming industry. They go under cover and all sorts, and they really get stuff done."

"So, what's it called, and where is it?"

"It is called Hillside, and it is in Norwich. They have over two thousand rescued animals there. Have a look at it on the Internet. I already have, and it is the best place for animals ever."

"Two thousand animals!" Susie gasped. "So, are you saying what I think you are saying?" Her voice was shaking with emotion. Though she was pretty sure what was coming, she needed to hear it. She absolutely needed to hear Tracey say it.

"I am saying that they love all animals: pigs and cows, horses and donkeys, sheep and goats, turkeys and hens, all of them."

"And Floss?"

"When I told Wendy about her, she was really nice, saying how awful it was that she had suffered so much and how good it was that we are trying to save her. I could just tell from talking to her how much she cares about animals."

"Yes, go on."

"Steady on, I am getting there. She went on to say that they have a very special Highland cow called Blondie, which came to the sanctuary recently. Well, she says that Blondie could do with a friend. And guess what? She thinks that Floss could be that friend. She wants us to take her there as soon as possible. Susie, love, we have found her a home. What do you make of that?!"

Overwhelmed by the relief of it all, Susie could not speak. Tears flowed down her cheeks, rendering her unable to respond. She was forced to blow her nose loudly on an already soggy tissue.

"Are you still there?"

"Yeah, I am still here," Susie replied, her voice now excited. "I don't know how to thank you for this, Tracey, truly I don't."

"Hey, there is no need to thank me, Susie. I am glad that you had the guts to start this off, and I am glad that you asked me to help. You really are quite some kid."

Susie laughed. "Mum says that I have grown up a lot doing this and that my confidence has returned."

"Well, you have certainly impressed me!"

"So, when can we get her then? Gosh, this is so exciting! I must ring John so that we can arrange to get her."

"Aren't you off school next week, half term or something?"

"Yes, I am."

"So how does this Monday sound?"

"Monday!" Susie said excitedly. Monday was just two days away. She simply could not believe how soon that was.

"Yes, Monday is fabulous," she said. "I'll ring John to make sure he is okay with it. I am sure that he will be, though."

"Monday it is then. Try to get him to agree to an early morning start. It is a long way down to Norwich. Oh, and get some directions to his place in Leeds. I don't know Leeds very well. In fact, I don't know Leeds at all."

It was early Monday morning, and Joe Devlin was on the beach with his black Labrador, Benjie. There had been a light snow fall overnight, the second fall that March. Most of it had melted, but now that it had turned to rain, white flecks remained dotted along the more-sheltered areas of the beach. He brought his camera from his pocket and took a few pictures of the scene. For some reason, there was something extremely emotive about snow on a beach. Glenda rarely came on walks with him now that the weather had turned cold – it played up her arthritis – but she loved to share his experiences through his photographs, and he was sure that she would enjoy this one. His thoughts turned to her. She would be waiting for him at their cottage; his morning newspaper would be on the table, and his toast in the toaster. His stomach rumbled as he thought of his breakfast, and then his eyes scanned the beach for a final pebble to fling. Spotting a large flat one in the shingle, he picked it up and skimmed it across the lightly foaming waves. It bounced three times.

"Here, boy," he called.

Benjie, who was at the water's edge, took a lingering look at the sinking pebble and then rushed to his master's side.

"Good boy," Joe said as he patted the dog's damp head. "It's time for our breakfast, lad."

They made their way across the beach and towards the steep stone steps that would take them up to the clifftops. From there, it was less than a mile's walk home. Joe and Glenda's was one of four detached cottages overlooking the sea. It had half an acre of land to the rear of it and a pretty little garden to the front, just enough land to keep his eight free-range hens happy.

Glenda was looking out of the kitchen window as Joe arrived at the gate, and he waved at her as he opened it. When he got inside the kitchen, he could see that she had already buttered two slices of toast and had cut them into ten narrow strips ready for dipping in the waiting boiled eggs. His tongue went across his top lip.

"Hi love," he said, and he leaned forward and kissed her on the cheek. "The eggs look nice."

Brenda smiled at him and made a grab for the dog's collar. "Good walk?" she asked as she wiped the dog's feet with a cloth.

"Yeah, a bit wet but enjoyable," Joe said, pulling off his boots. He then placed his cold hands against her cheeks. "Cold too," he added.

"Oh! You are freezing," she said, clasping his hands to warm them. "Has all the snow gone? The rain has melted most of it in the garden."

"There was still some down at the beach. It seemed strange seeing snow and sand together. I have taken a few pictures that I will show you after breakfast."

He took his camera from his pocket and placed it on the sideboard. Then he pulled a chair up to the table and picked up the newspaper, shaking it to straighten the pages.

"Cup of tea, love?" Glenda asked.

Joe nodded as he took the impressively sized mug from Glenda's hand. "Thank you, darling," he said.

The first strip of toast, dripping with egg yolk, went towards his mouth at about the same time as his eyes fell onto the newspaper. And there she was, almost as large as life, staring at him from the front page. The finger of toast went straight up the left nostril of his nose.

"Glenda!" he cried, pushing his plate away so that he could see the newspaper better.

His wife hurried to the table and began to dab at the egg yolk on his face with a piece of kitchen roll. "Do you need your eyes tested again, love?" she said.

"Yeah … yeah, I know that it went up my nose, but it has nothing to do with my eyes. Have you seen this?"

Glenda looked at the newspaper. "Yes," she said. "It is a picture of a Highland cow. I noticed it on the front page when it was delivered. Kind of took me back a few months."

"Well, it *would* take you back," Joe replied. "This cow, she was one of ours."

"Nah, she can't have been. Why would she be in the newspaper?"

"I am telling you that this was one of ours. I would recognise her anywhere. It's Floss, the one we hand-reared when her mother died."

Glenda, now showing more interest, took up the newspaper. She then began to read the story out loud. "It says that she has been a fugitive since escaping from a man who bought her at Thirsk market last year. Most of ours went to Thirsk market. Good grief, Joe! You may be right."

Joe nodded. "I *am* right. Go on," he said.

"They think she escaped because her calf was taken away from her, and they have worked out that she has travelled over sixty miles trying to find it," Glenda said, adding, "I feel terrible, Joe. It is dreadful to think of the poor thing looking for her baby like that."

Joe nodded again, and his head bowed down towards the table. He remembered the strong little calf that Floss had given birth to, a lovely thing it had been. If he had not been so ill, he would never have allowed the calf to have been taken away from her at such a tender age.

"Where does it say she is?"

"It doesn't mention where she is now, but it does say that some teenage girl has been responsible for rescuing her, and that she is being taken to a new home, an animal sanctuary in Norwich. Hillside it is called."

"Does it say when she is to be taken to this place?"

"Today."

"Today! Good grief! So little time then. Do you recall what happened to the calf, Glenda? I remember our Terry coming to see me in hospital and talking to me about it. I also remember telling him that I did not want it to go to the auction. You were with him, do you remember? Where did it go? We must call Terry and ask him where it went."

"We don't need to call our Terry because I remember who took it. It was big Bill Gatling, Joe."

Joe frowned and his heart sank. "Bill Gatling! What on earth was our Terry thinking of? I've never liked that man. He does not know how to look after or treat animals; never has done. He should never have been allowed to get his hands on my lovely little calf. Goodness, I hope that we are not too late. Do you know if any money changed hands?"

"I don't think so. I think Terry just gave the calf to him, sort of on loan. You cannot blame Terry if anything has happened to the calf, though. You were ill, Joe. Remember? Terry was just doing his best at a very difficult time."

Joe calmed down a little. "Yeah, you are right. He's a good lad, our Terry, and I am being unfair. Anyway, if Bill didn't pay for the calf, then he still belongs to me. Pass me the phone, love. Let's hope that I am not too late to right this thing."

Over in Ealand, at about the same time that morning, Susie had just stepped out of the house. It had rained throughout the night – and was still raining – but no amount of water would dampen her spirits. This was the day that she and Tracey were to collect Floss, and as Susie skipped through the puddles and towards the road, her energy was at an all-time high. She waved to Tracey, who was waiting for her in the jeep. The cattle trailer was in tow, all ready to go pick up Floss.

"I didn't think that this day was ever going to arrive!" Susie said excitedly as she sat herself down in the passenger seat and clipped on her seat belt.

Tracey turned her head and smiled at her. "Me neither. Are you excited?"

"Excited?! I've not been able to sleep a wink. I just cannot wait to see my lovely Floss happy in a new home, properly cared for by people who will love her as I do."

"Well, from the pictures that are on Hillside's website, it certainly looks the kind of place where an animal would have a good life. Anyway, we will soon find out. Have you remembered to bring some directions?"

Susie brought a piece of notepaper from her pocket and placed it on her lap. "Of course," she said. "It was nice of John to offer to take her to Goole for us, wasn't it? He really seems like a changed man – I mean when I met him, I couldn't stand him."

"Yeah, it was good of him," Tracey said. "It is much better that we can collect her from Goole. It's not that far, and I didn't fancy trying to tow this cattle trailer all through the centre of Leeds and then return the same way to start towards Norwich."

"Do you think he will have set off with her yet?"

Tracey looked at the clock on her dashboard. "Why don't you give him a call and see how he is getting on with loading her?"

Susie nodded and brought her mobile phone from her pocket.

"Hi, John; it's Susie. We are about to set off, so I was wondering how you're getting on with Floss."

She heard John sigh. "Not so good. Floss, as you call her, is galloping around in a frenzy, and I haven't been able to get anywhere near her. She seemed okay until I pulled the trailer into the barn and then she just went mad. It's like something whispered some terror in her ear, and now she is trying to push her way out of the pen I made for her. I can't understand it."

"Have you tried talking to her, John? She may be afraid of where you are planning to take her."

"Really, Susie, I think that's going a bit far, even for you."

"She understands more than you realise, John."

"Don't be silly, Susie. If she carries on like this, though, we will have to cancel today."

Susie's heart sank. Cancel today? They could not do that. Everything was in place, and the sanctuary was waiting for Floss. Maybe they should have gone to collect her in Leeds after all. She supposed that they could still go over, but that would take an awful long time.

"Just try it, John," Susie begged. "Tell her that you are taking her to me. Please. I will stay on the phone whilst you do it."

She pressed the phone close to her ear. John was obviously walking now as his breathing down the line had got louder and heavier. She then heard him yell at Floss.

"Floss! I have Susie here, and she wants me to tell you not to worry, and that I am taking you to her."

"Did it work? John, did it work?"

There came a moment of silence and then John came back on the phone. "You are not going to believe this," he said. "The instant I told her that, well she stopped running around, and she came to the fence. She is now staring at me and her expression – well you'd have to see it to believe it – bewildered doesn't quite cover it."

"Put the phone to her ear, John. Let her hear my voice. She won't understand phones. She won't understand that I could possibly be inside such a small object."

"Is it next to her ear?"

"Yes, Susie. Talk to her."

"Hello, Floss. It's Susie, sweetheart. I know it must be strange hearing me on the phone like this, but it really is me. I need you to be good for John, and he will bring you to me. You must not try to escape. You need to be good and trust me and then all will be well."

John came back on the phone. "It's working," he said. "She's just become quiet as a mouse. Hey, I'd best not say that around here. Mice are not quiet around here."

"What?"

"It doesn't matter. Right then, if she continues behaving like she is now, I should be able to load her. I will see you in Goole in about an hour."

"Can you remind me the way, John? I have it written down, but it won't hurt to double-check."

"Just head for the main road. Go straight through Crowle, heading towards Goole. Keep going on that road. You will pass through several villages. When you see a windmill, you need to turn left, and then Fred's farmhouse will come into view. Wait for me there."

"Okay, then, let's do this thing!"

Tracey started the engine, and Susie watched as the wipers crossed the windscreen at full speed. She wiped her hand over the misted side window and looked towards the house. Her mother was at the window and waving. Susie grinned, waving back. They were off at last; off to get her beloved Floss.

Using the main highway, they passed Susie's school, and they continued into Crowle. After Crowle, the road began to narrow, leading them into the countryside. The next village was Eastoft, and as they approached the village, the sky darkened and the rain became even heavier, each massive drop bouncing inches up off the road surface. Tracey slowed down, but even so, the jeep's chunky tyres sliced through the ever increasing puddles, casting water to either side in huge waves. After they had gone through Eastoft, the sky brightened somewhat, and the rain trickled to a drizzle, which was a welcome relief to both Susie and Tracey. By the time they reached the busier parish of Swinefleet, Tracey turned the wipers off altogether. It was just after that when a disused windmill came into view.

"Do you think that's it?" Tracey asked, glancing at Susie.

Susie shrugged her shoulders. "It might be," she said. "But I expected the farm to be a little further on than this. John said to take a left turn just after the mill and that we would then see a house, but I can't see a turn. Can you?"

Tracey shook her head, braking sharply as they reached the windmill, bringing the jeep to a halt at the side of the road.

"There isn't a turn," she said, screwing up her nose. "Hang on! There is a track. It's very churned up, as if tractors have been back and forth along it. Did John say that the turn was onto a farm track?"

Susie pored over her notes. "He didn't say," she said. "And I dare not call him, as he will be driving and Floss will be with him."

They spent a few moments fixating on the muddy state of the track. A row of tall conifer trees some way down obscured any farmhouse that could be hiding behind them.

"Well," Tracey finally said. "I suppose that we had better try it. I hope that we don't get bogged down, though. If we do, Floss will not be going far today."

Tracey's left hand went forward and grabbed the lever – engaging four-wheel drive. She then turned the jeep onto the track which was more of a quagmire than a useable road. Susie could see that she was doing her very best to avoid the deepest of the water-filled hollows, but it was a tricky task. The vehicle threw driver and passenger around in their seats like rag dolls, as it rose and fell, jerked and jolted. A particularly deep hole made the jeep skew sideways quite violently, and Susie was forced to cling to her seat. As it steadied again, she snapped her head around to check on the trailer.

"Is it okay?" Tracey said.

"I think so," Susie replied. "It nearly jackknifed."

"Yeah, I know. This track is in a right state."

The land became less churned up as they neared the tall conifers, where stone had been freshly laid. When they passed the trees, Fred's old house came into view.

"There is a house then," Susie said, ducking her head so that she could see the whole of the building through the windscreen. "This must be the right place, though it looks a bit derelict. I don't remember John saying that the house was derelict."

"Well, we had better try it," Tracey replied, and she pulled up next to the overgrown garden and pulled on the handbrake.

It was an old house, built in 1898, during the reign of Queen Victoria. In those days it had been very grand, the manor house of many hectares of land around it. Now, though, with many owners not having kept up with the expensive maintenance, it was a shadow of its former self. The window frames were rotten and peeling, and green lichen and sprawling ivy obliterated any signs of the beautiful stonework that lay behind. Some of the upstairs windows were broken and boarded up. Susie's eyes fell on the heavy and imposing wooden door which was right at the centre of the house, and she turned her head towards Tracey.

"It looks spooky," Susie said. "Like something out of a horror movie. I don't think that this can be the right place."

Tracey laughed. "Well, before we turn around, I think one of us should knock."

Susie took in a deep breath. "By one of us, do you mean me?"

Tracey gave a cynical smile and nodded. "I'll stay here with the jeep."

"Thanks!" Susie replied.

She climbed from the jeep and headed for the huge stone pillars marking the entrance to what had once been the garden and orchard of the house. There wasn't a gate, and so she passed through the pillars and into the jungle of rotten weeds. It was lucky that she had worn her toughest boots, as they saved her legs from most of the rotting thistles and brambles. When she reached the house, she climbed onto the single stone step, and looked up at the imposing door. Just within her reach there was a rusty old door knocker in the shape of a goat's head. It looked quite fearsome, with its blanked-out eyes and miserable expression, and she hesitated before reaching for it. Whoever lived in this house was sure to be as frightful as the knocker. She managed one rap and then waited nervously. It was a relief when no one answered.

"No one is in!" she shouted, jumping from the step and looking towards Tracey, who had taken leave of the jeep and now stood by the stone pillars. "This can't be the right place."

"Did John say Fred would be in?" Tracey called back.

Susie shrugged her shoulders. "I don't think we discussed it."

"Try looking in the windows. He may not have heard you."

Susie took a few steps backwards so that she could view all four of the dirty windows on the ground floor. They were huge windows with stone sills and filthy green curtains drawn right across three of them. She made her way to the one window to her right, which did not have curtains. After wiping rainwater from the sill with her sleeve, she leaned against it and pressed her nose to the pane.

Except for an empty antique bookcase on the far side of the room, it was completely clear of furnishings. Three of the walls had drab burgundy flocked wallpaper, which was peeling off in places; the gable end was a tumble of bricks, with a large black hole where a grand open fire once warmed the house.

Susie turned away, shaking her head towards Tracey. This could not be the right place. Though she didn't really want to call John when he was driving, she was going to have to, or he would probably be waiting somewhere else for them. Reaching into her pocket, she clasped hold of her mobile and pulled it out. She looked down at the keypad and searched out his number.

"Hey, John; it's me. We're at this old house, but we're not sure whether it's the right place."

"Take a look behind you, Susie. I am here – just coming around the trees now. I can see you. I will be with you in a minute."

Susie snapped her head around, and when she saw John's black pickup and trailer, she let out a loud shriek of delight. Floss was in that trailer, and soon they would be reunited. Everything really was coming together – finally. She did not feel the brambles scratching her legs as she ran through them again, and she was at Tracey's side as John pulled up.

"Now then, ladies," John said, winding his window down to greet them. "Terrible weather, uh! It was snowing in Leeds, and I almost had to turn around."

Susie's stomach did a somersault.

John smiled at her. "Don't look so worried. It isn't snowing here. You should be a very happy young lady today."

"I am. Just a bit nervous that something might go wrong," she said. "I will not be happy until I see her trotting off that trailer into the safety of Hillside Animal Sanctuary. How is she? Did she travel okay?"

"Go take a look." He waved his hand towards the trailer. "After you spoke to her she loaded like an angel, but I haven't seen her since she went in. I am sure that she is fine."

Susie did not need asking for a second time. She made a move for the trailer, quickly setting her eyes to one of the air vents.

"Oh, Floss," she cooed. "I cannot believe that you are really here. This is so wonderful. Who would have thought when we first met all those months ago – when you were limping and hungry – that we would be here in this moment, right now, about to take you to a lovely new home?"

A thunderous moo ensued, and the trailer rocked with the intensity of it.

Susie turned her head towards John and Tracey, who had moved in behind her. "Did you hear that? I think she is pleased to see me."

They laughed in unison.

Returning her eyes to the opening, Susie moved her fingertips into the vent so that she could caress Floss's nose. "Now don't you be afraid of anything. We have to move you into a different trailer, and then we are going on a long journey. But I promise you that it will be worth it."

Floss replied with a long moo that sounded almost like a sigh of relief.

John placed a hand on Susie's shoulder, making her jump. "So," he said. "She looks a bit better than the last time you saw her, doesn't she?"

Susie removed her fingers from Floss's nostrils and turned to look at him. "She looks great, John. Thank you so very much for all your help. I know that I have been difficult, and I know that it can't have been easy for you having to look after her in Leeds, but I am so very grateful for everything you have done."

John smiled. "I won't say that it has been easy, and I certainly cannot say that I haven't suffered. However, I am pleased with how it has turned out. She really is quite something, and so are you."

Susie bowed her head modestly. She then moved her hand to her pocket. "I have the money for you."

"And I have something for you. Wait here a moment."

He returned to his pickup, and after fiddling about for a short time, he brought out a small wallet.

"This is her passport," he said, holding it towards Susie. "Fred gave it to me last night; it must travel with her. I also got him to sign a receipt for you, just to make sure that everything is done properly. I have tucked it inside the passport. I thought you would want the transaction to be belt and braces."

"Belt and braces," Susie repeated. "Yes, that's what I like."

They swapped items, and Susie opened the passport up, poring over the content. It was the first farm-animal passport that she had ever seen.

"It tells us everything about her," Susie said. "Who her mother and father were, where she came from, how old she is – everything."

"Where did she come from?" Tracey asked, beckoning for a look at the passport, which Susie passed over to her.

"Reading in Berkshire!" Tracey exclaimed. "She has been on a right journey this past year then, hasn't she! And she's only four years old."

Tracey returned the document to Susie, who promptly kissed it. "For luck," she said before carefully placing it in her coat pocket and zipping it securely.

John laughed. "You cannot get any luckier than that cow did to find you," he said. "Some lucky cow, that." He turned to Tracey then. "Right, I guess that we should get on with moving her to your trailer. I will turn around in the field next to the house, and then I will pass by you and reverse the back of my trailer to yours. We should be able to make a gated walkway from one trailer to the other. What do you think?"

"Sounds good to me," Tracey replied. "What do you think, Susie?"

"I think that with me around, Floss will just do whatever we want her to do. She knows what is happening today; I know she does."

John coughed. "Uh, you weren't around the last time she was here on this farm. Let me tell you, she is good at wandering off, and she is also good at making fools of people. Fred ended up in one of these ditches; so he did."

Suddenly, Floss gave a strange moo that sounded almost like a laugh.

Susie giggled. "She found that funny," she said to Tracey and John. "Didn't you, Floss?"

The same odd moo came again, louder this time.

Susie, Tracey, and John all laughed.

"Back soon," John said.

They watched him turn the pickup around in the field. He passed them and then began reversing, lining the rear of his trailer perfectly with Tracey's.

"He's a good driver, isn't he?" Susie said.

Tracey nodded. "I couldn't have done it like that," she said. "I am rubbish at reversing trailers, and with all this soggy mud, we could have ended up in the ditch."

John opened his door and swung his legs from the pickup.

Tracey and Susie turned their impressed expressions towards him, but he seemed to take no notice.

"So," he said. "Let's see if we can make a better job than we did with her last time we were on this track."

Watching as John opened the catches on both ramps and keen on helping him, Susie and Tracey pulled the side gates of Tracey's trailer out.

John then did the same to his own trailer.

"Look at that," John said, smiling broadly. He seemed as pleased as punch with the sealed passage they had created. "Now, get ready, ladies, and don't do anything heroic. Watch out for her horns. Okay, here she comes."

Floss came to the top of the ramp. First, her eyes fell on Tracey, and then they settled on Susie, who beamed at her.

"Come on, Floss," Susie said, speaking calmly and softly. "Come on down, girl. No one is going to hurt you."

Floss came steadily down the slats of the ramp. But then, as she reached the intersection, her eyes suddenly widened with terror.

Susie instinctively knew the cause of her distress. "She's frightened of the trailer," she said, looking first at Tracey and then at John. "She remembers it from when she was darted by the vet."

John shook his head at Susie. "It's nothing to do with being scared of the trailer. She's just thinking of making a run for it again. All that mooing and stuff – she was fooling us all along. Quick, ladies, flap your arms about to put her off. If she does escape from here, she will be gone – make no mistake about that."

John and Tracey began waving their arms about frenziedly, and as Susie watched them, her eye balls shot up into their lids. They really were behaving like fruit loops, as it was all quite unnecessary. She turned to look at Floss.

"Take no notice of them, Floss," she said. "And do not be afraid of the trailer. This time I promise absolutely that I am coming with you. After all, I need to check that your new home is everything it should be."

Susie saw Floss take another apprehensive glance at the insides of the trailer. Her eyes then moved to John and Tracey who were still flapping about.

Susie kept her cool. It's okay," she said. "Really it is."

Floss looked at Susie once more, and Susie simply smiled at her. The smile seemed to do the trick because Floss suddenly leaped onto the ramp of Tracey's trailer and then with a loud clatter of hooves, she scrambled up and shot inside.

John immediately closed the side gates and lifted the ramp into place. He then looked at Susie.

"Phew!" he said, breathing out a long sigh. "That went better than I thought it would. I'd like to say that she went in because of our hysterical flapping, but I kind of got the impression that it was all down to you. She really trusts you, doesn't she?"

"I told you. She is a very special cow."

John laughed. "Yeah, you tell that sanctuary to look after her."

Susie smiled at him, knowing that Floss had got to his heartstrings too. "I will, John," she said.

John held his hand out then to shake hers.

"Oh, and one more thing," he said. "Don't go saving any more cows. Not near me, anyway."

Susie and Tracey both laughed at this.

"Well, I guess that this is goodbye then," John said, releasing Susie's hand. "Take care. It's a long journey down to Norfolk."

They watched him return to his pickup, and, knowing that he was checking his mirrors, they continued waving until the rear of his trailer was halfway between them and the trees.

Susie then turned to Tracey. "Pinch me, Tracey, in case I am dreaming," she said. "I honestly cannot believe that we actually have Floss here with us."

And then Floss let out a loud moo, just to let them know that she was there.

Susie smiled. "Hear that?" she said, opening the passenger door to Tracey's jeep. "I think she is ready for Hillside."

The first half of the journey took them just short of two hours, passing through Lincoln and Sleaford, where they stopped to refuel and to check Floss. After a quick sandwich each, bought at the service station, they then took up the A17, passing through Boston and Kings Lynn. The weather had turned for the worse again, raining much of the way, but it was lighter than it had been in the morning and not heavy enough to make the journey bothersome.

Hillside Animal Sanctuary was in the village of Frettenham, and it was easy enough to find the village. However, now that they had arrived, they were lost. A maze of country lanes seemed to go off in all directions, and after going around in circles, Tracey pulled up at the kerbside.

"What about asking her?" she said, nodding towards an elderly woman walking down the pavement on her side of the jeep.

"Nah," Susie replied. The woman looked to be in a hurry and was fighting with an umbrella that had half turned inside out. She doubted that she would want to spend time stopping to give them directions.

"Him," she said, nodding her head towards a dark-haired young man who had just left his house to walk his black Labrador. Tracey lowered her window and hollered over to him. "Excuse me! Can you help us? We are looking for Hillside Animal Sanctuary."

The man hurried over, pulling the dog with him. He then leaned in towards Tracey. "Hillside? Yes, of course, I know it. Everyone around here does. It's the place that looks after animals. The main entrance is on Hall Lane. You are not far away now."

He swapped the dog's lead to his left hand so that he could indicate with his right.

"At the end of this lane, turn right. You will come to a pub. Turn at the next left and keep going. You should soon pick up signs for the sanctuary. The road will take you out of the village and into the countryside. The sanctuary entrance is on the right. It's a huge place; you can't really miss it."

After thanking the man profusely, Tracey closed her window, and they set off again – reaching the end of the lane in just a few seconds. The right turn was sharp and Tracey took it slowly and carefully. She was obviously conscious that the road was wet and that the tightness of the turn might knock Floss off her balance. They took the turn after the pub then, just as the man had said, and soon the wide entrance to the sanctuary came into view. Tracey flicked up the jeep's indicator lever.

"Oh my goodness!" Susie exclaimed excitedly as they turned in. "We have arrived at Hillside."

Despite the drab weather, the place looked amazing. There were extensive fields on either side of a long lane, which Susie was guessing would eventually take them to the main part of the sanctuary. The fields were carefully enclosed with posts and wooden rails, and the grass was neat and free of weeds. There were cows grazing, along with a large flock of sheep. Pretty shrubs were dotted here and there, breaking up the picturesque scene.

"My goodness!" Susie exclaimed again. "I never expected it to be as good as this. It's a hidden gem, this place."

Tracey nodded. "Looks good, doesn't it? I guess we just carry on down the lane and see where it takes us."

They took up the lane between the fields, continuing for about a minute before reaching a closed farm gate. Tracey pulled the jeep bumper up to it and pulled on the handbrake. She and Susie then took the opportunity to stretch their legs.

SUSAN JAYNE MCAULEY

It had been a long journey, over five hours, and they were stiff and sore.

"I won't be a minute," Susie said, suddenly making for the trailer behind them. If it had felt like a long journey for her, then she felt sure that it had been an epic one for poor Floss. She anxiously pressed her eyes to an air vent.

"Hello, darling," she cooed. "We are here. We are at your new home, and it looks absolutely fantastic. We will have you out soon, and you are not going to be disappointed."

Floss mooed gently, and Susie smiled at her. It seemed that she was more than ready to get out of the trailer and stretch her legs too. "I will see you again in a few minutes," she told her. "Not long now, I promise."

Susie hurriedly returned to Tracey who, with her back to her, was in the process of opening the gate.

"How is she?" Tracey asked, glancing over her shoulder.

"She looks absolutely fine, but I imagine she's feeling pretty fed up in there."

"She'll not be in much longer. Can you hold the gate whilst I drive through?"

Susie nodded, holding the gate back until the jeep and trailer had passed her. When both were clear she closed the gate and secured the latch. Then she took in the scene beyond.

The yard was large and concreted, obviously intended for those bringing livestock boxes and trailers in to be able to turn around safely. To the left of the concrete yard, there was a spacious paddock, fenced with wooden rails. It had a field shelter to one side of it and a metal water trough. Two white-haired llamas and a sandy alpaca were responsible for the neatness of the grass, and they lifted their heads, chewing thoughtfully as they checked out their latest visitors.

"This just keeps getting better and better," Susie said softly to herself. Even the sun had come out to welcome them to Floss's new home. Though it was low in the sky now that it was getting late, it sparkled at her through the trees. "Nice of you to finally show yourself," Susie said fully out loud, laughing. "But I bet you always shine here at Hillside."

She looked up then. Tracey had parked the trailer up and was on her way over.

"So, what do you think now that you have seen a bit more of the place?" Tracey asked her.

"I think that this is the best place ever," Susie said. "We simply could not have done any better for Floss. It's as if she was always meant to be here. This place is her destiny; I am certain of it. This is the start of the rest of her life."

"Well, I have to say that I agree. It is certainly amazing. I mean, you have to have your doubts about places before you see them for real, but there are no doubts here. Floss is going to be very well looked after indeed."

Susie felt her eyes begin to tingle, and she sniffed away a tear. A strange feeling of sadness had come over her. It wasn't a feeling that she had been expecting.

"You know, Tracey, it will still be a sad farewell for me. I mean, Norfolk isn't exactly next door to where I live. When will I ever get to see her?"

"Hey, at least you can rest easy that she will have an excellent life, and that is something that neither you, nor I would have been able to give her – not like this place can."

Blowing her nose in a tissue, Susie nodded. This was no time for her to feel sad. Everything was turning out just fine, but it still hurt knowing that she was soon to let go of something that she loved so very much.

The sanctuary office was signposted down another lane from the yard, though they could not see the building from where they were standing. For a moment, they deliberated, wondering if they should go on foot or use the jeep. Not being certain that there would be room near the office to turn the trailer around, they finally decided on walking. There didn't seem any point taking Floss with them until they knew where she would be going.

They passed another paddock on the way. It was home to three black-and-white calves, each just over a year old, which were happily grazing in the late sunshine, their backs steaming from the earlier downpours. Susie and Tracey paused to read the sign that had been fixed to the top rail of the calves' fence. It seemed that the poor creatures had been condemned simply for being the wrong sex, but they were lucky: the sanctuary rescued them. The calves, playful youngsters in the sunshine, lifted their heads and frolicked alongside Susie and Tracey as they walked.

Susie turned to Tracey. "Aww," she said. "I truly cannot believe the wonder of this place. Seeing the animals so happy, it just makes you feel so good inside. Thank goodness not everyone is awful to animals." Her eyes began to fill up again. "I am so glad that you found it, Tracey. Floss is so very lucky."

Tracey smiled and nodded. Floss was very lucky indeed, and in many ways.

As they rounded the bend in the lane, they caught sight of a smart brick building with a grey slate roof and white framed windows. Conscious that the sun was setting fast and it wouldn't be light for very much longer, Susie and Tracey hurried towards the building.

Just as Tracey had moved her fingers to the door handle, they both heard a voice calling from behind them.

"I am here. I am here."

They both turned simultaneously. A dark-haired woman in a thick green sweater was dashing down the lane towards them. She had a feed bucket in one hand and what looked to be a grooming brush in the other. The smile on her face went from ear to ear. Following a few steps behind her was a much older man. He wasn't hurrying quite so much.

"Good afternoon," the woman said, panting as she reached them. She then placed her bucket on the floor so that she could hold out her hand. "I am Wendy. Are you the two ladies who have brought dear Floss to join us? We have been looking forward to meeting you and to receiving her. Quite the celebrity she is."

Tracey turned to Susie and whispered, "Wendy is the founder of Hillside."

"Oh!" Susie exclaimed, shaking Wendy's hand vigorously. "We are very pleased to meet you too. And can I just say that I think you and all the people who work here are absolutely wonderful. When you see a place like this, it makes you realise that there is hope after all."

Wendy's face flushed pink. "We do our very best," she replied. "There are a lot of needy animals out there, and it is a very cruel world. The sad reality is that not all are as fortunate as Floss, but we help as many as we can."

"If it wasn't for you agreeing to take her, we do not know where she could have gone. Her time was running out."

"We don't turn our back on any animal," Wendy replied. "Someone has to protect them, because the laws in this country often fall very short of doing so. We, however, are here for them all – domestic or farm animal, great or small. We have over two thousand, you know."

"Yes, I know," Susie said. "It must be very hard work."

"It is, but it is also very rewarding."

Susie noticed then that the older gentleman was edging forward.

Wendy turned to him. "Well," she said, moving her hand to the small of his back and gently pushing him forward. "I think it is time that I introduced you both to someone. This is Joe Devlin."

Susie and Tracey looked equally bemused at Joe's wizened, grey-bearded face. Were they supposed to know him?

Wendy smiled. "I had better explain," she said. "Joe used to own Floss. In fact, it was Joe who bred her."

Susie's bottom jaw dropped. Why was this Joe person here? Had he some legal claim on Floss?

"You look worried," Joe said. "But you needn't be. I am not here to cause trouble; in fact, quite the contrary. Now let me tell you a little story of what happened. This morning, I was sitting at the kitchen table about to eat my breakfast and enjoy my morning newspaper. Well, I hadn't even managed to get a mouthful when suddenly I found myself with egg up my nose, staring at a picture of a so-called fugitive Highland cow. There was this heart-warming story that went with the picture about two young ladies who had rescued her from the abattoir. Well, it was the most unusual thing, because that cow was Floss, and I recognised her straight away. I knew every bit of her; you see, she was hand-reared after her mother died."

Susie's eyes urged him to continue.

"Well, now, I went on to read that it was thought she had escaped to look for the baby calf that had been taken away from her."

Susie couldn't help but interrupt. "Well, *did* her calf get taken away?"

"I am afraid that he did."

"How could you do something like that to her? It's evil and cruel separating a mother from her baby."

"I agree, and I never intended for it to happen. My little herd of Highland cows were my pride and joy. I did not breed them to eat them; I bred them to show them and to enjoy them, and the male calf that Floss gave birth to, well, he was an absolute treasure. But I became really ill, and my son had to look after things. He had a lot to do and simply did the best he could."

"And so why are you here now?"

Joe smiled. "I am here to right the wrong that was done to Floss," he said. "Can you see the barn just a little further down the lane?"

All eyes turned towards the barn, which was about a hundred metres past the office, and Susie nodded.

"Well, we should all head on to the barn as quick as we can, because there is something very special inside," Joe said. "Oh, you'd better go and get Floss; she will want to see this."

Susie and Tracey looked at each other, too astounded to speak or question what might be in the barn. "Come on then," Susie finally said, pulling at Tracey's arm. "Let's get her."

They ran the length of the lane to the car park where they had left the jeep and trailer. Panting breathlessly, they opened the doors to the jeep and climbed inside. Tracey started the engine.

"Quick!" Susie said. "They're waiting for us."

"They're not going anywhere, Susie. Calm down."

"I can't," Susie said. "I just cannot believe that this is happening. Are you thinking what I am thinking about what is inside the barn?"

"Probably," Tracey replied. "But let's not get carried away, just in case we have got it wrong."

Wendy and Joe were already at the barn as Tracey circled the trailer across the front of it. The doors were on metal runners, and as Wendy slid them open, she beckoned Tracey to wind her window down.

"Pull into the barn. We will unload her inside."

Tracey completed the manoeuvre and drove in through the big open doors. When she was certain that the back of the trailer was clear of the entrance, she brought the jeep to a halt.

Susie and Tracey both climbed out of the jeep.

Inside, the barn was enormous, spanning a good forty metres from end to end. Except for the area where they had pulled in, which was gravelled, a thick covering of straw filled the entire barn floor. The straw smelled fresh, clearly inviting to any animal that might want to lay on it. A fence divided the barn into two separate enclosures. There was a gated opening at the far side, and a grassed paddock could be seen beyond.

Susie's eyes set on what appeared to be the only occupant of the barn: a blonde adult Highland cow. Her heart sank. She had been rather hoping for something else.

"Have you seen him yet?" Wendy asked.

Susie nodded. "Yes, she's really nice." She tried to hide the disappointment in her voice, but it wasn't easy. "It's good that Floss will have a friend," she added.

"Ah, so you have seen Blondie," Wendy said. "Yes, she will make a good friend to them both, but I wasn't talking about Blondie. Look over there, in the corner on this side of the barn. Just a minute – it's getting a bit gloomy in here. I will turn on the lights."

Wendy turned and made her way to the wall behind them. There came a brief flicker, and then the barn lit up.

Susie and Tracey immediately set their eyes on one corner. A juvenile Highland, a calf not quite a year old, was looking over at them. He looked extremely nervous, like he really did not know what was going on.

Susie turned to Wendy and Joe. "Floss's son?"

Wendy nodded. "We think so," she said.

Tracey hurried to the rear of her trailer and began to undo the catches. "Well," she said as she lowered the ramp. "There is one way to find out. Floss will know."

Floss came to the top of the ramp, and her eyes immediately fell on Susie's smiling face. She mooed loudly.

"Hello, my darling," Susie said softly. "Come on down so that you can see your new home, sweetheart. We think it is going to be a lot more special than we could ever have known."

Floss did not come down straight away. Instead, she blinked a few times, her eyes adjusting to the barn's interior. She seemed to look at Blondie first, greeting her politely; and then, when her eyes set on the calf, they did not move from him.

"What do you think?" Susie said, speaking quietly to Wendy. "Does she recognise him?"

Wendy shrugged.

Joe smiled and it was a knowing smile. "Give her time," he said. "It's been a long while."

"Go on," Susie whispered to Floss. "Go and take a look at him."

Still not taking her eyes from the calf, Floss slowly made her way down the ramp.

"It's okay," Susie soothed. "Go on."

Floss walked towards Boris, but then, when she was about halfway to him, she stopped, looking this way and that, her expression uneasy.

"What's the matter with her?" Susie said anxiously, speaking to Joe. "If he is her long-lost son, then why doesn't she go to him?"

"I expect she just cannot believe what she is seeing," Joe said. "She will go to him, though. He is her son; I am certain of it."

The calf then began to step backwards, as if he were looking for somewhere to run.

Susie was horrified. "It's not her son," she cried. "It can't be."

But then something magical happened. Floss began smelling the air, and the calf did the same. He stopped moving backwards and let her approach him. She walked around him then, sniffing at him from head to toe and back again.

There was no mistaking it now: the scent, the one that had cemented their bond at the instance of his birth, was all over the calf – and it was a smell his mother could never forget. And then as Floss saw the calf wiggle his left ear, she let out a moo that was so loud it shook the roof of the barn. She had found him. Somehow and in such an unusual way, she had found her beloved son.

"Boris?"

"Mum!"

Overwhelmed, she began to cry massive sobs that made her sides heave. Tears streamed down her face, so much so that they blocked her nose.

"My son, my beautiful boy, it really is you."

Though he was now too big to get beneath her belly, Boris huddled against her, his eyes full of love.

"I never thought that I would see you again," he said.

"Oh, my beautiful, handsome boy, I cannot believe this is really happening, but I know it is because this time I can feel your breath. I have been looking for you ever since they took you away."

She took a step back then so that she could get a proper look at him. "Just look at you! Oh, would you just look at you! You are so grown up, so big now."

"You've kind of grown too, Mum. Or at least your head has."

"My head?"

"Yes, it looks kind of lumpy and bumpy, and there are some strange long things sticking out of your hair. I hate to say this, but they look like rats' tails."

Floss began to laugh. "Ah," she said. "Not quite rats. Nibble, Gnaw, it is safe for you to come out now."

Out from her hair popped two tiny noses, whiskers twitching excitedly.

"These are my little friends. Nibble, Gnaw, I would like you to meet my son, Boris."

The two mice squeaked excitedly, and Nibble hurried to Floss's ear.

"I am so happy for you, Floss," she said. "This is one dream that you can stay in forever. No animal deserves this more than you."

Floss gently lowered her head then so that the mice could slide down her face.

"I hope you like it here," she said.

"Oh we will," Nibble replied. "We are going to leave you to your moment now, whilst we take a look around, see where we can best make a new home for ourselves."

Floss smiled at them. "Thank you for helping me," she said. "I don't think that I would have made it here without your help."

"You are very welcome," Nibble said and then she turned to Gnaw. "Come on. Floss has a lot of catching up to do with her son. We'll leave her to get on with it."

After their worm-like tails had disappeared into the straw, Boris turned to look at his mother, his face bemused. "Rats," he said. "Most definitely rats. I know a rat when I see one. Why do you have them crawling about you?"

"They are field mice, not rats," Floss said. "And they are my very good friends. You know, Boris, something I have learned on my long journey to find you is that friends come in all shapes and sizes. They also don't always have four legs."

"Do you mean that you made friends with … ?" he said haltingly, scarcely able to bring himself to say the words that followed. "Mum, did you make friends with horrible humans?"

"Not all humans are horrible, Boris. Though some may have torn us apart, others have been very kind. In fact, it is a certain young human who is responsible for bringing us together again."

She looked over towards the barn doors, where Susie and Wendy already had tissues to their noses.

"I won't be long," she told Boris. "There is something that I must do."

She trotted towards Susie, who held her arms out to greet her.

"Hey, Floss," she said lovingly. "I bet you did not expect this! I said that you were going to like it here, didn't I?"

Floss mooed gently and let Susie caress her face.

"I am going to miss you when I leave, Floss," Susie said. "I am going to miss seeing you an awful lot, but I am going to miss you in a good way, knowing that you will have such a happy life with your son here at Hillside. Whenever I have a bad moment, I will think of you here, and it will lift me from it."

A tear came to Floss's eye, and Susie reached out and gently wiped it away with her tissue. "You really are an amazing animal," she said. "Truly amazing! I am so glad that neither of us gave in."

And when Floss smiled at her, Susie saw that the sadness which always clouded the cow's eyes had finally lifted. They were now as bright as buttons and full of joy for the wonderful life she was about to enjoy.

"I will visit you soon, Floss," Susie said.

"Thank you, Susie," Floss said with a soft moo. "My dear old friend, Ned, was right. Not all humans are bad after all."

And at that exact moment, in a beautiful green meadow more than a hundred miles away, Ned the Donkey looked up from his grazing. As the late March sunshine warmed his face, he smiled and nodded at his friend, Gertie the Goat.

"Floss and Boris are together again, Gertie," Ned said.

Gertie smiled too.

Somehow, someway, Ned knew that mother and son had found each other, just as he had always said they would.

Lightning Source UK Ltd.
Milton Keynes UK
UKOW04f1801270915

259349UK00001B/1/P